Jose

"This i[barcode: D0013549] n Hopi and I belong [PT-ARY-578] The snipers' helicopter veered over their shelter behind the hogan. "These guys may not hesitate to shoot an armed white stranger, but they'll at least think about shooting another Indian, especially one who's not carrying a weapon."

"What makes you think I was going to stop you? It's a good idea."

He spun around, surprised, and saw the smile on her face. "It wouldn't have hurt to argue the point with me." Walking to the door of the hogan, he kept his hands out where they could be seen. "Hello?" The door swung open on its own. He looked inside the room, then turned to Glenna, his face ashen. "Don't look in there."

"Joe, I'm a Federal cop, remember?"

She peered inside. All of her FBI training was forgotten with the sight that met her eyes.

ABOUT THE AUTHOR

Aimée Thurlo's *Breach of Faith* was inspired by her long-standing respect of the Hopi culture, and admiration for its peoples' struggle to remain true to their heritage. Aimée reminds us that her knowledge of Hopi traditions and theology is that of an interested outsider, and is based on what she has been taught after a long and respectful study. In *Breach of Faith*, the hero and heroine are searching for a balance point between their disparate cultures. Aimée and her husband, David, have spent twenty-two years blending their own different cultural backgrounds into a strong and happy marriage. The Thurlos live in New Mexico and, when not writing, devote their time to their extensive family of pets.

Books by Aimée Thurlo

HARLEQUIN INTRIGUE
131–BLACK MESA
141–SUITABLE FOR FRAMING
162–STRANGERS WHO LINGER
175–NIGHTWIND

HARLEQUIN SUPERROMANCE
312–THE RIGHT COMBINATION

Breach of Faith

Aimée Thurlo

Harlequin Books

TORONTO • NEW YORK • LONDON
AMSTERDAM • PARIS • SYDNEY • HAMBURG
STOCKHOLM • ATHENS • TOKYO • MILAN
MADRID • WARSAW • BUDAPEST • AUCKLAND

To Margaret, who showed us that
distance is no obstacle to friendship

Acknowledgment:
With special thanks to Richard Bucher of the
Southwest Museum for his time and help

Author's Note:
*The Native American rites depicted in this work
have been abbreviated, to avoid offending those
whose religious beliefs depend on the secrecy of
the rites.*

Harlequin Intrigue edition published October 1992

ISBN 0-373-22200-9

BREACH OF FAITH

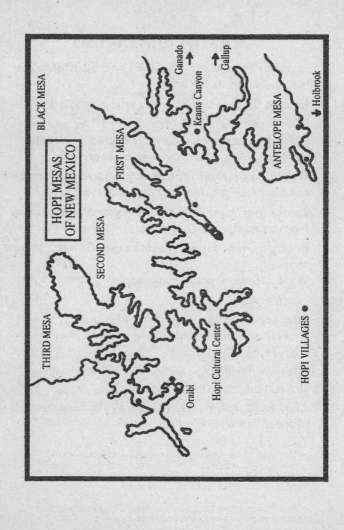

HOPI MESAS
OF NEW MEXICO

BLACK MESA

THIRD MESA

SECOND MESA

FIRST MESA

ANTELOPE MESA

Ganado ↑

Keams Canyon •

Gallup ↑

Holbrook ↓

Oraibi •

Hopi Cultural Center

HOPI VILLAGES •

CAST OF CHARACTERS

Joseph Payestewa—Violence and disaster follow him—will they catch up?

Glenna Day—This FBI agent was interested in Hopi culture, and one Hopi in particular.

Gilbert Payestewa—He stole sacred garments from his own mother, but was he coerced?

Wilma Payestewa—Each day the sacred garments remain missing brings her closer to death.

James Morris—He had a history of dealing stolen Hopi artifacts.

Bobby Shaw—Honest businessman or hungry loan shark?

Murray White—Shaw's lawyer . . . and innocent pawn?

Michael Newton—A British anthropology professor who had something to learn from the Hopi Nation.

Nigel Penhalligon—Billionaire investor with a stake in the Hopi healing rites.

Charles Murphy—He was always in the wrong place at the wrong time.

Glossary

Masau'u	War God of Fire and Death	Hopi
Dineh	Navajo People	Navajo
piñon	type of evergreen	Spanish
chindi	evil side of man's soul	Navajo
hik'si	soul-breath body	Hopi
kahopi	unHopilike	Hopi
nicho	recessed shelf	Spanish
kikmongwi	village father	Hopi
wuye	clan's nonhuman partner	Hopi
chongo	bun at back of head	Spanish
tusqua	Hopi ancestral land	Hopi
paho	prayer stick	Hopi
ikwaatsi	good friend	Hopi
bilagáana	white person	Navajo
túhikya	medicine man	Hopi
tihus	small effigies	Hopi
na'atsi	standards/flags	Hopi
dumalaitaka	spirit guide	Hopi
tochi	men's moccasins	Hopi
Marau-vaho	special prayer stick	Hopi
Kwan	men's religious society	Hopi
Tao	men's religious society	Hopi
Navotciwa	purifying rite	Hopi
tiponi	fetish	Hopi
pahana	white man	Hopi

Prologue

Gilbert Payestewa stood next to his pickup in the fading light and checked the tie-down on the tarp that covered the back. The last thing he needed was for a late February breeze to break it loose at the wrong moment. If there was any hope of repairing the damage his actions would cause, he'd need to use the few tricks he had up his sleeve.

He studied the sagebrush around him nervously. The vast, sandstone-littered mesa appeared empty save for a solitary jackrabbit that had come out to forage, thinking himself hidden among the tall bushes. In another ten minutes it would be completely dark. He listened, but no other sounds reached him. Shoulders hunched in resignation, Gilbert walked to the cab of his truck and gathered up a black plastic garbage bag. This had been the quickest and most practical method to transport the items, but it seemed the final insult to the sacred objects that lay inside.

He lifted the sack carefully and positioned it over his shoulder. It weighed only a few pounds at most. The real burden lay in knowing that he was about to betray those he loved and everything he believed in. He stood still for a moment, desperately trying to think of another solution. But the mask of *Masau'u*, the War God of Fire and Death, had been the only payment they'd accept. He worried most about his mother and how the loss of the precious items entrusted to her care would affect her. If only there had been another way to keep his family safe!

Finding comfort in the knowledge that his plans were more complicated than his enemies expected, Gilbert walked down the left-hand rut of the dirt road. His bruised ribs felt as if they were on fire with each step he took. He still couldn't see out of his left eye, it remained swollen from the beating he'd taken. Accepting it as the consequences of his actions, he'd remained firm despite the punishing attack. He'd known the risks of dealing with the *pahana*, the white man. Yet the threat to his elderly mother and father had finally evoked the response they'd wanted. His parents wouldn't have survived long if men like these caught them away from the village.

As he continued across the Joint Use area shared by both Navajo and Hopi, he considered the price his weakness for gambling had exacted.

Even so, he'd soon make things right again. With the motorcycle and his own modern day "bloodhound," he'd be able to track everything, and hopefully recover the items before anyone even realized they were missing.

Hearing the sound of a vehicle, he moved quickly, hiding the trash bag in the middle of a large clump of brush. Five minutes later he saw headlights approach from the Navajo side of the desert. In the muted glow of the moon, he identified the four-wheel-drive Jeep. They were on time.

Gilbert watched two men step out and stand by the doors. Finally a third emerged, their boss. The man was thin and unimposing, yet the bruises that marked Gilbert's body were a powerful reminder of the threat he represented.

"Keep your hands away from your pockets," the man ordered calmly. He remained behind the glare of the headlights. "I'm sure you'll understand if I have one of my boys frisk you. We don't want any accidents."

"You brought the markers?" Gilbert gritted his teeth as rough hands spun him around and patted him down, oblivious to the injuries they'd inflicted earlier. His searcher removed the small folding knife from his pocket.

"He's clean *now*," the muscular-looking *pahana* pronounced, and tossed the knife to his employer.

"We're ready to trade then," the boss said. "Where are the things we asked for?"

"I need to see my markers first," Gilbert insisted.

The man reached into his jacket pocket and held the papers up. "Do we get down to business now, or do we play?"

Gilbert knew from firsthand experience that the *pahana's* definition of "play" meant inflicting a great deal of pain. Wordlessly he reached over into the clump of brush and brought out the sack. "Everything you asked for is here."

"Open the bag with one hand, then set it down so we can see inside."

Gilbert followed his instructions, moving slowly.

The man glanced inside the sack, then nodded, satisfied. "Okay. Fasten it back up, then bring it over to me."

"My markers," Gilbert repeated as he approached.

"Here you go." With a flair, he tore the papers in half and handed the pieces to Gilbert. "Consider yourself paid in full."

As they stood face to face, Gilbert glanced down at the sack. "These objects are dangerous—particularly to those who don't know how to protect themselves. Any outsider in possession of them is in great physical and spiritual danger. Let me work my debts off some other way."

"Sorry, but I've got a new backer, and I have to answer to him. He wants the mask, the robe and the medicine pouch, so that's what I'm here to get."

Gilbert nodded, then carefully placed the sack down in front of the man. He held the torn markers, staring at the bits of paper. How had things gotten so out of hand? Anger and frustration tore through him as he shuddered.

Crouching down on the sandy track, Gilbert took a cheap lighter from his pocket and set fire to the papers. He watched them turn into gray ashes and then glanced up. Seeing the thin man raising his gun, he suddenly realized it was a double cross. He spun around and started to run, but it was already too late.

Three shots rang out and ripped into his back. His chest exploded in incendiary pain. As an oily darkness began to spread over the edges of his vision, his knees buckled and he dropped to the sand. He struggled to stay conscious, clinging desperately to life. Without him, there wouldn't be anyone to bring the objects back. The curse would follow each female member of his family and wipe out his clan until its blood legacy was fulfilled.

As pain gave way to numbness, the image of the death god, tall and horrible, seemed to rise out of the sand before him. He realized that his time had run out. *Masau'u* was about to claim his first victim. He wondered how many more would die before it was over.

Then as the darkness of *Masau'u's* great shadow settled over him, he wondered no more.

Chapter One

Special Agent Glenna Day drove north along the slender desert highway with her window open, taking advantage of the clear but cold winter day. The refreshing breeze blew through her light brown hair and helped keep her extra alert that early in the morning. Even though she had one of the best arrest and conviction records in the Bureau, she wasn't optimistic about her assignment. This time, getting the cooperation of those involved was going to take diplomacy, skill and lots of patience.

Hearing her call sign over the radio, Glenna picked up the mike and responded. She recognized the man's voice immediately. Special Agent Justin Nakai, a Navajo, usually worked the regional cases inside the Navajo reservation.

"I just want to let you know that the Navajo police are actually eager to turn this case over to the Bureau," he said, his clear voice coming over the radio. "Everyone is very touchy because the body of the Hopi man was found in a section of the Joint Use area that borders Navajo land."

"I'm aware of the tension that exists between the tribes," Glenna answered, "but what is the origin?"

"It's all due to the way the land was divided a century ago," Nakai answered. "Many Navajos believe that the Hopis never made proper use of the land, so they shouldn't have had so much of it apportioned to them."

Glenna smiled. "I hear that there are others who say that the Hopi were there first," she spoke into the mike, "and that the land *is* being used, but in a different way."

There was a lengthy silence. "Yeah, some do say that. And by the way, I'm not totally unsympathetic to the Hopi claim. I just think the Navajos have a better case."

"I'd have never guessed. But don't worry, I know I'll be walking a thin line. I do have some knowledge of the Hopi Way so maybe I can be a buffer between the tribes during the investigation."

"I'll meet you at the crime scene in case you need help with the Navajo police, but I won't be able to stay long. If you need me later, you've got the numbers where I can be reached. I'll be available."

"I appreciate it," she said, and signed off.

As she left the Navajo reservation and entered the Joint Use area, she felt her body tense. So much could go wrong. She remembered her Hopi friend back in college. At one time she'd hoped the teasing and flirting between them would lead to something more, but it never had. Slowly she'd come to accept it and learned just to enjoy their time together. Then, out of ignorance, she'd made a mistake that had caused their friendship to come to an abrupt end. She'd learned then just how private the Hopi could be about things that pertained to their lives and culture. She'd also found out the hard way that to the Hopi, forgiveness was a futile gesture that did not, and could not, cancel an injury. A wrong against another stood forever, unlike a debt of money, for example, that could be paid and then forgotten.

Forty minutes later Glenna turned off the road and drove down a deeply rutted dirt track that ran parallel to a shallow wash. Two vehicles were already parked just outside a large area of waist-high, gray-green sagebrush that had been marked off with yellow tape. Quickly Glenna removed her sunglasses and placed them in her purse. Her light amber eyes were sensitive to the desert sun even in winter, and she knew making eye contact was a tricky subject around Native Americans, but the appearance of hiding your eyes behind lenses was worse than either drawback. Leaving her own vehicle beside the others, Glenna strode over to the men, both Navajos. One she recognized as her fellow agent, the other was a Navajo policeman. The officer held a clipboard in his hand and was sketching the crime scene.

She saw them look casually in her direction, nod, then resume their conversation. Glenna began to pick her way forward carefully, concerned about disturbing any undiscovered evidence.

"Gentlemen," she said as she approached. Silently she noticed that Nakai was as fit as ever. The much older officer beside him contrasted sharply with the agent's tall, athletic build. She made a mental note of the name pinned over the officer's shirt pocket. Harry Benally's facial features and body were somewhat rounded, attesting to a case of middle-age spread. She refrained from extending her hand, remembering that those of their tribe preferred to avoid touching anyone who was not a close family member.

With relief, she noted that the cultural details she'd learned in college were coming back to her now that she needed them. She'd minored in anthropology, with most of her course studies focusing on Native American cultures of the southwest. That was one of the reasons she'd been assigned to this area.

As she approached the shallow grave where the body lay, Glenna hardened her expression. She still remembered the first autopsy she'd viewed after she'd become an agent. The ravages of death were never easy to view. Glenna scrutinized the ground, careful not to disturb tracks and marks already there. "Has an M.E. been called?"

"The closest thing we've got to a medical examiner is one of the regular doctors at the PHS—Public Health Service—Clinic," Nakai answered. "But at least she's done this before. She'll collect all the organic evidence for testing and tell us what she can from her postmortem."

Glenna spotted signs that a large canine had been digging around the grave, which explained some of the tracks she'd seen. The animal had unearthed a considerable portion of the torso. The corpse's head had also been exposed, though from the marks on the ground, she judged that part had been uncovered with a small shovel. Taking a closer look, Glenna crouched down beside the body. She was grateful for the first time today that it was winter. The cold had guaranteed that the only odor reaching her nostrils was that of the freshly exposed soil.

Glenna studied the blackened eye and the recently scabbed-over cut on the victim's eyebrow. "Looks like he was in a fight recently. Do you know who he is?"

"We think so," Benally answered, "but we're waiting for confirmation. We found what we believe to be the victim's truck about fifty yards from here, just over that rise." Benally pursed his lips in a characteristic Navajo gesture indicating direction. "There was no registration in the glove compartment, but we found it stuck in a paperback Western underneath the seat. I called the Hopi police and they're checking it out. They weren't able to get hold of the owner of the truck, probably because this is his body. Anyway, they're trying to find a relative to come out with a Hopi officer. We'll have him ID the body when he gets here, if he can. If not, it's possible we'll find a driver's license in the victim's pockets once we dig him out. But we thought we should leave things where they are until you got here."

"I notice you've been sketching the scene. Have you taken photos, including the tracks and footprints? I'm going to need that type of documentation and also plaster casts, if possible."

"Photos are already done, along with notes on angles and exposures. As for the casts, I can use plaster of Paris. Our department's budget doesn't allow us to use dental stone."

With a nod, she stood up, resisting the urge to dust off her clothes. "Who found him?"

"One of the local *Dineh*...Navajos...named Jerry Todacheene. He was out here at dawn with his sheep. While he was looking for a lamb, his dog dug out most of what you see here. He called the tribal police. I arrived at about 8:00 a.m. and cleared the sand away from the head and face to try to identify the body. When I realized he was Hopi, I stopped and called Agent Nakai. Since the FBI is responsible for investigating murders on the reservation, I figured I'd bring you guys in right away."

"How certain are you that Todacheene didn't add anything besides his tracks to the crime scene, or for that matter take something away?"

Officer Harry Benally gave her an incredulous look. "Jerry's an old Navajo. He stayed as far away from that body as he could. Count on it. And he wouldn't want to touch anything associated with it, either. He's moved on with his sheep."

Glenna spotted an area of sand stained crimson. She started toward it when something else caught her eye. She stopped and crouched down to see it. A small pile of ashes lay next to a good-sized rock. "What's this?"

Justin crouched by her. "We saw it, took a few close-ups, and left it there for you. There's no breeze so we figured it was safe. Do you want some help gathering it up?"

"No, let me do this while you continue checking the rest of the scene." She retrieved a small box from her car trunk, then began to systematically pick up the thin gray flakes by carefully sliding a piece of stiff paper beneath them. Once they were all in the box, she placed the lid back on and labeled the top with the date, location and her initials. Making sure the find was recorded in Benally's sketch, she continued toward the blood-soaked patch of sand. "They didn't even try to hide this."

"They probably didn't think they had to. It's isolated out here, so they weren't worried about someone passing by. Also, in a day or two, either snow, wind or animals would obscure it. Their problem was the body. They couldn't afford to leave it uncovered. If buzzards started gathering, the sheepherders around here would have grown curious."

She stood to one side and studied the ground. "Are those tire tracks ahead from either of your vehicles?"

Justin shook his head. "We stayed clear. The footprints around it indicate that the victim met three other people here."

Moving slowly, she scoured the ground for evidence, and recorded her impressions in a small spiral notebook. Glenna looked up, hearing the sound of a vehicle approaching. It was the Hopi police officer with whomever they'd found to identify the victim. "When they get here, could you ask the relative to wait until the M.E. comes? I want her to be there before we disturb the remains." Seeing Benally nod, she continued, "I'll be checking out the truck next."

"He can show you the way," Benally gestured toward Nakai. "I better go meet the Hopis," he answered. "There's only one thing that makes them more nervous than a Navajo, and that's the FBI."

As she walked with Nakai to the battered old pickup, she zipped up her jacket. The cold, dry air of the desert seemed to chill her right down to the bone. Seeing that the door to the truck was open a crack, she pulled it from the bottom and opened it further. "I'll have to make sure everything's dusted for prints," she commented, looking inside. "Then after that, maybe the Navajo police can take this truck apart and search it for contraband." She glanced at the glove compartment, but didn't touch it. There'd be time to inspect its contents later.

Noticing a canvas tarp covering something in the bed of the truck, Glenna left the cab and walked to the back. Grasping a rope tie-down, she loosened it enough to look underneath. A well-maintained Harley-Davidson motorcycle, minus a license plate, lay there. She studied it for a moment, then unfastened one of the saddlebags with her pen. Without actually touching the leather, she glanced inside. "There's an AM-FM radio and a set of headphones in here. About all that tells us is that he liked music."

As she jumped off the back, her gaze turned to the men approaching. Her heart leaped to her throat. There stood

Joseph Payestewa, the most unforgettable man who had ever entered her life.

He stopped in mid-stride as his eyes captured hers. For a second neither of them moved. He stood taller than most men of his tribe at five foot eight, and had a lean but powerful build. His jet-black hair touched the upper part of his shoulders and emphasized his square jaw and the strength inherent in his features. He wore a white turtleneck sweater, a denim jacket and jeans. The combination accentuated everything she'd remembered about him. He looked like a very tempting blend of modern civility and the wildness and freedom that made up his heritage.

Joseph approached her slowly, his back ramrod straight. "What are *you* doing here?"

Chapter Two

Out of the corner of her eye, she saw Justin's eyes narrow slightly, but he said nothing.

"I'm a Special Agent for the FBI. This is my case," she managed. Meeting him like this had thrown her completely, but she was going to do everything she could not to let it show. "Have you been briefed by one of the officers?"

"Yes," Joseph said without inflection. He caught her eyes again in an unfeeling steady gaze. "I'll wait for the Medical Examiner."

Glenna felt the sting of his gaze. Then her attention shifted toward a large, white hospital van speeding noisily toward them. "We have company."

"That's Doc Wanda Shapiro, the acting M.E." Nakai spoke.

"Let's go meet her," Glenna said, anxious to do something that would ease the awkwardness she felt.

Wanda Shapiro was a large, heavy-set woman with salt and pepper hair. Her eyes darted around as she approached, medical bag in hand. There was a no-nonsense air about her that precluded the need for small talk or protocol. "Let me get through this as quickly as possible," she said. Taking a step toward Glenna, she lowered her voice to a whisper. "Keep the Hopi man back until I've done my initial examination. After we retrieve the body and place it in a better situation for viewing, then we can have him take a look.''

Wanda walked off toward the body as Glenna quickly asked Joseph to wait another few minutes. He nodded, a cold look in his eye.

Glenna almost had to run to catch up with Wanda, and when she did, her reception was somewhat less than cordial.

"You're going to want answers fast, so I might as well warn you. I'll do my best, but I'm no miracle worker." Wanda ducked beneath the yellow tape line, then crossed over to the sandy grave. Kneeling beside it, she studied the position of the body and its surroundings, then rose to her feet. "So who's going to shovel him out of there?" she demanded, staring hard at Glenna.

Glenna, not wanting to waste precious time, picked up the shovel that she'd seen propped against a clump of piñon and started toward the grave.

Nakai placed a hand on her shoulder. "Let's keep it fair. Harry can do the shoveling. Then you and I can lift him out." He glanced at Harry. "Unless you'd rather I do the shoveling, and you help lift him out."

Benally shook his head. "Your original suggestion suits me fine. This is one time I don't mind having the FBI take over."

"How cooperative of you," Nakai muttered.

Glenna watched the two men. The Navajos had an almost instinctive aversion to death and everything connected with it. Fear of the *chindi,* the evil side of a man that lingered earthbound after death, was strong among them. According to tribal beliefs, that half of a man's nature was incapable of merging with universal harmony, and so became an uncontrollable force capable of doing much harm. The Hopis, by contrast, held the belief in an afterlife and saw death as an important change of status for a person. One simply went on to better things. She found that view much more reassuring than the Navajo one.

After the sand had been removed, Glenna glanced over at Joseph, who still stood fifty feet away. His face was set and impassive. Crouching by the body, she carefully examined the victim's hands then fastened a paper bag securely around each. With Nakai's help, she then lifted the corpse out onto a stretcher Benally had retrieved from the medical van. The instant it was possible, Nakai moved away from the body. Benally, in turn, kept a discreet distance from Nakai as well as the victim.

Seeing the look of concern Glenna gave him, Justin shrugged. "It's part of the job so don't give it a thought. Preference has nothing to do with duty."

"I'll second that," Wanda said, kneeling next to the body. She switched on a tape recorder and began to detail her findings. "The victim is in his early thirties, and appears to have been shot three times. Bullets entered through the back. The relative absence of blood around the grave indicates he was moved after he died."

She continued recording for another five minutes, then finally stopped. "He was probably killed about twelve hours ago, but that's only a guess. From the partially healed marks on his body, I'd say he'd been beaten up about a day before that. I'll know more once I get him to the clinic." She covered the body with a plastic sheet. "I imagine you'll want to have fluid and tissue samples taken to labs in the city."

"Yes," Glenna replied. Realizing Joseph had started to come forward with the Hopi policeman, she signaled Benally to intercept them. With effort, she tried to push aside her concern for an old friend and concentrate on the job. "Can I search the body now, Doctor Shapiro?"

Wanda nodded and watched while Glenna went through the victim's pockets for a wallet. She didn't find one.

"I don't know about you, but I hate this part of the job," Wanda said, putting her gloves back into her bag. "Personally, I'd rather think of myself as a doctor for the living, not the dead. I got elected to do this because I happened to take a few courses in forensic medicine at school. Lucky me."

"If I had a choice, I'd just as soon get a detailed report from an extremely qualified crime scene investigator,"

Glenna said in a barely audible voice. "The first time I saw a body, I couldn't keep my food down for three days."

Wanda gave her a quick, candid smile. "Good. I'm glad you can admit that you're human. Some women in male-dominated professions tend to acquire a chip on their shoulders." She chuckled softy. "I admit it's in self-defense, but having one of us who's like that around here is enough."

Glenna found Wanda's candor, particularly in the midst of a murder investigation, refreshing. "You're a rare one, Doc. A camel that sees its own hump."

"It saves time when you don't need anyone else to point out your shortcomings," Wanda replied.

Finally Glenna nodded to Benally, letting him know it was okay to let the men pass.

"Ready?" she asked softly when Joseph came up. She crouched by the victim and lifted the sheet away from his face.

Joseph moved closer, then gazed down. His lips tightened into a thin line, and he tore his gaze away. After a long pause, he spoke. "It's my brother, Gilbert."

"I'm so sorry, Joe," she said, covering the body once again. "I know this is difficult for you, but I'm going to have to ask you some questions."

"Don't you always?" His eyes flashed with anger and he lowered his voice slightly. "If you don't mind, I prefer to speak with your Navajo associates."

She was aware that he'd meant it as an insult, but she refused to take the bait. "I'm the case agent, Joseph. You'll have to deal with me."

"I trusted you once. Why should I do that again?"

"You don't have a choice. I'm here to solve your brother's murder."

Joseph stared across the vast plateau. "I wonder what kind of choices Gilbert had," he said quietly.

Glenna watched the officers carry the body to the hospital van. "Why don't you ride with me, Joseph? I have to make a stop at the hospital, then you and I can sit down and talk."

Before he could answer, the Hopi officer approached. "I'll be glad to take Joseph to the hospital so he can make the arrangements—that is, if you're through with him," the young man offered.

"I'll ride with him and leave you to your business," Joseph said and walked off.

He was challenging her, but for now she'd let it pass. She'd pick her battles carefully.

Glenna followed Doc Shapiro back to the highway through a cloud of dust, but her mind stayed on Joseph. Earlier this morning she'd been determined to make time to track him down. She'd never dreamed he'd find *her,* and that it would be under circumstances like these!

One thing was perfectly clear, however. Time had not worked any special magic on the old hurts. The past still stood between them like the Grand Canyon.

As she pulled into the parking lot of the Public Health Services Clinic, a low, long adobe building sitting below the mesa-top village, Glenna forced her thoughts back to the grim business at hand. She was here to solve a murder and she had every intention of solving it. After her work was finished, perhaps Joseph would finally see that she wasn't his enemy and never had been. Yet it was likely that things would get worse before they got better. Her job seldom made friends.

Glenna followed two orderlies who were taking the body inside on a gurney. "We'll need to inventory all his personal effects," she said to Justin, then glanced at Doc Shapiro.

"Go through the first door on your left, that's our morgue. I'll be there shortly," Wanda answered.

As Glenna stared down the hall, she felt a hand on her shoulder. Turning, she saw it was Joseph, his features distorted by grief. "We must have Gilbert's body back as soon as possible. According to our Way, my brother has to be buried within four days of his death. If this doesn't take place, his *hik'si,* his breath body, won't reach the Underworld. This is very important to us. Now, more than ever, we need our rituals."

"I understand. I'll do everything in my power to get the body to you on time." Glenna walked down to the morgue and found Doc Shapiro. "How soon do you think you'll be able to release the body? There's a matter of burial rites we're going to have to take into account."

"I know. I've dealt with this before," Wanda answered. "I'll take all the fluid and tissue samples we need and do a full autopsy right away. We're not that busy here at the clinic now, so it shouldn't be a problem."

Working with Justin, Glenna cataloged the victim's personal effects. "His wallet's gone, but he's still got his watch," Glenna commented. "Maybe his killers were just hoping to delay identification of the body."

"It's possible, and fits in with the evidence so far. There's nothing else with which to make a quick ID. The vehicle registration wasn't where it should have been, so if the killers did a fast search, they probably missed it," Justin conceded readily. "They might have assumed he'd never put it in the truck." Nakai moved away from the body, then stood by the door for a few minutes staring into space. "From your conversation I gather you've met the victim's brother before. Does he have a criminal record?"

"Not that I know of, but I'll check it out. The last time I saw Joseph was back in college." She smiled wryly. "And that was more years ago than I care to admit." She was thirty-two now, and although ten years had passed, graduation seemed like it had been just yesterday.

"Unless you need me, I'm going to head back to my office," he said.

"Okay. I know how to reach you."

Lost in thought, Glenna watched Nakai leave. It was time to question Joseph. She hoped he wouldn't try to make her job too difficult. If he did, he'd find she'd become a great deal tougher than she used to be.

As she reached the reception area, she saw Joseph standing by the window staring outside at a stunted juniper. Glenna exchanged a few words with Harry Benally, then a moment later approached Joseph. "We need to

talk, Joe, in private. Is there someplace you'd prefer to
go?''

He turned and met her gaze. ''Why don't you take me
to my car? It's at the gas station near here. Then you can
follow me to my home. It's not far away if you measure it
in time instead of miles.''

The suggestion surprised her, especially in light of what
had happened between them in the past. Maybe the anger
she'd detected earlier wasn't as deeply ingrained as she'd
feared. ''All right. That's fine,'' she answered. His house
was probably quite a distance from here, but travel across
the thinly populated desert would be speedy.

''My home is the best place to go, believe me. There are
things you have to be told, only they're very private and
difficult to discuss with an outsider. To begin with...'' his
voice dropped to a barely audible whisper, ''I think I know
why my brother was killed.''

JOSEPH DROVE DOWN the narrow asphalt road that passed
near his home in the broad flatland between Antelope and
First Mesa. There were a few junipers and an occasional
patch of piñons on the north slopes, but the ground cover
was mainly brush and wild grass. It was isolated by city
standards, but when he'd come back from the *pahana*
university, this was the one place that had suited all his
needs. It was near his clan's ancestral shrine, his father's
corn fields, and close to the electronics firm where he
worked as an engineer.

Living out here and tending his father's small field had
helped him reconnect with the ancient ways. He'd been
able to make the transition then, acknowledging that he'd
become part of two conflicting worlds. Some thought he'd
become *kahopi,* unHopilike, but he didn't see it that way.
In his heart, his tribe and his culture would always come
first. Now that he'd finally attained the peace of mind he'd
worked hard to find, the unthinkable had happened.

He glanced in the rearview mirror. Having Glenna come
back into his life just added to the turmoil his usually calm
life had become. He couldn't quite believe Gilbert was

dead and that the woman he'd once loved was here to investigate the crime. He half expected to wake up and discover it had only been a vivid nightmare.

Joseph parked in front of his home, and watched
Glenna as she came toward him. There had been a time
when he'd fantasized about bringing her here, but now he
realized the past could never be undone. As an FBI agent,
Glenna was only a means of dealing with the problems
Gilbert had left for them. Any feelings he'd had for her in
the past had long since been buried by the bitterness he'd
felt after her betrayal. Nothing could be allowed to interfere with what had to be done. The consequences of Gilbert's actions were already exacting a price, and more lives
hung in the balance.

Glenna met him at the door. "It's beautiful out here."
She looked at the steep sides of a red sandstone mesa rising up behind the house. A small arroyo leading down
from the heights ran parallel to the back of his home,
serving to drain runoff away from the property. Weathered piñons stood among the thick clumps of sagebrush.

He opened the door and led her inside. The white-
washed stucco walls were barren except for the few kachina dolls he'd made. The one he'd carved for Glenna so
many years ago, but had never given her, stood in a *nicho*,
a shelf built into the wall.

Glenna glanced around and walked directly to it, even
though she'd never known it had been meant for her. A
stab of sorrow pierced him, but he quickly forced it away.
He'd always known she'd like it. Her tastes hadn't
changed, even if the two of them had. "Make yourself
comfortable," he gestured to the brown leather couch in
the center of the room. "What I have to say may take some
time."

Out of habit and practice, she sat at an angle with the
door. Retrieving a small notebook from her purse, she
patiently waited for him to begin.

He paced the room like a caged tiger. "This isn't easy to
say, so bear with me." He stopped by the window, then
turned toward her. "I loved my brother," he said slowly,

"but I wasn't blind to his faults. Gilbert had a way of finding trouble and this time it cost him his life." He clenched his fists as anger and sorrow settled over him like an impossibly heavy burden. Despite all his good intentions, he'd failed Gilbert and that knowledge would haunt him forever. Perhaps if he'd refused to help him, forcing his brother to face the consequences of his life-style, this could have been avoided. Yet it was difficult to turn away when someone you loved was in trouble.

He struggled to find the right words. "Gilbert has taken some things from my mother's house that he had no right to even touch. These items are of ceremonial significance, not only to my clan, but to the tribe. As a result, my mother is very sick. I'm afraid that unless our property is returned soon, she will die."

The statement had been delivered without drama and it was the matter-of-fact tone that had chilled her. It took her a moment to gather her thoughts. "Your mother has had some terrible shocks. She needs some time to adjust to what's happened," she said.

"No, you don't understand. Yes, she's experienced the loss of a son, but there's more to it than that. Stealing these objects carries a curse, not only to the thief, but all the women of our clan, starting with my mother. If the legend of the curse is true, as she believes it is, it could wipe out our entire family."

"Do you believe in it?"

He could tell that her question came from genuine concern rather than an attempt to patronize him. That made answering her easier. "A part of me does, I suppose. My brother is gone and from what I've seen so far, my mother will be next. Whether or not it's due to a curse or her own heartbreak is irrelevant. The outcome will be the same."

Chapter Three

Joseph returned to the couch and forced himself to sit down. "This is a very sensitive issue for the tribe as well as my family. You see, as many as two-thirds of the clan pieces have been stolen over the years. Holy objects that have been handed down for generations and form the framework of everything we believe in, are disappearing. In this particular case, my mother will shoulder the heaviest load of all. As the head woman of our clan, she was in charge of keeping the objects safely hidden and she's failed at that task. Soon word will get out and everyone will know what Gilbert has done. Her embarrassment..." He paused, then shook his head. "No, *shame* is a better word, will be difficult for her to bear."

"Will your family be ostracized by the others?"

"That's too harsh a word, I think. But there's going to be a lot of anger directed at us. Remember, also, that according to our beliefs, our clan will be the focus of an ancient curse. Evil is supposed to overshadow all of us in one form or another until everything is returned. People will want to avoid us since they don't know when or how the gods are going to hand down their punishment."

"Exactly what was stolen?" She'd hoped he would mention it on his own, but his reluctance to be specific was obvious. She had to force him to clarify even if he loathed talking about it.

He let out a sigh. Finally, after a long pause, he answered. "The mask of the *Masau'u*, our war god. Also his robe, which is made from rabbit pelts, and includes a belt decorated with shells and such. A small medicine pouch the impersonator carries with him during special ceremonies was also taken."

"I can check on the collector's value of the artifacts," she said quietly. "I know there's a very active illegal market for that. But what about the medicine pouch? What did that contain?"

"Nothing particularly valuable to anyone except maybe a medicine man. It was filled with common herbs that are used in conjunction with certain rites."

"Could the pouch itself be significant to a collector?"

"I don't think so. There's nothing unique about it."

"What makes you so sure that the theft is connected to Gilbert's murder, or for that matter, that it was your brother who took the items? Did someone actually see him do that?"

"No, but he was the only one who could have. They were kept in a secret place in my mother's home and Gilbert knew how to get them without injuring himself. Gilbert had visited them the day before yesterday. My parents left him alone while they helped out a neighbor, then by the time they returned, he was gone. Shortly after that, my mother discovered the theft. She contacted me right away and I've been looking for Gil ever since." He tried to block out his feelings. She needed facts and logic, not emotions. "There's one thing I'm certain of. This isn't something Gil would have done lightly. He must have been coerced somehow. What I need to do for our own peace of mind is find out why he did this to us."

"His reasons could be very important to my case, so you can count on my learning what they were. Then, as soon as I can, I'll tell you. Just don't get involved in the investigation, Joe, please. You'll only complicate matters and possibly slow down my progress." When he failed to answer, it occurred to her that he was going to disregard her request. "You're not going to do as I ask, are you?" she observed.

"You already know the answer to that," he answered quietly. "My mother only had two sons. I've taken a leave of absence from my job already. It's up to me to undo the damage Gil has caused."

She sat still, measuring his words. At last she glanced up and with one look managed to convey both disapproval and acknowledgment of the inevitable. "I'll need to speak to your parents and see the place the items were taken from," she said. "Also, I could really use sketches or photos of the objects, if there are any."

"I'll ask my mother about that when I take you over there. As a matter of courtesy, by the way, you shouldn't question them inside their home. That should only be done when you're outside. I know it'll test your patience, but out here on the reservation different rules apply."

"I appreciate your help," she answered honestly.

"There's something else," he added with a trace of reluctance. "My parents are very elderly. Go easy on them, please. I'm not asking you that as an FBI agent, but as a person. And maybe, too, because you owe me one." He saw her stiffen, and knew she didn't agree with his recollection of the past.

"Joe, it's time I made something clear to you. I won't hurt your parents or anyone else unnecessarily, but I intend to do whatever I have to in order to solve this case. As far as my owing you something . . ." She shook her head. "It's obvious we have different interpretations of what happened."

"What's to interpret?" he countered evenly. "When you asked me about our women's societies and their special rites, I told you much more than I should have. I trusted you with a story that no one outside my tribe ever knew. It involved my mother and my own birth. How could it get more personal than that? Yet you used it as part of your psychology class term paper. Do you deny what you did?"

She exhaled softly. She would have preferred to talk about this some other time, but he wasn't going to give her a choice. It would hang over their heads, and maybe cause him to withhold information unless she got it out into the open. "I kept your name and your family's out of it completely. My paper was on how thought can affect physiological states. Your mother's inability to have children, and the curing rites that later resulted in the birth of two sons was a beautiful example of that. If you recall, I also cited other instances where cures were effected through methods other than the Hopi Way, yet remained unexplained medically."

"I never objected to the paper, Glenna, just the manner you used to get your information. You should have told me where your questions were leading. I had no reason to be on my guard around a friend."

"Do you really remember that night?" she asked. "You'd said that the white world had forgotten how to see with their souls instead of just with their eyes. When I asked you to explain, you told me a little bit about the Hopi Way and then about your mother's cure. At the time, I wasn't even thinking of writing a paper. That didn't occur to me until months later. I never dreamed you'd be upset as long as I kept your name out of it."

"Maybe that was the problem. You never understood friendship carried certain obligations," he replied quietly. "For instance, after you met Brad you never had time for me, even though we'd been friends for quite a while. That evening we were just talking about was a rare instance. And you were only with me then because Brad was out of town with the football team."

"I was barely twenty when I met Brad. Everything was all-consuming back then. Surely you remember the first time you fell madly in love."

His jaw clenched. Yes, he remembered only too well. It had been with Glenna. He'd agonized over it. She wasn't of his tribe. The implications of a serious relationship with her had been grave. According to their customs, for a child to be considered Hopi, the mother had to be Hopi.

Yet, even knowing the cost, he hadn't been able to get her out of his mind. Then she'd met Brad and he'd been forced to admit he'd seen far too much in her playful flirting. She hadn't really been interested in him at all. His feelings for her had tricked him into believing his own fantasy.

He avoided her eyes. "Whatever happened between you two?"

"We got married," she said in a tight voice, "but it didn't last."

He could sense her pain and wondered if she was still in love with Brad. The possibility bothered Joe and he realized that a part of him still cared for her. Maybe that was why he felt better holding on to his anger. "It seems we see the same event from very different perspectives."

"Let it go, Joe," she said, a trace of sorrow in her voice.

He wondered if he could. Still, she was right. The past wasn't as important as what was happening to those he loved now. His tribe was the center of his world, and his future would depend on how he handled the legacy Gilbert had left for them.

"I shouldn't have brought this up. We have other things to attend to. Let me take you to my parents' house."

Glenna followed him out. "I better check with the Hopi police chief first. He wasn't at the scene of the crime, or at the clinic."

Joseph shrugged. "He's not exactly on great terms with the Navajo police," he paused, then added, "nor with our own tribe, either, for that matter. He's stuck between the traditionalists and the progressives, just like the Tribal Council."

"I don't understand. His job is to uphold the law. That's not political, that's clear cut."

"Administratively the police is an arm of the Bureau of Indian Affairs, a Federal agency. His department has to enforce both white and Hopi law. The man answers to quite a few people."

"All the more reason for me to pay him a visit before I go any further on this case. My supervisor told him I'd be here, so I'm sure he's expecting me to drop by. Jurisdictional things are tricky and a little courtesy goes a long way. If you can give me directions to your parents' house, I'll meet you there in a few hours.''

''Directions have a way of sounding vague out here. Why don't I lead you to the police station, then wait for you there? Once you're through, you can follow me to my mother's home.''

''Okay. Let's get going.''

Glenna stayed several car lengths behind Joseph as they drove down a long stretch of empty blacktop. Neither the years nor the strain between them had diminished the effect he had on her. Everything about him seemed imbued with a natural, totally unpremeditated sensuousness that would take any woman's breath away. It was there in his stance, the slant of his belt, the smooth, bronzed muscles that strained beneath the fabric of his shirt. He seemed unaware of it and openly skeptical when it was pointed out to him. Back in college she'd had fun teasing him about it. Yet now that he'd matured, its effect had become even more potent, much like fine old wine versus new. There was a new strength in the way he carried himself that went far beyond his good looks. Joseph had acquired the easy grace of a wildcat moving along the rocks on the mesa. There was also an unmistakable calm and confident air about him that attracted her like a magnet to steel.

Glenna pulled her thoughts away from him. The case was going to be complicated enough. This was no time to indulge in speculations that were bound to create more trouble for her. She forced her mind on to her driving and concentrated on avoiding the potholes in the road. A half hour later they arrived at a modern-looking village near the foot of one of the mesas and entered the stone and stucco police headquarters. A young Hopi woman manned both the radio and the front desk. She looked up, gave Joseph a glance, then focused on Glenna. ''May I help you?''

Glenna displayed her badge and identified herself. ''I'd like to speak to the police chief.''

The woman stood. ''Captain Kywanwytewa's been expecting you. He's in his office.''

Glenna glanced at Joseph, who'd seated himself on a pine bench, then followed the woman down the hall. She wondered if they'd managed to pinpoint the time of her arrival, or if he'd just expected her to come in sometime today. "Did you know I was on my way here?"

The woman smiled. "You'll find that in all the Hopi villages, even the ones without telephones, news travels *very* fast."

As they entered a small office at the rear of the building, a short, stocky man stood up from behind his battered desk. Pulling a chair out from against the wall, he invited her to sit down. "I'm glad you're here."

"I want to keep you informed on what I learn, Captain," she said. It wouldn't be reasonable to expect him to cooperate with her unless she also extended him the same courtesy. "My preliminary investigation shows that Gilbert Payestewa's murder might have been connected to some missing ceremonial items."

"Yes, I've heard about the Payestewa's problem. Do you have any suspects?"

"Not yet."

"Then consider the possibility that Joseph Payestewa is involved in this."

The news took her completely by surprise. "What makes you say that? Does he have a police record?"

"No, Joseph's clean, but the two brothers were always very close. Gilbert loved to gamble, which is legal on the reservation, but he'd get into fights over the games. That's when we'd step in and make arrests. We hauled Gilbert in many times, but he never cared. He knew Joseph would come and bail him out. He was very dependent on his brother. That's the reason I find it hard to believe he would steal the kachina costume without even giving his brother a clue. He'd want to make sure he could count on Joseph's help. You watch Joseph very carefully, he may try to lead you astray."

"We're going to have to get more evidence before we know what happened, but I appreciate the tip. At least it's a start."

"By the way, how much help will you be wanting from us? In my opinion, you're wasting your time around here. The objects and Payestewa's killer are miles away from Hopi land by now."

"Possibly," she conceded. That is, unless another tribal member was responsible for Gilbert's death. The buyer and the murderer didn't have to be one and the same. She met the captain's direct gaze, and decided against pointing out something he already knew. "No matter how we look at this, the trail starts here. If you could assign one of your people to me as an interpreter, that would be a big help."

The captain stared out the window at the dark gray clouds forming overhead. "That might backfire. The old ones who are normally more comfortable speaking Hopi are often hard-core traditionalists. They're not too fond of the police department. You'd be better off talking to the village father where Joseph's parents live. If you can get him to help you, then you'll really have an asset. His office is considered to be such a holy calling that the villagers attribute the success of their crops to his prayers. He wields considerable influence and can open doors that would otherwise remain shut to you. He's also Joseph and Gilbert's uncle, by the way, and as the head of the *Kwan*, he wears the *Masau'u* costume to the society's ceremonies."

"Thanks, Captain." She stood and shook his hand. "If you need me I'll be staying at this motel," she scribbled down a name. "It's in Keams Canyon. I also have a radio in my car should you want to get hold of me quickly during the day."

After saying goodbye, Glenna walked down the hall to the reception area. Unable to find Joseph, she opened the door and walked outside. He was leaning against the stone wall to the south, his eyes focused on the clouds spreading from horizon to horizon. "It's a little cool to be hanging around outside, isn't it?"

He shrugged. "Not to me. The cold helps me think."

She didn't comment, but wondered if his reluctance to stay inside was due to other reasons. He certainly hadn't made a friend of the captain. "I'm ready to go to your parents' home. Will you lead the way?"

He accompanied her to the Bureau's vehicle. "I'm not sure what the captain told you about me or Gilbert, but I'm certain it wasn't flattering. The captain disapproved of my bailing Gil out whenever he got into trouble, but Gil had no one else to turn to." He stared at the ground. "My brother and I were close and that's going to lead some people to believe that I knew what he was going to do. But you see that's precisely why he wouldn't have told me. He would have known I'd stop him any way I could."

"The captain is entitled to his opinion, Joseph."

"And what's yours?"

She remained silent for a moment. "I haven't formed one yet."

He couldn't expect anything else, but it still hurt to see the uncertainty in her eyes. Yet it was his own reaction that bothered him more than anything else. He really shouldn't have cared what she thought. Wordlessly, he strode back to his own car.

As they drove among the weather-sculpted Hopi mesas, his thoughts turned to his mother. At the rate her health was deteriorating he wasn't sure how long she'd remain alive. This morning when he'd gone to the house in answer to his father's summons, he'd found his mother pale and extremely weak. Her hand had trembled violently even while resting on the table.

Joseph had offered her what little comfort he could, but more than the loss of the sacred items was haunting her. It was knowing that her youngest son had committed the crime.

A short time later they approached the ancient highlands that had originally housed the entire village. Now a collection of stone and adobe buildings appeared amid the jumble of boulders at its base as well. He drove to the farthest tip of the cliff extending into the valley, and parked in front of a modest dwelling made of cinder blocks and cut stone.

Joseph stood by his vehicle as Glenna pulled up beside him. "Give me a moment to talk to them, okay?"

"That's fine." Glenna stayed in her car as Joseph went inside. It was colder now than it had been earlier. With the engine off, the heat dissipated quickly. She zipped up her jacket and studied the home before her in an effort to distract herself. Earth had been piled on the flat roof for insulation. She noticed a thin curl of smoke coming from a single masonry chimney. In winter, she'd been told, many of the villages burned coal from local mines for heat.

Glenna watched as Joseph came out five minutes later. He belonged here, yet he also seemed aloof. She wondered what he saw when he looked at the village his parents called home. Did he feel at ease here, or did it seem alien to him after having lived in the white world for so long. She opened the car door and stepped out to meet him.

"They know you're here," he said, "and that you want to ask them questions. Normally they'd meet you outside, but my mother's health is very bad. They've agreed to talk to you in the house. I have to warn you, though, there are things they'll never discuss with a *pahana*."

"I understand. I'll be as quick as I can so your mother can rest."

As she walked inside the home, she saw that even here in the ancient village the old and the new coexisted in an uneasy truce. The house had electricity, but judging from the large galvanized can in the adjoining kitchen, not running water.

Dan Payestewa greeted them from the corner of the living room where he sat weaving a brightly colored blanket. His skill in the traditionally male profession seemed evident. In respect to their customs, however, she refrained from making any comment on it. Praise was seen as making comparisons that might cause someone else to be unhappy.

Wilma Payestewa sat very still in an old wooden chair and regarded Glenna warily. As her husband introduced her, she merely nodded in weary acknowledgment. The woman's eyes were heavy with fatigue.

Dan left the loom and moved closer to the group. "I remember hearing my son speak of you many years ago."

Glenna nodded, wondering how much they knew. "Yes, we were friends in college."

Dan Payestewa looked up at her. "I remember him saying that you were learning about the Hopi, and understood us better than most *pahanas.*"

"I've tried. I've been interested in your traditions since I learned that Oraibi was occupied over three hundred years before Columbus discovered America. Your ways have helped the Hopi withstand almost every kind of hardship."

As Wilma Payestewa managed a thin smile, Glenna noted how frail the woman appeared. She wondered how Dan and Joseph managed to conceal their true feelings. Hopi customs prohibited them from showing any undue concern, or even acknowledging that there was a problem with her health. According to their beliefs, sickness needed to be deprived of the power thinking about it would give.

Wilma smiled hesitantly as Joseph went into the kitchen. "I know there are questions you want to ask, but we know very little," she said, her voice whisper soft. "My son Gilbert was a heartache to us. He was a good man deep inside, but he never learned the discipline a good Hopi needs. To the last, he refused to change. The day he came here his face was bruised and swollen. He'd been fighting again." Her voice broke and she turned away for a moment.

Glenna hated to ask her to elaborate, but she had no choice. "Do you know with whom, or what it was about?"

Wilma glanced at her husband, then shrugged and stared at the floor.

"His gambling perhaps?" Glenna insisted, looking from one to the other. She could see the anguish on the woman's face and wished her job didn't sometimes force her to be so direct.

"I just don't know," she managed. "The truth is, Gilbert tried to solve everything with his fists."

Wilma looked at Joseph as he stepped back into the room. "Take her down to where the objects were kept," she said quietly. "She hasn't asked yet, but she'll want to see."

Glenna thanked her, then followed Joseph. He rolled aside an area rug in the middle of the living room that hid a trap door, then led the way down several narrow steps into a tiny chamber. "This is where the mask and robe were hidden. As you can see, there's nothing here now." The enclosure was carved from a cleft in the rocky mesa floor. "It's impregnable in every direction except the stairs," he said in a hushed whisper, his voice echoing in the darkness. A large pouch on top of an adobe brick captured her attention.

"He left this behind," she commented, placing two fingers on the adobe.

Suddenly, Joseph lurched toward her and pushed her against the wall. As she tumbled backward, she heard a sharp thud. A long-bladed knife had shot downward with incredible force, cutting through the pouch and imbedding itself in the hardened mud.

Chapter Four

Glenna stared at the knife gleaming in the half light coming from above. "What happened? I barely touched that adobe."

"It's an antitheft device," Joseph answered, trying to even his breathing. "My father installed it years ago after several ritual items were carried off by visitors our people had trusted." He offered her a hand up.

"Very effective," she said, trying to gather her wits. "Thanks. I could have been a few fingers short. Next time I'll ask before touching."

He nodded. "Obviously, my brother replaced that bag there to offset the weight of the mask and robe, then took the items with him."

"Did you ask about sketches or photos?" she added, struggling to return her voice to its normal pitch.

"My mother said that there aren't any drawings or pictures available, although some of the other *Masau'u* masks have been photographed in scholarly books. Our clan's kachina mask is very special and sacred. It's that of a *wuye*. That means it's the clan's non-human partner, the one who gives us protection. There are other masks owned by individuals, but a *wuye* is irreplaceable. It's only brought out for special ceremonies. Other masks are scraped and repainted for each dance. Ours is refurbished only when it becomes absolutely necessary, and it is never stripped."

Out of deference to Wilma Payestewa's condition, she'd refrained from asking before, but there was something she had to know. "Do you think your mother or father have any idea who might be responsible for Gilbert's murder or where the objects may be now?"

Joseph felt a sharp stab of sorrow. "No, and I'm glad they don't. If they had, my father would have gone after the things himself, believe me."

"All right. Then let me say goodbye to your parents for now. I want to go speak with the village father next. The Tribal Council has already been notified that I'll be handling this case, so I don't need to touch base with them until the next time they convene."

"The father of our village, my uncle, is a traditionalist and views the council as a *pahana* invention. It would probably be a good idea for you not to mention the council," Joseph warned as they returned upstairs.

Glenna said goodbye to Wilma and Dan Payestewa, then walked outside with Joseph. "Does your mother feel comfortable visiting the PHS doctors in Keams Canyon? Maybe they could help her."

"That's not her way," Joseph answered. "On the same subject, I appreciated your not mentioning anything about her illness when you were with them. Were you being polite, or did you remember our customs?"

"I remembered."

He nodded, barely managing to conceal an approving smile. "I should warn you that I don't know how welcome I'll be with our *kikmongwi*, even if he is my mother's brother. He never approved of the way I tried to help Gil. Anyway, I'll show you to his home. We can walk there."

Actually, it would have been impossible to drive. The road leading to the stone house was blocked by large ragged boulders that had dislodged from the mesa recently. As they strode along, the people they passed were seemingly engrossed in their tasks, but Glenna was aware of the suspicious glances that darted their way. She could feel Joseph bracing himself as they walked up the dirt path leading to the house. "You don't have to go any further, Joe. Let me take it from here."

"No. I'll have to talk to him before I leave you to your business. There's too much at stake for my family and he should know I intend to rectify what Gilbert has done," Joseph knocked, then opened the door when the invitation was issued from inside. He introduced Luther Coyama to Glenna, then helped the man bring out two chairs for them to sit on.

"I've been expecting a visit from both of you," Coyama said.

Glenna saw him shift his attention to Joseph. As the two spoke, she watched the village father. He was dressed in ordinary work jeans and a wool sweater, yet there was an air of distinction about him. His long gray hair was fixed *chongo* style and he wore several large turquoise rings on each hand.

"I know that you'll do your best to make amends for your brother's actions," he said after listening to Joseph. "It's unfortunate that the task has fallen on you, but I don't see how you can avoid it." He turned to look at Glenna. "Now tell me what I can do for you."

Glenna identified herself as the case agent. "As village father you know the people here better than any outside official. My job is going to demand I ask some very difficult questions, and I must have everyone's cooperation. Without it, I have little chance of success."

"You're bound to encounter resistance," Coyama admitted. "You're *pahana* and some of our people are going to see your presence here as an intrusion. Between the *pahanas* and the Navajos, much of the original Hopi *tusqua*, our ancestral land, is now held by others."

"I'm aware of the problems, believe me, but if I can solve this case, everyone will benefit. My knowledge and training can be an asset to the tribe."

Coyama nodded slowly. "You're right, but you also have to understand our viewpoint. Centuries of trying to coexist with the *pahanas* who come to observe us as if we're insects inside a jar, have made our tribe very skeptical of outsiders. That attitude is based on a hundred broken promises and it can't be swept aside simply because it's now expedient to do so," he answered.

Glenna regarded him thoughtfully. He was obviously as intelligent as he was educated. She wanted very much to enlist his help, but there wasn't anything else she could say. She waited, sensing he was gauging everything before making up his mind.

After several long moments he glanced up and trained his sharp eyes on Joseph. "I appoint you to be her guide and interpreter as long as she's here."

"I don't understand. My help isn't likely to make her job any easier. Depending on who she's dealing with, it might even make things worse."

"You're going to be looking into this matter on your own anyway. By placing you two together, I'm making sure that you don't obstruct each other by working at cross-purposes."

Glenna looked at Joseph and saw the surprised look on his face. She'd intended on asking Coyama for his help finding an interpreter, and a guide would be useful. But surely he didn't expect her to share her investigative responsibilities.

"I'm very grateful for the help you've offered me, but there will be certain decisions that I'll have to make alone. I'm not trying to minimize the help Joseph can give me, but the legal system is complex. I have to follow many rules and procedures. It won't do us any good to catch whoever has committed these crimes, for instance, if it's done in a way that won't hold up in court."

"Joseph will work with you, not supersede your authority." The elderly man's features remained tranquil. "You should also work with him and accept his judgment on matters that concern our religious practices."

She sensed the iron will behind the eyes that sagged at half mast. "Thank you for taking time to see me," she said, conceding that the matter had been decided.

As they left the house Joseph fell in step beside her. "My uncle has an amazing gift for reading people. If you look at it, all he's really done is cement the working arrangement we already had unofficially.''

Joseph was right, but she wondered if he was just trying to make things more palatable to her. There was no doubt that the villagers would not react favorably now if she tried to conduct the investigation alone. Coyama had given her no choice. ''We'll see how things work out,'' she said, deliberately being vague.

Joseph matched her strides. ''What next?''

''I need to learn everything I can about your brother. Was Gilbert married?''

He nodded. ''His wife and young daughter live at the base of the mesa where everything's more modern. Gil liked being comfortable. Shall I take you there?''

''Lead the way. I'll follow you in my car,'' Glenna answered.

It took fifteen minutes of travel over a rough winding road to get to the gray cinder block home. Down here the houses were equipped with electricity and running water, but they lacked the style and traditional look of those atop the mesa.

She left the car and went to meet Joseph on the wellworn path leading to the house. Abruptly a small girl, about five years old, threw open the door and ran right between them.

Joseph caught the little girl, then tickled and released her as she squealed with delight. His eyes remained on her for a second longer as she skipped down the road and joined another child, who was approaching from a neighbor's house. ''That's Juanita, my niece. She's got more energy than you can imagine. She's never still for more than a second.''

Glenna saw the love reflected in his eyes. ''She's adorable, Joe.''

''She's the best thing that ever happened to my brother, I envied him. I wish she'd been mine.''

Glenna's heart constricted as she remembered her past and the heartbreaks there. She wanted to say something, but the words became lodged in her throat. The appearance of a young Hopi woman at the door of the home gave her a few precious seconds to gather herself.

The woman glanced at her daughter, verifying she was all right, then waved at Joseph. "Come in," she invited softly.

As they entered the small living room, Joseph made the introductions.

Sara Payestewa met Glenna's gaze, held it for a moment, then finally looked away. "I have work to do in the kitchen. Why don't you come in there with me?"

Glenna followed, wondering if she should have stayed outside. She wouldn't be able to question the woman inside her home. As she entered the kitchen, she noticed the room had all the modern conveniences, including a microwave oven. Maybe the same rules didn't apply here, Sara was obviously one of the progressives.

Almost as if reading her mind, Sara shrugged. "Some say that if we enjoy things like these—" she gestured around the room "—we become just like the *pahanas*. I don't think so. As long as we hold onto our beliefs, there's no reason for us to make it harder on ourselves. Would you like to sit down?"

Glenna nodded, hesitant to begin.

"I know there are things you want to ask me, so go ahead."

Glenna got down to business. "Some say that your husband took ceremonial objects from his mother."

"So I've heard." Sara retrieved several green chilies from the refrigerator and began to dice the vegetables on an oak breadboard. "I can tell you one thing. My husband wouldn't have done that unless someone had forced him, you can count on it."

"Perhaps he was trying to get some money for you and your daughter," Glenna suggested. "Everyone has bills and things they need."

"Yes, that's true, but Gil could always hustle some business when he wanted to. Gilbert was one heck of a repairman. There wasn't anything he couldn't fix." She met Glenna's eyes. "I know that you're going to hear many bad things about Gilbert, but he was trying to change. Lately he'd been working very hard at his shop."

"But what about the missing items? Do you think Gilbert's being unjustly accused?" Glenna deliberately kept her tone soft. She wanted information, not a confrontation.

Sara took a deep breath, a trace of moisture starting to appear in her eyes. "I've thought about this, and I believe that someone blackmailed Gil into doing what he did. Trouble followed my husband, I'm afraid."

"What leverage do you think they could have used to blackmail him?"

Sara just shook her head. "I don't know. You'll have to find those answers on your own."

Glenna said nothing for a moment. If Sara knew more than she was saying, she gave no indication of it. For now, she opted to leave matters where they stood. "Thank you for your help, Sara." She placed a card in front of her. "If there's anything you can think of that might help, please let me know. You can reach me at this number."

Glenna walked outside with Joseph. "Is Gilbert's workshop around here?"

"No, it's in Keams Canyon, but it's probably not worth the drive. There's nothing much to see there except a colossal mess of parts."

"I'd like to take a look anyway, but you don't have to go with me if you'd rather not. Just give me directions and the keys."

"I'll go." He paused, his voice tense. "I wasn't trying to keep you from going, just warning you about what to expect." He stared ahead, lips pursed in a thin white line. "No, that's not it." His stomach clenched as he struggled to explain what he didn't want to put into words. "The truth is, I was worried about what you might find there. If Gil stole from us, his own family, it's possible he's been stealing from others long before this. We've all taken for granted that Gil did legitimate work at his shop, but now I'm not so sure."

She wanted to offer some comfort, and it saddened her to know there was nothing she could do or say. "I'll go by myself. There's no reason for you to have to come."

"There's every reason," he countered. "Finding the answers and facing the truth is the only way I can help my family now."

"At the beginning of a case, people are generally eager to learn what happened," she tried to explain. "Then, when the evidence begins to surface, the picture that emerges is very often the last thing they want to see."

"I'm very aware of that," he countered. "I'm not going blindly into anything out of loyalty, if that's what you're worried about."

She shrugged, refusing to argue the point any further. "Do you want to ride with me?"

"Sure, but instead of leaving my car here, let me drop it off at home. It's on our way."

Fifteen minutes later Joseph joined her in the Bureau car. "I wish there was some way to speed up our progress on this."

His pain touched her heart. "Why don't you tell me more about Gilbert's gambling?" she prodded gently. "I'm getting the idea that it was the major problem in his life. Do you know if he owed money to anyone in particular?"

"No, I really don't," he snapped. Taking a deep breath, he continued in an even voice. "Gil knew that I disapproved of the way he was throwing his money away, so he never talked to me about it. Whenever his debts got out of hand though, he'd come to my home and tell me what he thought I wanted to hear. He knew I wouldn't let his family pay for his negligence."

"Did you ever turn him away?"

He fought the shriveling emptiness that tore at him. "No," he whispered, "and I realize now what a mistake that was," he said. "By always helping Gilbert, I made it possible for him to continue doing the things that were destroying him inside. I believe the modern term for it is co-dependency," he added bitterly.

There was no denying the courage behind his brutally frank admission, despite his tone. His vulnerability filled her with compassion. Joseph had the strength of tempered steel and the gentleness of one who knew intimately the frailty of the human heart. "It's very easy for people to find labels that make everything fit into neat little niches, but don't be so hard on yourself. Nowadays, sticking by someone who's in trouble is immediately regarded with suspicion. Yet loyalty and commitment to family have their place. What you were trying to do wasn't wrong, it was just human."

Her answer surprised him. Maybe she did understand exactly what was in his heart. Still, it didn't lessen his guilt, or his pain. He drew back into himself, needing to refocus his thinking away from her. "Small time gambling is commonplace on the reservation," he said after a moment. "I wish I'd bothered to learn if Gil had a favorite hangout."

"Are there games just outside the reservation that are more accessible to the white population?"

"I've heard there are, but they're high stakes. Our people are too poor to take part in them, and that by the way, includes Gilbert."

He struggled between the desire to protect his family from an outsider and her need to know. Yet he had to be open with her. She was his best chance of retrieving the missing objects. Even though he was quick to learn, she had the experience.

As they entered the small town of Keams Canyon, Joseph guided her to his brother's workshop. It was a stucco building located at the end of a row of old, run-down business shops.

Glenna parked near the side and pointed out a broken window. "Was it always like that?"

"No way. It's too cold out here and there's very little to stop the wind. Gil would have covered it with plywood, if nothing else." Glenna checked her pistol. "But this area has had problems with vandalism lately. I don't think there's anything to be overly concerned about."

Glenna picked up the radio mike and called in a report. "Give me the keys and stay here. I'll go take a look," she said.

Glenna moved silently toward the building. Stepping closer to the shattered window, gun in hand, she peered cautiously inside. A shadow crossed over the far wall and then disappeared in the blink of an eye.

Scarcely breathing, she made her way around to the back, looking for the rear exit. The door was open. She started quietly toward it when she heard a sound somewhere ahead of her. Glenna flattened against the wall. Surprise was her best tool. If she could get the drop on the intruder now, then she might keep the confrontation from escalating into something far worse. Her skin prickled with anticipation and a touch of fear as she froze, waiting.

Suddenly Joseph appeared from around the far corner of the building.

"Damn it! I told you to stay put!" she said in a harsh whisper.

Joseph stopped suddenly, peering ahead until he saw her outlined in the shadow of the building. "I went around the front and wedged the door with a board. Then I figured I'd come around this way and we'd catch him in the middle."

The sharp mechanical stroke of a shotgun slide intruded on his words. Before Joseph could take a step, the big ugly muzzle poked out from around a tree less than ten feet behind him. Glenna raised her pistol, ready to defend him, and knowing she'd need a miracle to succeed.

Chapter Five

Before she could take a breath, a man's clear voice rang out. "Police! Don't move," he ordered.

Glenna quickly slipped her pistol back into her holster and stood. The last thing she wanted to do was surprise the officer while holding a gun in her hand. Bringing out her ID, she slowly stepped clear of the shadows. "FBI Special Agent Day," she said, holding up the gold badge. "I was the one who made the call."

The young Hopi police officer never took his eyes off Joseph, his shotgun still trained on him.

"This man's with me," she said, "but someone was inside the building. I think he might have taken off already since by the time I came around, the rear door was wide open."

The officer lowered the barrel of his shotgun. "I'll go take a look inside."

"Don't you have any backup?"

"It'll be a while before they get here. There're not that many of us," he replied matter-of-factly.

Glenna reached for her own weapon. "Then I'll be your backup. Lead the way."

She followed the uniformed officer and helped him begin a methodical search of the premises. They went through each doorway buddy-fashion. The tremendous clutter slowed their progress.

Finally satisfied no one was there, Glenna placed her gun back inside the holster. "It must have been the tarp over there," she reasoned. One corner of it lifted, then settled back down as the wind rushed through the shattered window. "It throws a shadow on the wall as it billows outward."

The officer walked to the broken window. "Either way, someone *did* break in here. That glass was smashed from the outside. Most of the pieces are on the floor."

Glenna walked to the door and gestured for Joseph to enter. "Will you take a look around, and tell us if anything's missing?"

Joseph took a deep breath, puffed up his cheeks, then let the air out slowly. "I'll try. The office is the only place with some semblance of order, so it'll be the easiest place for me to start."

"Lead the way," she said.

A small television set had been placed on a shelf made out of bricks and pushed flush against the wall. The cash register on the opposite side of the room was open and nearly empty, save for a handful of change.

"Someone cleaned him out," the officer commented, studying the open drawer.

"It could have been Gilbert himself," Joseph replied. "From what I can tell nothing else has been stolen."

Glenna studied the yellow self-adhesive notepad beside the phone. That would have to be checked later. There were some impressions left from a previous message.

Joseph opened the door that led to the restroom and swore softly.

Hearing him, Glenna turned and followed his line of vision. On the floor was a towel laden with bloodstains. "Don't touch anything," she warned. Stepping to Joseph's side, she glanced into the tiny room. An open bottle of aspirin was on the sink, a drinking glass next to it.

"He must have come here after a fight to clean himself up. I wonder how close it was to the time he got killed," Joseph muttered.

"Doctor Shapiro should know today," Glenna replied, then addressed the officer. "We're going to need to have this place sealed off and carefully searched. We need photos of everything, and I want this towel and the notepad by the telephone analyzed."

"I'll call our team," the officer said, then walked off.

Glenna glanced around, studying the area carefully. There seemed to be a bit of animal fur that had snagged on the edge of a file cabinet drawer. "Did your brother have a pet?"

"No." Joseph came toward her and studied the small piece of soft gray-white fur. "May I pick it up? I'd like to take a closer look. I think I know what it is."

She nodded, and Joseph lifted it free.

He held it between his thumb and forefinger, studying it intently. "There's hide on the back and it's been cured." He showed her the reverse side. "It's rabbit skin," he said, his voice muted. "I can't be one hundred percent sure, but the color and type matches the robe of *Masau'u*. It's made of rabbit pelts."

"Then your brother must have brought the items here first, and later moved them elsewhere," she muttered thoughtfully. "He probably stashed them in the drawers to keep them out of sight. We'll search them for confirmation." As she glanced at Joe, the expression on his face cut through her like a knife. Had she sounded callous? She hadn't meant to. "Are you all right, Joe?" she asked gently.

"I know it doesn't make sense," he said in a strangled voice, "but until now I'd held onto the hope that somehow it would all turn out to be a big mistake."

She saw the pain etched on his face. Deep lines framed his eyes and creased his mouth in a way that made him appear much older. He wasn't trying to hide how he felt like men often did. Yet he wasn't asking for her sympathy, either. The inner strength his honesty portrayed stirred an undefinable emotion inside her.

"I'm sorry, Joseph," she said. "I'll use everything I know to get those objects back where they belong. The

Bureau has considerable resources and I'm very good at what I do. My job keeps me working night and day, and it usually pays off. You can expect results.''

Despite her confidence, Glenna's words had betrayed a vulnerability that touched him deeply. Maybe once you know pain, you become more attuned to it in others. He, too, had been successful in his work, and the satisfaction he'd found there had helped him fill the void in his personal life. He started to speak when the policeman came back into the room.

Glenna's attention shifted to the officer. He held some paper bags and a manila envelope to be used for holding evidence. ''Let me know what you get from the impressions on that notepad. Also, I'd like to make sure that the blood on that towel is Gilbert Payestewa's,'' she said quietly. ''Were you planning on taking it to Doc Shapiro?''

The officer nodded, placing the towel into a paper bag, then labeling the outside with a permanent marker.

''In that case, I'll take it over to her myself. I was going to the clinic anyway.'' The officer handed her the bag, and she signed a receipt for the evidence. Glenna started out the door, then stopped and turned to the policeman. ''I need to locate a truck impounded from a crime scene in the Joint Use area. Do you know where it might have been taken?''

''If you're referring to the one belonging to Gilbert Payestewa, I expect the Navajo police have it. I'll call and find out where it is.''

''Thanks, I'd appreciate that.'' She walked with the Hopi policeman to his car, and waited for the information to be relayed back.

Joseph stood outside by the open doorway, watching. All his life he'd been taught to suppress anger and to avoid emotional excesses of any kind. Yet the need to exact revenge for his brother's beating and murder was tugging at him right now. He wanted to let go and stop demanding more from himself than he would have expected from anyone else. Yet as his eyes wandered to the Hopi officer, he drew strength from deep inside himself and years of discipline prevailed. To repair the damage that had already been done, he'd need to restrain his instincts and keep his thinking clear.

Glenna came up, interrupting his thoughts. "I'm going to the clinic, then to Navajo police headquarters in Window Rock. They've got your brother's vehicle there. I'd like you to come take a look at it," she said in a gentle voice. "You might be able to tell if something's been added that doesn't belong there, or if there's anything missing."

He followed her wordlessly, consciously keeping his eyes off the brown paper bag she held in her hand. He knew the towel with his brother's blood was inside it. "I'll help any way I can. The truck used to be mine. I sold it to him last year."

They were quiet during the trip, but he felt no compulsion to break the silence. As he stared out the window he became acutely aware of Glenna's perfume. It permeated the air, tempting his senses with its delicate floral scent. There had been so many possibilities for them once. Every day around her had been sparked with excitement and life. He remembered a picnic they'd had on a stormy day. She'd brought a basket of food and a blanket, and insisted they go on with their plans, despite the weather. He'd held her against him that afternoon for hours as they'd watched the rain from his apartment window. Her hair had smelled of lilacs.

But now it was death that brought them together. He withdrew into his thoughts, lost within himself and the burden he shouldered.

"Have you lived here since you left college?" she asked.

Joseph knew she was trying to divert his thoughts, and he was grateful for the distraction. "Yes. This area's always been home to me. Everyone and everything I love is here. What about you? How did you end up back in Arizona?"

"The FBI thought my college background made me the perfect choice for this area."

"You were attracted to careers in law enforcement, but after Brad came into your life you seemed to lose interest in that kind of work."

"Only temporarily. After Brad and I split up, I knew it was time to go after my own dreams. I wanted a career with the best, so I applied for the FBI. There were background checks and tests first, then fifteen weeks of hell at the academy. But I finally made it."

"Has it been what you expected?"

"It's more consuming than I initially thought, but that's fine with me. I know I'm doing something worthwhile and that's what really matters."

He suspected there was much she wasn't saying, but it was clear she wasn't ready to tell him any more.

Glenna slowed the car as she entered the clinic's parking lot. After a few moments she found a space near the visitor's entrance. "This shouldn't take me long. Then we can go on to Window Rock."

As they entered the building Glenna spotted Doc Shapiro coming down the hall. "Wait here. I'll be back in a moment." Discreetly handing the doctor the paper bag, she explained. "I'd like you to verify whether this was the victim's blood."

Doctor Shapiro signed the receipt Glenna handed her for the labeled bag. "I'll get to it as quickly as I can. In the meantime, I've got a few interesting things to tell you. We knew Payestewa had been in a fight, but he was apparently beaten up badly. He had a freshly cracked rib, and contusions I believe were inflicted about twelve hours prior to his death. Also, whoever shot him came to that meeting prepared to kill, or maybe the person was a pro who believed in always being prepared. The bullets I extracted from the body had been modified. The copper-jacketed lead nose of each round was cut in a crisscross pattern so it would expand on impact."

Joseph, standing about six feet behind Glenna, heard the doctor's words clearly. He'd never suspected the fight had occurred that long before Gilbert's death. The news made his stomach clench into a knot. Why hadn't Gil come to him for help as he'd always done? His body shook and for a moment he couldn't say a word. Then as he struggled for control a coldness swept over him, numbing him from the pain and rage. He stepped forward. "Doctor, when will you release my brother's body?"

"By noon tomorrow."

"And his personal effects?"

Wanda glanced at Glenna. "They bury the deceased with his possessions," she explained.

Glenna nodded, remembering. "I'll have to document them and get clearance for this."

Joseph stared at the floor, then glanced up. "If nothing else, may I have his pocketknife? He always carried it with him. I gave it to him when he graduated from high school."

"I don't recall seeing that," Glenna said slowly.

Joseph looked at Glenna, then the doctor. "He kept it in his pocket."

Glenna glanced at the doc. "Let's get the envelope with his effects out of your safe. We'll check, just to make sure."

Glenna followed her to the office, then scattered the items on top of the table. "It's not here," she said, looking at Joseph. "How big was the knife, and did it have any monetary value?"

"It was about three inches long when closed, and it wasn't worth much to anyone except him. It's really not the type of thing someone would bother stealing, and it was too small to use as a weapon."

"Maybe it fell out of his pocket at the crime scene," Glenna suggested. "We'll check with the Navajo police."

They returned to the car, and he rode in silence next to her for twenty minutes. "What's on your mind? Let's have it," she said at last.

"It seems to me that you now have evidence that my brother was *forced* to steal our ceremonial objects. Someone beat him into compliance," he said, his voice tight.

"Whoa! You're jumping to conclusions. We don't *know* that at all!"

"Gilbert had been worked over. Judging from the doc's timeframe, he went to my mother's house soon afterward, took the things he needed, then delivered them. Once he did that, they killed him. It's fairly obvious."

"You're trying to force the pieces to fit. Don't impose your theory on the evidence yet. Wait until the facts themselves reveal what happened."

He took a deep breath, then let it out slowly. "I have one advantage over you. I knew my brother, and this is the only thing that makes sense."

"Your feelings for your brother may be clouding the issue," she said quietly.

The statement cut deeply, but he tried not to show it. "No, not in this case."

Glenna watched him out of the corner of her eye. Instinct and knowledge warned her to be careful. Joseph's emotions were being kept under a tight lid and the pressure was obviously getting to him. Yet if she refused his help, that would create more problems than it would solve. Her actions wouldn't sit well with the *kikmongwi*. The tribe would also be far less likely to cooperate with her if she defied one of the elders. Of course, the capper would be that Joseph would investigate on his own. As an agent and as his friend, she had to do everything in her power to prevent him from doing that.

By the time she pulled into the Navajo police station, she had acknowledged to herself that she was stuck. "Let me get permission to take you to Gilbert's truck. Hopefully you'll be able to find a clue none of us would know to spot."

Before long they were heading outside, a Navajo police officer at their side. "It's at the back of the lot," the officer told her. "We ran all the checks, but have only two new pieces of information to give you. The transistor radio in the motorcycle saddlebags doesn't work and it had a tag from the victim's repair shop taped on it. That's it."

"Did you say motorcycle?" Joseph asked, puzzled.

Glenna started to explain when the officer beside her suddenly spurted forward. "Hey you, stop!" he ordered loudly.

Glenna glanced ahead. A man had rolled the motorcycle off the truck with a plank and was trying to get the engine started. A large hole had been cut in the chain-link fence behind him. "Don't let him get away!" she yelled, breaking into a run.

Chapter Six

Glenna sprinted after the man, cursing herself for not having taken a closer look at the motorcycle. Was there important evidence hidden somewhere in it?

They were almost upon him when the young Hopi gave up trying to start the machine and jumped off. He slipped through the fence quickly and took off across the desert. The stout Navajo officer gave up after a few strides, realizing he didn't have a chance.

Glenna glanced around quickly. "Joseph, help. We can't let him escape!"

Joseph nodded and ducked through the opening in the fence. With the skill of a natural athlete he ran across the desert terrain. Runners were traditionally valued by his tribe and he'd been one of the best. Nowadays, however, he did it mostly for fun or as part of their ceremonies. Hitting his stride, he left Glenna and the officer behind in a matter of seconds.

Joseph kept his mind focused on the pursuit. He would catch up. The thought that this man could be linked to his brother's death gave him strength. Joseph hurtled past the rocks and low clumps of rabbitbrush as he continued the chase, his feet barely touching the ground. Then, as the man cleared a small hillside, Joseph temporarily lost sight of him. Calling upon all of his energy reserves, he pushed himself forward even faster. A moment later, from the crest of the hill, he saw the would-be thief heading toward a cluster of houses.

Joseph took advantage of the downward slope to pick up more speed. Slowly the distance separating them dwindled. It wouldn't be long now, the man was tiring. They ran across a tiny lawn and the man disappeared around the corner of a house. Chest heaving, Joseph followed, then stopped short.

Glenna and the Navajo policeman were there with the thief, who was on the ground, gasping for breath. As Joseph stared in surprise, the officer handcuffed the suspect.

Glenna smiled at Joe, then helped the policeman load their prisoner into a police car. "You can run like the wind, you know that Joseph?" she observed.

Feeling sheepish, he avoided her gaze. "For all the good it did me." He leaned over, hands on his knees, trying to even his breathing.

"Hey, you did a great job. By staying with him, you bought us enough time to get the vehicles and head him off."

"I still don't understand what the motorcycle has to do with Gilbert," Joseph managed.

"We found it in the back of Gilbert's truck, tied down and covered with a tarp. There were no papers on it."

"I don't know what it was doing there. Gil doesn't own a motorcycle."

"I might have some answers after I get a chance to talk to the suspect. Come on." She cocked her head, motioning toward her vehicle. "We'll ride back together. Then I'd like you to look over that cycle and see what you think. Maybe Gilbert bought it without your knowing."

"If he did, it would have had to have been very recently. But even that doesn't make sense. He was broke, or darn near so. I had to loan him some money to get by just two weeks ago."

"Was it enough cash, do you think, to make the purchase?"

"No, I never gave my brother a lump sum. He'd only gamble it away."

They entered the station five minutes later. The Navajo officer was already in the lobby, waiting. Glenna strode up to him. "I'd like the gentleman with me," she said, respecting the Navajo custom for not using names, "to go over the motorcycle as well as the truck. He may be able to spot something for us."

"We'll give him an escort," the policeman replied. "The suspect is in the first room to your left," he added, anticipating her next question.

Even though Joseph had made no attempt to go down the hall, the officer moved in front of him, blocking his path. "You can wait out here," he said. "Someone will take you out to see the motorcycle and truck in a few minutes."

Glenna gave Joseph a nod, then followed another of the officers, Lieutenant Yazzie, to a small room in the back. The young Hopi prisoner had been uncuffed and allowed to sit down.

The first twenty minutes passed slowly. The Hopi man refused counsel, in fact, he refused to say anything at all. Yazzie stared at the small notepad in front of him for a while, then flipped it to the section that pictured a twelve month calendar. With precision, he began penciling over each of the numbers, darkening each. "We'll be here until you tell me what I need to know. I'm on duty anyway, so it doesn't matter to me if it takes all night. Then the next shift will take over for me tomorrow morning."

The Hopi man glowered at him. "I just wanted what was mine."

"What *was* yours?"

The suspect shrugged as if dismissing the question and silence stretched out again. Glenna watched Yazzie work absently on each numbered date. He was already up to April. She had a gut feeling that when he finished all twelve months, he'd just go back to January and start again. Realizing that her fingernails were digging into her palms, she forced herself to stop.

The Hopi stared for what seemed an eternity at the gathering darkness just outside the high, narrow window. She tried not to roll her eyes when Yazzie's pencil moved back to the month of January.

"My name's Don Koinva," the man said at last. "Gilbert was my friend. I wouldn't steal from him."

The Navajo shifted uncomfortably, but said nothing.

"If the man was your friend, then maybe you'll give us some answers," Glenna said. "His brother is outside. How do you think all this makes him feel?"

"I don't know. I haven't asked him," the Hopi man replied in perfect seriousness.

She kicked herself mentally. She should have remembered that in both the Navajo and Hopi cultures, no one *ever* spoke for someone else. It was a breach of that person's rights and a matter that was taken very seriously.

Yazzie gave her a casual look, but even though his face was void of expression, the message was painfully clear. She leaned against the wall and waited. She'd keep her mouth shut and let them proceed at their own pace.

The silence stretched out, then finally Yazzie spoke. "It looks like you're going to be a guest of the Navajo Nation for a while."

"I didn't do anything wrong," the Hopi man answered.

"You damaged the fence, and tried to take what didn't belong to you."

"I'll pay for the repair of the fence, and I didn't steal anything."

"It wasn't because you didn't try. I was told that the motorcycle wouldn't start."

"It's mine. Check the key I left in the ignition. I loaned it to Gilbert because I owed him a favor."

"So why didn't you just tell us? You didn't have to steal what was yours."

"I didn't want to pay a fine for getting it back," he grumbled. "I don't have any papers on the cycle. I bought it from a friend years ago, and never registered it."

"Give us the previous owner's name and we can clear this up," Yazzie said.

"You'll still want me to pay for the registration."

"Better than sitting in jail," Yazzie countered, then changed the subject. "The transistor radio in the saddle-bags, is that yours?"

He shook his head. "I took all my stuff out of the bags before I gave the cycle to Gilbert."

"Did he tell you what he wanted the cycle for?"

"No, just that he needed it."

They were still getting nowhere, she noted, but if Don Koinva was Gilbert's friend, there might be another way he could help. "Can you give us the names of any of the people Gilbert gambled with?"

"He gambled with just about everyone. He was in it for the game, not to make friends."

"Do you have any idea who might have murdered him?" she pressed.

He shook his head. "Whoever beat him up, maybe. When he got the cycle, his face was all swollen up and he had some cuts. Gilbert was always in fights. He'd forget to pay people back and that made them mad."

"Is there anything else you can tell us?" Yazzie insisted. "Like who worked him over, or who he owed money to?"

Koinva shrugged. "That's all I know. Can I go now?"

Yazzie shook his head. "We need to run a few things through our computer first, so you'll be here a little longer. If you think of anything else, just let us know." He handcuffed Koinva, then led him out of the room.

Koinva glanced back at Glenna. "Tell Joseph he's a good runner."

Glenna walked down the hall to meet Joseph. On the way, she checked the report listing everything found inside Gilbert's truck.

A moment later Glenna delivered Koinva's message to Joe, then turned her attention back to business. "Did you get a good look at the truck and cycle?"

He nodded, gesturing toward Harry Benally who was behind one of the desks. "I went out with him, but saw nothing unusual, except for what I've already told you about the motorcycle."

She nodded, disappointed. "Okay, let's go. I'll drop you off at your home."

"Did you find Gil's pocketknife?"

She shook her head. "Sorry."

As Glenna drove away from the station, Joe remained quiet and stared out into the arid darkness. The moon had ducked behind a layer of clouds, and only the glow of the car's headlights cut through the oppressive gloom. Somehow the landscape matched his mood. "What's next on your agenda?"

"Tomorrow I'd like to talk to your brother's neighbors."

"You can use his name," he said pointedly, the strain of the day evident in his voice. "I'm not Navajo."

She exhaled softly. Pride was a difficult thing to deal with, and so was stress. "Also, I'd like to speak to Gilbert's close friends."

"I'll help you as much as I can. My influence might be limited, but it'll be the best asset you've got. Remember that."

"I agree, but don't start thinking you're indispensable, Joe," she warned, uneasiness creeping over her. "If I had to, I'd find a way to do it without you."

They rode in tense silence until she pulled into the driveway of his home twenty minutes later.

He got out of the car and spoke wearily. "I'll meet you tomorrow at your hotel. I'll help you find the people you want to talk to. Then we'll see where we stand and where you want to go from there."

As soon as he shut the door, she pulled out and headed back to town. Joe was trying to make himself an equal partner in the investigation. She didn't blame him, under the circumstances it was natural. Yet he'd have to learn that certain matters entailed a responsibility that could not be shared.

Her own thoughts startled her. After the case was closed, she'd intended to ask for his help on the one matter that was dearest to her heart. Yet he'd have the right to refuse her on the same grounds.

The knowledge stung. Joseph was not part of her future, but he was the only person in a position to help her. Her own world could not give her the answers she needed, but maybe the key she'd searched for was there, in the Hopi Way. She clung to that hope with everything that was feminine in her.

Glenna awoke at six-thirty sharp the next morning. Her alarm hadn't gone off, but she'd never been able to sleep soundly when working on a new case. This time, she had even more than the normal pursuit of evidence to worry her. The danger to the Payestewa family filled her with a sense of urgency.

Joseph's mother was obviously quite ill. She had a terrible feeling the elderly woman would die soon unless the items were returned. Psychology classes in college had proved to her that belief could accomplish things that transcended logic.

She rose reluctantly and dressed warmly in a steel blue sweater, black slacks and a cream wool jacket. Standing before the mirror, she studied her reflection. The new pancake holster made it easier to conceal her pistol, an advantage when dealing with the general public. People often felt uncomfortable around an armed person in street clothes.

She'd just finished a quick breakfast when she heard a knock at the door. "Yes?"

"It's Joe," he said.

She unlocked the door and joined him in the hall. "Let's take my car. While I drive, you can give me directions."

He guided her through the canyon lands until they arrived at the village. Once there, she remembered the way to the dirt road where Gil had lived.

Glenna left the car and walked down the street with Joseph. At first she wasn't sure if her perceptions were right, but by the time they visited the third house, it was obvious. People were choosing to speak to her instead of him. Most would meet them outside, as far from their homes as possible. Then, deliberately ignoring Joseph, and oblivious to the icy wind, they'd answer her questions.

By the time they were finished two hours later, she felt frustrated and so cold she'd stopped feeling parts of her face. She touched her nose to assure herself it was still there, then glanced at Joseph. The lines on his face had deepened. All morning long he'd been snubbed by the people he cared most about, and it wasn't difficult to see the pain he felt. "What a frustrating morning—for both of us," she said gently as they got back into her car.

"At least we found out one thing we didn't know before. People saw Gil carrying a black trash bag the evening before he was killed. If he was handling it as carefully as they say, maybe he had the things he'd taken in there. According to the time the witnesses gave us, it was after he left my mother's house."

"Yes, but it's hardly conclusive. It might mean something, then again not. For all we really know he could have been carrying leaky garbage."

Joseph thought for a moment, then spoke. "Something occurred to me earlier as we were walking around. The person who had Gil steal the *Masau'u* costume must have gathered enough information about our village to know whom to approach. If he hadn't specifically asked for those items, Gil would have claimed that he didn't have access to ceremonial objects. It would have been easy to convince most people that only the leaders of religious societies knew where those were kept and that someone with Gil's history would not be taken into their confidence. That makes me think there's a very motivated, and highly knowledgeable collector behind this."

"There is some sense to that. The buyer would not only have to know a great deal about the Hopi religion, but also be in a position to have learned who the clan leaders are. Of course it is possible Gilbert volunteered that information."

Joseph shook his head. "No way. It just isn't a subject any of us discuss. Besides, if someone had asked Gil about his religious society or our mother's or father's, he would have shrugged it off saying that he'd never bothered to learn about stuff like that. It wouldn't have been a lie, either."

"All right, then let's go from the standpoint that the buyer knew about these objects and who might have access to them. Where could Gilbert have met someone with specific knowledge of that kind?"

He thought about it. "Anthropologists must have been coming to the villages to study our ways for decades, and art dealers are always hanging around. It's got to be someone who's an expert. Keep in mind that if Gil thought he could have pawned off a replica, I'm certain he would have. There are ways to make forgeries look authentic. He could have taken it to one of our artisans, for instance."

"Have there been any dealers or professors visiting on a regular basis lately?"

"We have a steady flow year round, but let me check with the cultural center. A friend of mine, Clyde, works for the tribe watching tourists and trying to spot trouble before it happens. He's sharp, but I doubt he'd tell you anything he couldn't substantiate legally. He likes to be careful. I've known him for years, though, so I'm sure I can get him to talk to me. He'd be able to tell me who seemed to ask too many questions, or looked as if he might be inclined to record or take photos."

"Okay, you follow that up. In the meantime I'll have the motel in the area give me a list of all their guests this past year. I'll make a note of any names who show up frequently, and have them checked out through Bureau files. The Latent Descriptor Index in the Identification Section's computer compares the details of a crime under investigation to the techniques used by criminals already in our files. If it finds any similarities, it'll suggest a suspect and provide us with fingerprints."

"It sounds promising."

"I'm not just going to sit around and hope for the best, though. I'm going to start talking to art dealers in this area." She started the engine, and turned back onto the main road toward Keams Canyon. She'd elected to stay at the motel there because of the availability of telephones. "I'll drop you off back at your car, then you can—" Hearing a call come over her radio, she reached for the mike. A second later the Hopi police captain's voice came over the air.

"We've received an anonymous tip about the stolen artifacts. They're at a village on Third Mesa," he said, giving her the name of the village and the location. "I'm on my way there now. I thought you'd want to come."

"Of course I do." She reached for the map in her glove compartment.

Joseph sat ramrod straight. "I can get you there more quickly than your map."

"You're not coming, sorry. I'm dropping you off right here. It isn't too far for you to walk back to Gil's home."

"No. I'm going one way or another. I'll beg, borrow or steal the transportation I need, but I *will* be there."

She gave him a hard look. He wasn't bluffing. She could see the determination etched on his face. "All right. I don't have time to argue, so make yourself useful. Tell me exactly how to find the house we're looking for."

They sped down a two-lane road to the third spur extending out from Black Mesa. A short time later they approached the new village at the foot of the rocky escarpment. Two police cars were parked a short distance from a small cinder block house.

"Stay out of the way, Joseph, or I'll have you arrested. Is that clear?"

"My interest is only in the items. Any criminals are your responsibility."

"Good. We agree. So when we get there..."

A sudden blast rocked the earth, tossing two policemen to the ground. As the shock wave slammed against her vehicle, Glenna hit the brakes and swerved, but the explosion threw the car out of control.

Chapter Seven

Debris slammed down over the roof like giant hail stones. Glenna regained control of the car and braked immediately. She ducked below the level of the seat pulling Joseph down with her. The sounds continued for several seconds, then an ominous quiet descended. She peered out cautiously. Bright orange flames licked skyward in an erratic, hellish dance that all but obscured the entrance to the house.

She sensed rather than saw Joseph trying to sit up. "Stay down and open the door on your side. We'll use the car to shield us."

Joseph slipped out, Glenna a split second behind him. "Wait for me," she said. "I've got to get those policemen out of danger."

Moving forward in a crouch, she scrambled to the side of the officer closest to her. The officer appeared dazed, but unhurt. Draping his arm over her shoulder, she hurried with him back behind the closest patrol car. Out of the corner of her eye, she saw Joseph and someone else moving toward the other man. The police captain and Joseph returned a moment later steadying a young Hopi cop who seemed more embarrassed than injured.

The captain glanced down the gravel street and saw some residents hurrying toward the scene. "The people are anxious to try and put out the fire, but we can't let them approach just yet." He nodded his approval as one of the officers hurried to intercept a group cautiously moving closer.

Keeping low, Joseph moved to Glenna's side. "I have to go inside that building. If the mask is in there, it's my duty to do all I can to save it."

"You can't! Look at that place!" she said, cocking her head toward the billowing smoke streaming from the door.

"This is his decision to make. He has much at stake." The captain nodded to Joseph. "There's a fire extinguisher in the back of my car. Maybe you can clear a path inside through the back."

Suddenly a second explosion rocked the ground, nearly knocking them off their feet.

"Like I said, going inside is not a good idea," Glenna repeated, crouching behind the car with the others.

"You better wait, Payestewa," Captain Kywanwytewa conceded. "The gods will decide the outcome of what happens here today. It's out of your hands now."

Joseph nodded, but said nothing. His brother had unleashed a nightmare. No matter where he turned there was only chaos. He struggled for the discipline that sustained him as a Hopi. Thoughts had power and needed to be channeled down the right paths to achieve results. He could not yield to his fears.

A Hopi patrolman came rushing up from where a group of people had gathered some distance away. "Captain, gotta talk to you."

The captain met with the officer, and exchanged a few quick words. "I have an interesting development," he said, returning to where Glenna and Joseph stood. "Someone was seen staggering out the back door just before the second explosion. My man recognized him as Lewis Secakuku. It appears that the impact and some flying debris caught him before he could get away. He's out cold. My men are transporting him to the hospital right now."

"I know Lewis," Joseph admitted. "He was a friend of Gilbert's. We all went to the same high school. They were freshmen when I was a senior."

The captain shot him a speculative glance, but remained silent.

"How badly hurt is he?" Glenna asked.

"It's hard to tell, but he was unconscious when they dragged him away from the scene of the explosion. The doctors at the clinic will notify us if he wakes up."

Joseph's eyes remained on the burning building. No more explosions had occurred, but fire had spread to both ends of the cinder block structure. If the mask and robe were inside, he had almost no chance of finding them intact now.

Seconds ticked by with agonizing slowness. "Unless people are allowed to work on the fire soon," Joseph said at last, "it's likely to spread to the neighboring houses. All it'll take is one spark."

The captain stared at the blaze, which was already starting to diminish. "Go ahead and give them the okay."

Joseph jogged toward a group of villagers who'd been waiting for permission to proceed. Without hesitation, he shed his jacket and worked alongside the men fighting the blaze.

Three garden hoses were linked in order to reach the house. Water coursed inside through holes where windows had once been. Joseph squinted against the sting of smoke that enveloped the building. The fire was being suppressed quickly. The second there was a clear path leading inside, he'd have to risk entering. There was still a chance, though admittedly very slight, that the mask and robe had been spared.

It took another ten minutes before the last glowing ember was extinguished. Joe went inside with the captain and Glenna flanking him. Glenna photographed the small building's interior, then started collecting evidence at the site of each of the explosions.

The captain stayed beside Joseph. "You know the mask and robe better than I do. If you see anything that indicates they were here, then let me know."

Joseph glanced around the acrid-smelling, humid interior, now illuminated by a battery-powered lantern as well as sunlight. "Who used this building?" he asked, studying what appeared to be the remains of someone's woodworking shop.

"No one recently. It was part of Riley Sakmoisi's shop, but he's been sick for the last two years so it's been abandoned. Since he sold off most of his tools, there was nothing here of any value."

Joseph crouched by a badly scorched table and searched through the debris, poking and separating the soot and ashes. Unable to find anything there, he continued around the room.

An hour later he was finally willing to admit he'd done all he could. "I don't see anything that indicates the robe and mask were ever here, but that doesn't mean anything. There's not much left to sift through."

"Then it's time to leave," the captain said with an air of finality.

Joseph nodded and started to follow the captain out. Suddenly he froze in midstep. On the wall, held by water left from the hoses, was one black-tipped, white feather.

Sensing something was wrong, the captain stopped and followed Joseph's gaze. "Do you recognize that?"

"I'm almost certain it came from the mask. The feathers used on it are very distinctive," he answered. Reaching down, he lifted up a large piece of the ruined door. Beneath were several more feathers, a piece of leather, and the crushed, flame-charred remnants of a mask. "It looks like we were too late."

"So the objects were here," Glenna said softly. Her gaze drifted over Joseph, knowing the impossible weight the newfound knowledge placed on his shoulders. He stood tall, despite the brutal awakening, reaching out to no one for help. Her heart went out to him. She understood that kind of pride, but also knew the loneliness it carried.

The captain's hand-held radio brought her out of her musings. He stepped away from Glenna and Joseph, and exchanged a few words with someone at the other end. While she waited, Glenna placed the remnants of the ceremonial items into storage bags.

"Secakuku seems to be regaining consciousness," the captain said, after finishing his conversation. "We better get to the hospital quickly. The doctors have no idea how long he'll stay awake in his condition."

They headed to their cars, and with Captain Kywanwytewa in the lead, sped toward Keams Canyon. "Don't give up, Joe," she said, never taking her eyes off the road. "We might be able to get some answers from this man."

"For my family, the battle's over. I was more interested in righting the wrong than in catching the criminal. Our Way teaches that justice is inescapable. The criminals behind the theft can't avoid paying the consequences for their actions. Unfortunately my family will also be penalized now that the objects have been destroyed."

She started to reply, then stopped. A moment later she began again, measuring her words carefully. "I don't want you to get your hopes up, Joe, but I think we're being purposely misled. You sifted through everything inside that building, yet all you found were a few feathers and a portion of a mask. Don't you think that at least some part of the robe and the belt should have survived, too?"

"You're right," he said slowly as the import of her words sank in. "The belt is decorated with hooves, bones and shells. Even if nothing else had survived the fire, the shells should have. They're made out of calcium carbonate. That's like limestone." An immense feeling of relief flooded over him. He gave her a weary but grateful smile. "I owe you one, Glenna. You've given me reason to keep searching."

"We're up against some very clever and ruthless people," she said. "Maybe Secakuku will be able to tell us more about them."

They arrived at the hospital a while later. Joseph and Glenna entered the building a few feet behind the captain. Before they even reached the desk, a nurse hurried out to meet them.

"He slipped out of bed and escaped, Captain. A deputy and one of our orderlies are out looking for him now."

"Did he say anything when he regained consciousness?" Glenna asked.

"A few words, something about a 'short fuse', but it was very difficult to understand him. Then he seemed to go to sleep, so I stepped over to another patient behind a screen in the emergency room. When I came back less than a minute later, he was gone."

While Joseph and the remaining deputies joined the search for Secakuku, Glenna followed the captain down the hall. Working together in one of the doctor's offices, they searched through Secakuku's personal effects.

"I was hoping we'd find a clue among his things, but it looks like we struck out," Glenna said. "We're not completely empty-handed, though. I've got a theory about the fire and the ceremonial objects presumed lost in it," she said, and recounted her conclusions.

The captain nodded thoughtfully. "I agree with you, but do you think the trail ends with Secakuku?"

"Unfortunately that's what we still need to find out. We know he set off the explosion, but was that to protect himself or someone else? And what connection did he have to Gilbert Payestewa?" She shrugged and shook her head. "It's too bad we didn't get here before the man got away."

"My deputies will be searching for Lewis Secakuku in every village and on every mesa. If we get a lead, we'll let you know right away."

"I appreciate that, Captain. And on a related matter, I'd like to meet with you at the station in about an hour. I want to get a list of art dealers in this area who might be tempted to deal with objects of questionable background. Also, I'll need a copy of Gilbert Payestewa's record. If it's possible, I'd like your people to cross-reference and find out who else was arrested along with him. That might lead me to some of his gambling associates."

"I'll have an officer working on it by the time you arrive."

Glenna strode back to the lobby. She'd have to check with Agent Nakai to see if he could send a courier to pick up the evidence they'd gathered at the fire. Maybe he'd also received word about the lab tests they'd already requested. It was a bit soon, but she could get lucky. As she reached the lobby, she saw Joseph coming down the hall from the clinic side.

He came up to her quickly. "They've released Gilbert's body to my family and the job of ritually preparing him for burial falls to my father and me. Could you give me a ride to Gil's home? My father is probably already there."

Throughout the drive, Joseph remained quiet. Glenna respected his silence though a dozen questions raced through her mind. She couldn't hold off on the investigation now, even if she'd wanted to. If the rituals that comprised their burial kept Joseph away for very long, she'd have to proceed without him. Perhaps the village leader could assign someone to act as an interpreter if one was needed in the interim.

As they neared the village Joseph shifted in his seat to face her more squarely. "Normally I'd stay with my family for a while, but these aren't ordinary circumstances. Since most of our time has been taken up by the requirement of the medical investigator, it's imperative that we complete the burial before sundown. By tomorrow morning my duties will be finished. I'll go speak with Clyde at the Cultural Center then and see what I can learn about recent visitors to our villages."

"I appreciate your help, Joe, but I don't want to rush you away from your family at a time like this. Maybe I should ask the village leader to appoint someone else as my interpreter for a few days."

"I don't think he'd allow it. Remember that as a people, we don't view death as a tragedy. I'll miss my brother, but neither my village nor my family will tolerate having me neglect my duties because of what's happened. My brother has gone to a better place. From there, he can still help our tribe by bringing rain and making our farms fruitful. That's the way we've been taught to deal with this."

"All right. You know how to reach me when you're ready."

He stepped out of the car. "I'll see you tomorrow sometime."

He stood outside in the cold, needing more time to himself before he faced the others. As Glenna's car disappeared from view, he found himself wishing she could have stayed. Being around her might have made the task ahead of him a little easier.

Almost as quickly as it had formed, he banished the thought from his mind. He had a duty to perform. As he turned around ready to enter the house, his mother stood at the door.

"Gilbert!" Her face broke out in a wide smile. "I knew it was a mistake. You're all right!"

Chapter Eight

Joseph turned around without thinking and looked behind him. No one was there, of course. It was obvious that his mother, in her wish to see her youngest son, had mistaken him for his brother. Finally, as the elderly woman came toward him, Joseph forced himself to respond. "Mother, it's me, Joseph," he said gently, then led her back inside the house.

It was hours before Gilbert's body was prepared. A masklike layer of cotton, with openings at the eyes and nose, covered his face. Prayer feathers were tied to the string that held it in place. His body was bound with yucca strips and wrapped in blankets secured by ropes.

With Gilbert's body fastened over the back of a sturdy horse, they led the small procession to an unmarked grave on the slope of the mesa. After the grave was sealed, Joseph placed a double-stick *paho,* prayer stick, with painted green sticks and black points near the grave. While his mother and aunts set other prayer offerings above the grave, he positioned a single eagle-breath feather on the west side. A line of cornmeal pointing that direction indicated the continuation of the road to the Underworld.

He found comfort in the rituals. At least these made sense and held purpose and order.

His father came to stand beside him. "By sunrise, Gilbert's *hik'si* will rise and travel to the Underworld. He will find peace now."

Joseph was surprised when his mother approached the grave and pronounced the ritual words releasing her son. Her eyes were clear and her expression one of sorrow as she came toward Joseph and placed one hand on his shoulder. "I know my youngest son is dead. I wanted to forget, but it seems I won't be allowed to escape that knowledge."

"We all need you now, you know. Father most of all," Joseph said as they returned to the village.

The elderly woman nodded. "That's why I'm going to fight this and hold on. I know you won't fail us. You never have."

The words had been meant as encouragement, but Joseph felt their weight. As they walked through the solitary roads, he thought of Glenna and all she was doing to find answers. Just having her around to talk to helped him bear the burden he carried. It occurred to him just how alone he'd been up to now. Even in the midst of everything that was happening in his life, thoughts of her filled him with a host of other gentler emotions. He couldn't help but wonder what it meant and where it all would lead.

GLENNA DROVE to the Hopi police headquarters. She'd met with Justin Nakai earlier, but that meeting had been disappointing. All she'd managed to learn was that lab tests on the paper ashes found at Gilbert's murder were still pending. Maybe she'd have better luck with Captain Kywanwytewa. When she arrived at the station a short time later, she was ushered to the captain's office.

He pulled out a chair from near the wall, offering it to her, then walked to his desk. "Still no sign of Secakuku. It seems he has few acquaintances in the area, and we're having to come up with new places to check. But I pulled the paperwork on the break-in at Gilbert Payestewa's workshop. I thought you might like to see the official report."

Glenna took the folder from his hands. "Thanks, Captain." She read it, then glanced up. "I'm interested in this vehicle witnesses claim to have seen in the area."

"The black, four-wheel-drive Jeep," the captain acknowledged. "Unfortunately that's all we have. We questioned everyone in the area, and then asked Sara Payestewa, Joseph, and his parents. No one could tell us anything about it, or who the driver might have been."

"It's too bad that the impressions on that notepad we found in Gilbert's office didn't pan out. I was hoping that would give us a lead."

The captain turned his palms upward. "That's the way it goes sometimes. All it ended up being was a repair order for a TV." He went to the top of his file cabinet and retrieved another folder. "I've also got Gilbert Payestewa's arrest record for you."

She studied the rap sheet. "Were you able to cross-reference and find the names of other suspects who were arrested along with him?"

Pressing the intercom button on his desk, the captain asked the secretary to bring in a copy of the printout. Moments later he handed her what she'd asked for. "This is the list. We categorized it by dates. As you can see, most of the names appear only once or twice."

Glenna studied the paper. There were two names that caught her immediate attention. One was the man who'd been arrested for trying to steal back the cycle he'd loaned Gilbert. The other belonged to a Navajo who'd been repeatedly arrested with Gil. "I'll follow these up as soon as possible. What I'd like to do first is check out the art dealers in your area. Can you give me the names of any you think might be tempted to deal in black market objects?"

"There's one who comes to mind," he said, jotting down a name and address out of a phone book. "My guess is that she's legit, but you never know. If the price was high enough...." He shrugged.

"Does she have a record?"

"Frances Martinez was arrested once, about three years ago, for selling stolen merchandise. She claimed she didn't know the pieces were hot, and after everything was returned to the rightful owners, the charges were dropped."

Glenna drove to Keams Canyon, and went to Martinez's shop. Even though it was after hours, the woman was still at the store.

"Frankly, I'm surprised you're here," Glenna said, after introducing herself. "I have your home address and I was almost tempted to try that first."

"I spend more time here than I ever do there. I'm single and I've put everything I've got into this business." She led the way to a small back office and offered Glenna a chair. "Now tell me what I can do for you."

"Do you know a man by the name of Gilbert Payes-tewa?"

Her gaze was wary. "He was murdered, right? I believe that's what the newspaper said." She leaned back in her chair, and studied Glenna cautiously. "If you're here now, then you must think it's linked to art objects possibly stolen from one of the villages."

Glenna decided to play it out. She remained quiet, neither confirming nor denying. Most people found that unnerving and would eventually start talking just to break the silence.

"I knew Gilbert," she admitted at last, "but I never bought anything from him."

"Did he ever approach you with items to sell?" Glenna had sensed the woman's intelligence. She was someone who weighed everything and would not easily incriminate herself.

"His wife made some nice jewelry, but that's not what most of my buyers are looking for. I deal in pottery, and kachina dolls, the unusual or antique ones." She hesitated briefly, then in an instant that flicker of uncertainty was gone and her expression closed.

"If you know something, now's the best time to tell me."

Frances nodded slowly. "What I could tell you would only be based on my own observations. I don't know anything you could take to court."

"Why don't you let me decide that."

Martinez stood and began to pace. "Gilbert could have made lots of money, if he'd been willing to steal from the tribe. If he'd been involved in that, he would have been much better off financially."

"Let's say, hypothetically, that he was stealing. Who around here can come up with enough cash to entice him to do that?"

"Not me, if that's what you had in mind. It would almost have to be a private collector, but the ones in this area have limited resources. The rest of us make our living trading with the Hopi so we can't afford to do anything that might alienate them. If there's ever any hint of impropriety, the tribe could shut us down."

"Still, thefts do happen. There would have to be buyers somewhere."

She stopped pacing and faced Glenna. "If I knew more, I'd tell you. The last thing I want is trouble with you guys."

Glenna nodded and accepted Martinez's word. She asked the shop owner to remain available should she be needed again and Martinez repeated that she was nearly always at the store. They parted amicably.

As Glenna drove back to the motel, she considered Frances Martinez as a suspect. The woman was either a natural liar or had been very open with her. Whatever the truth, Glenna admired what she perceived as the woman's directness. Being straightforward was a quality people were sometimes hesitant to demonstrate around an FBI agent.

Joseph certainly didn't have that problem. He had managed to get under her skin right away with his honesty, and it was having an effect on her.

It was getting increasingly difficult to push him from her thoughts for any length of time. His loyalty to those he loved made her heart ache with longing. Had anyone, even Brad, cared that much for her? Her ill-fated marriage had taught her one very important fact of life. A man usually wanted a woman who'd love him with her whole heart and soul. Yet few knew how to give with the totality they asked for. Now when she'd finally met someone who was capable of that, there were other factors that were destined to keep them apart. What made it worse was knowing that there was nothing she could do about it.

Glenna walked inside her motel room and prepared for bed. With a sigh, she crawled beneath the covers. The bed seemed impossibly large and empty. She was a strong woman, but strong women needed to be held, too. Brushing the feeling aside, she drifted off to a restless sleep.

Glenna awoke before dawn the next morning. She had a plan in mind by the time she stepped out of the shower and that made her feel much better. After a quick breakfast, she stopped by the motel's office and obtained the guest register for the last three months. She then drove to the motel adjacent to the Cultural Center and repeated the procedure. She was glad to note that the visitors weren't as varied as they were frequent. It wouldn't take long to identify them.

Pleased with the results, she headed to the Cultural Center's office. With any luck, she'd find Joe there. She'd just entered the courtyard when she saw Joe coming out of an entrance marked Employees Only.

Seeing her, he smiled and walked over. "I've got good news. Clyde's got a ledger where he keeps notes on visitors who catch his attention. He'll let me know if any fit the profile of the person we're looking for."

"That's great." She filled him in on the list she'd received from the captain. "There are only two names that stand out. One, since he was often arrested with Gilbert. The other, because he's the man I questioned at the Navajo police station." She gave him the names.

"I know Don Koinva, of course, but I've never met the Navajo." He stood there for a moment and appeared to consider something. "I might be of help to you with Don. You won't be able to get any information from him that might put him in danger. He won't do that for a stranger, particularly a cop who's not from the reservation. But he might for me."

"Okay, let's go. My car's parked outside. Koinva told the captain he didn't know why Gil was beat up, but he probably has other information that could help us. If Gil had a big gambling debt, he could have found himself being manipulated into almost anything."

"Gil always owed money, but around here it isn't like you see in the movies. People work things out by trading services if they don't have the money. Hoods aren't waiting to beat up a person who's welshed."

"Yet there were lots of fights," she commented without specifically mentioning Gilbert.

"Well, in my brother's case, that's because he liked proving himself in that way. He was good with his fists and could always make the other guy look far worse." His voice was flat. "Which clinches one thing. If Gil was beaten up, it wasn't a fair fight. Either he was up against someone built like a mountain, or he was outnumbered. And there's something else, too. The men against him must have known exactly what they were doing to inflict all the damage they did."

She concluded from his expression that he had prepared his brother's body for burial. Realizing what fulfilling that duty must have cost him personally, her respect for him grew. "I wish there was something I could say that would make things easier on you." She reached out and placed one hand on his forearm.

Her gesture must have taken him by surprise. The quick unguarded look he gave her betrayed his pain. But there was also an awareness of her touch, and of her as a woman.

His response made her heart race, but this was no time to indulge in those feelings. Reluctantly she pulled her hand away. "There's something that occurred to me," she said, forcing their minds back to business. "There has always been tension between the Hopis and the Navajos. Getting ceremonial items like the ones that were stolen could be one way for a Navajo to get even for what they term the 'Hopi Land Grab'. Someone who had been forced to relocate because of the boundary question would certainly have a grudge to settle."

"Gil would have cut off his hands before he turned those objects over to a Navajo. He barely spoke to them," he said flatly.

"Maybe his opinion was swayed by the leverage used against him." She opened the car door and slipped inside.

"My brother wasn't stupid. If they threatened his family, for instance, he would have found a way to appear to cooperate while holding a few cards up his sleeve. I can't see him meekly handing over the objects. That's not like him at all."

"He may not have had a choice. He was outmatched, like you said before."

Joe shrugged, but instead of answering he gave her directions to the shop where Don Koinva worked. "How do you keep your work from getting to you? Your time is spent dealing with the worst side of human nature."

"Yes, but there's also a sense of rightness about my work that appeals to me," she admitted. "You can go through life closing your eyes to all the inequities you see daily, or you can try to do something about it. I can't change the world, but maybe I can make it a little more livable. I restore order, and in that way I'm making a contribution. When I look back someday, I'd like to know that my life was something more than long."

Ten minutes later they arrived at a small warehouse at the edge of the village limits. Don Koinva sat outside on a large rock, eating a sandwich. He smiled at Joseph, but the expression faded instantly the second he spotted Glenna. Jumping up, he ran for the warehouse door as if he'd been shot from a cannon.

"Not again," Glenna groaned, springing from the car.

Chapter Nine

Don Koinva disappeared through the dark warehouse door, with Glenna and Joseph five seconds behind him.

Wary of a trap, Glenna forced Joe to slow down as they entered the building. Large slat-sided wooden crates filled the warehouse. Hearing footsteps, they flattened their backs against the wall. Light appeared somewhere across the cavernous room, and Glenna heard the sound of a door opening. Cautiously, they moved toward the light. As she approached the partially opened door leading out the back of the warehouse, she placed a hand on her 9 mm Sig Saur. She was ready to pull it clear of the holster at the slightest hint of danger. Joseph, a few steps behind her, stopped and watched.

Glenna cleared the door, then stared down the back road toward a row of houses. "He sure must like to run."

"Let's see if we can spot him." Joseph suggested. Glancing at the ground, he tugged at her sleeve, calling her attention to the tracks.

She smiled slowly. So Koinva hadn't gone anywhere. He was only trying to fool them into thinking he had.

"It looks like neither of us will be catching him this time," Joseph said in a normal tone, then winked.

"Let's go back to the car," Glenna said, playing along. "If we drive around for a bit maybe we'll spot him."

"Good idea," Joseph answered, walking back with her through the warehouse.

Glenna tossed Joseph the keys, but as they stepped outside, she quickly ducked back to the side of the building. There, out of view of anyone still inside, she crouched low and waited.

Joseph opened the passenger door and slammed it loudly knowing Koinva would be inside listening. He then walked around to the driver's side, started the engine and drove off with a spray of gravel.

Glenna ducked down behind a barrel close to the door. Five minutes went by, but she kept perfectly still. Finally a familiar face peered out of the warehouse doorway and then emerged, still carrying his sandwich.

"Don't run, Mr. Koinva," she said, clasping his arm quickly. "All we want to do is talk."

Koinva looked at her, surprise mirrored on his features. "I haven't done anything," he protested.

"I'm not here to cause problems for you," Glenna assured. "Relax and finish your lunch." She wanted to put him at ease, but the man continued to regard her suspiciously.

A minute later Joseph appeared from around the building. He walked up, nodded to Glenna, and sat on the ground. He regarded his brother's friend casually. "You ran well the other day," he said, as if oblivious to the reason they'd come.

"So did you. You're in good shape. Gilbert said you liked to stay fit." He grew thoughtful as he took a large bite of his sandwich. "You know, he often said he wished he could have been more like you. But he knew he could never be anyone but himself."

"That was the way it was meant to be," Joseph said.

Glenna noticed that Joe was trying to keep Don Koinva's attention focused away from her. He had a plan in mind, though she wasn't certain exactly what it was yet.

Finally Joseph spoke. "Gilbert called you *ikwaatsi,* his good friend, but he's gone now. If he was here, he'd want you to help me. Will you do it? Will you tell me who, if anyone, covered Gil's bets when he was broke? His gambling caused him problems and now I've got to undo what he's done."

"I understand that," Don answered. "You won't tell anyone I spoke to you?"

"No one."

He glanced at Glenna and shook his head. "Maybe later."

"No one has to know you helped," she assured.

Koinva shook his head. "No, thanks. Who of my tribe believes promises from the government? I'll talk to Joe alone, or not at all."

Joseph glanced at her and shrugged, making it clear that he was leaving it up to her.

She'd always hated the good ol' boy bonding, and this new version didn't appeal much to her, either. Yet Joe's approach was getting more results than hers, despite her training.

"All right," she conceded at length. Pride wasn't an issue now. Results were all that mattered, and this was the fastest way of getting some.

She retraced Joseph's path around the building. The car was parked down the street. Finally after about five minutes, Joseph joined her. "We got some good leads. He told me about a white man who runs the biggest gambling operations in the area. He's supposed to have some very powerful backers. Koinva said that Gil played cards on the man's boat on Lake Powell and worked for him on occasion to pay off what he owed. Secakuku worked for the guy, too. Don didn't know the man's name or what the name of the boat was, but he suggested we speak to the Navajo man you were looking for, Pete Atcitty. I was told he doesn't speak much English, but I speak Navajo so I should be able to help."

The drive to Chinle where Pete Atcitty lived was longer than she expected. The barren, rock-strewn desert looked chillingly isolated as snow flurries began to fall. "How does anyone get through these roads when it snows?"

"Sometimes tractors and horses have to be sent to pull cars out," he said matter-of-factly.

She shook her head as she stared at the road. "If no one knew to look for you things could really get rough."

"You have a car radio, but even without that, you have nothing to worry about."

"Are you kidding? Without it, we could be frozen solid by the time someone finally drove by."

"No, ma'am, you wouldn't freeze. I personally guarantee I'd do whatever was necessary to make sure you stayed warm."

Glenna caught his eyes as she glanced over and felt her cheeks burn. "If I pretended that I had no idea what you meant, would you believe me?"

"I may not be the winner of an Albert Einstein think-alike contest, but I'm not *that* dim."

She chuckled, but avoided his gaze. "Okay, never mind. The snow's stopping, so you don't have to worry anymore."

"Who worried?"

It was good to see him smile. It reminded her of college days. Unfortunately her feelings for him had matured and were more dangerous now under the present circumstances than they'd ever been. Something was happening between them, and neither of them was ready for it. She could not allow herself to get sidetracked. She'd learned self-discipline over the years, and it was time she started exercising it.

They rode in comfortable silence for the next twenty minutes. Despite the relaxed air she tried to project, she was extremely aware of Joseph as he sat beside her. With his legs stretched out before him, the casual angle of his hips and the masculinity just beneath the faded jeans were enough to tempt any woman's imagination. With a burst of sheer willpower, she forced herself to focus on the road.

They arrived at Atcitty's house, an unfinished, gray stucco frame dwelling, a while later. She'd started to get out, when Joe put his hand on her arm. "If you want him to cooperate, you'd be better off waiting here for a bit."

"In the car? Why?"

"It's the way of the Navajos. You don't go up to the door until you're invited." He gestured toward the side of the house where a woman was hanging laundry in the icy breeze. "Someone will come out in a minute."

True to what Joseph had said, Atcitty came out seconds later. He waited by the front door.

"That's the invitation, though a guarded one."

Glenna walked up to the door, Joseph half a step behind her. She pulled out her badge and added, "I'd like to ask you a few questions." The man looked at her incomprehensively, so she asked Joseph to translate.

The man nodded, then led the way inside the house. He sat across from them behind a Formica kitchen table and regarded her in silence.

Glenna formulated her questions simply, then waited for Joseph to translate. After learning that Lewis Secakuku and Gilbert were frequent visitors at his games, she tried to find out about any other close associates Joseph's brother might have had. Atcitty, however, claimed that Gilbert hadn't made any friends. According to him, the only person Gilbert was ever friendly with at the games was Secakuku.

"Ask him about the game on Lake Powell."

Atcitty shook his head in response to Joseph's question.

"Tell him that unless he cooperates, I'll have him picked up by the Navajo police and questioned at the station," she insisted. "It's up to him."

As Joseph translated, anger flashed in Atcitty's eyes and his arm flew out as if to strike her. In the blink of an eye, Joseph intercepted him, grabbing the man's index finger and bending it back.

Glenna recognized Joseph's defensive move. Radical extension of the index finger could incapacitate any man, regardless of his size. It strained the digital nerve on the front of the hand, while simultaneously pinching the median and radial nerves on the back. The intense pain would then travel along other nerves from his shoulder into his neck.

When Joseph released him a moment later, Atcitty held his injured hand close to him. Glenna quickly had Joe repeat her question.

Joseph translated the answer. "He says that it doesn't pay to give out names, particularly to those who aren't of his tribe."

"Tell him that he can take his choice of Navajo cops at the police station."

It took twenty minutes before they could extract the necessary information. From Atcitty's tone and the frequent use of the word *bilagáana*, the Navajo word for white person, it wasn't hard to guess the focus of their conversation. She was nearly certain Atcitty was using very colorful language to describe what he thought of Joseph's alliance with the FBI. Giving Glenna a vicious look, Atcitty finally scribbled down an address.

Joseph took the small piece of paper and slid it across to her. "He claims that Gil used to drive illegal liquor onto the Navajo Nation for an Anglo with red hair. He doesn't know the man's name. All he's got is the address where the booze is kept. He says that if we find that man, we'll have all the answers we need."

As they left the house Glenna was acutely aware of the vast gulf that separated her from Joseph's world. This was the only time she'd ever conducted an interview exclusively through an interpreter and she couldn't deny a strong feeling of isolation. She wondered if Joe had felt that way when he'd left the reservation for the first time.

"What's wrong? Do you resent having to depend on my help?"

"No, you handled things very well. Dealing with Atcitty just reminded me of all the differences separating your culture from mine."

"It's harder on the whites to come to the reservation than it is on us when we leave," he said, answering her unspoken question. "Most of us are bilingual, though very few whites speak our language. We're also more attuned to what to expect."

He watched the shoulders of the road for foraging jackrabbits as they drove. "The address Atcitty gave us isn't far from here. It's near Ganado. We passed through there on the way. Are we going there next?"

She shook her head. "This is one place I'll have to go without you. Since your presence isn't necessary, I'd be endangering you without sufficient cause."

"There is an advantage to having me along," he countered. "I can provide you with an excellent cover that will decrease the risk you're taking. If you stake that place out and use the cops to help, you'll probably tip your hand. People get to know who the cops are really fast around here. If you're parking with a local man, they'll just think we have something romantic in mind, and never give it a second thought."

"You may have a point," she conceded.

"Once you're ready to follow a delivery truck, I can also guide you into the reservation and, even more important, back out. If the Navajo police are involved, they'll want to make a bust right away and that's likely to leave you without the leads you need. You're interested in far more than liquor smuggling. With me along, we can tail them wherever they go. Then, if we get spotted, I can always say I was taking you out into the desert to see the stars."

She gave him a long look. Joe's intelligence and aptitude had qualified him for every honors program there'd been back in college. His mind, now mature and deductive, was sharper than ever. She questioned him. "What if they don't believe you?"

"That's a risk, of course, but we'd still have an ace in the hole. If we're up against a wall, I can admit that Gil was my brother. They'll see the resemblance, I'm sure, once I point it out. I'll say that I'm trying to find the red-haired man Gil worked for since he was one of the people my brother owed money to. I'll explain that I'm trying to square things so they won't hassle his widow. Considering my brother's money troubles, I'm sure it's a story they'll believe."

"Okay, you're on," she said after a minute. "You'll go with me and we'll stake out the warehouse. If we get spotted, we'll pose as lovers."

"It does have a nice ring to it, don't you think?"

She swallowed involuntarily. "The operative word here is *pose*. Those people could have *guns* and if we get caught in a shoot-out, you might lose very dear parts of your anatomy."

"If we're going to pass ourselves off as lovers, you're going to have to be a little friendlier," he said. Joe saw the icy look she shot him and started to laugh. "No one's dared to tease you recently, I see."

She smiled slowly. "Okay, I'll prove I'm a good sport by not hitting you. Instead I'll buy a big stuffed ape, then I'll call it Joseph and rip the stuffing out of it."

Minutes later she took the turn leading to Keams Canyon. "I'm going to make a quick stop by the motel and pick up my surveillance equipment." Shortly afterward, they were on their way to Ganado again.

Joe had warned her that the warehouse was on the outskirts of town. She'd expected it to be a lonely place five miles from nowhere, and she wasn't wrong. The old portable building had been hauled in and set up at the base of a small hill. The only illumination around came from lights that had been installed near the driveway. Two cars were parked there, but the sliding doors that led into the building were closed. An armed man served as a sentry, but he didn't seem overly concerned. He was sitting down on a large rock, smoking a cigarette.

"We'll park the car south of the building and keep watch through a starlight scope." She selected a spot near a cluster of bushes. In the distance, maybe their outline would meld with the surrounding pines and shrubs. She took out the starlight scope, telephoto lens, and camera from a small briefcase, then assembled the equipment. Resting the camera against the bottom of the open window, she waited.

The minutes ticked by but there were no signs of activity at the warehouse except for the restless sentry. The fleeting streak of a shooting star momentarily diverted her attention to the blackness of the desert sky. It would have been an idyllic spot for romance, but the circumstances were all wrong. She gathered her jacket around her tightly. "Aren't you cold with just your sweater on?"

"No, not really," he answered with a shrug. "I'm used to the weather around here. If I was sitting outside, I'd wear my jacket, but in the car, we've got two heaters on."

She glanced at him. "What heaters? I'm not running anything."

"Our bodies. We're warming it up."

"Oh, right." The thought that flashed through her mind had little to do with business. She glanced away, feeling her cheeks burning. At least it was too dark for him to notice her blushing.

"How well can you see through that scope?" he asked.

She handed it to him. "Here, why don't you see for yourself? Just hold down the switch to activate the electronics."

He took it from her hands, and aimed it out his own window. Their surroundings looked amazingly clear, though everything seemed shrouded in a light green cast. He swept the mesa behind him, then suddenly froze. "We've got trouble. There's a big guy uphill from us. He's either watching us or the people in the warehouse."

"Did he see you looking at him?"

"I don't think so. He was glancing behind him at the time."

"Then there might be more than one up there." She paused for a moment. "I want to know what's going on. If they're planning on causing some trouble, we've got to do something to turn the tables. Let's walk downhill into those piñons, like we're going to have a closer look at the warehouse. Once we're out of sight, we'll cut back to the left and circle around the hill behind them." She glanced at Joseph. "You'll have to stick close. I'm armed and you're not."

"Sounds good to me."

They moved downhill, staying behind cover, then switched direction. They'd almost reached the road when a familiar rumbling vibrated through the trees.

"Look out!" she shouted as a car came hurtling around the bend toward them.

Chapter Ten

As they dove for cover, the blast of a shotgun roared in their ears. Buckshot peppered a tall piñon in front of them, blowing splinters and bark everywhere.

Joseph hugged the ground until the vehicle had sped past them and disappeared. "There are more cars taking off down the hill," he said, scrambling to his feet. "Hear them?"

"Run! We've got to make it back to ours and tail them. The guys at the warehouse must have heard the shotgun blast and decided to split."

No matter how hard she tried, she couldn't quite keep up with Joe's rapid strides. When she arrived at the car, he was already inside, seat belt fastened.

Using the starlight scope, Joe focused on the house below. "I think we're too late. The cars that were parked outside are gone. No, wait a second." He saw the garage door open. A heartbeat later they both heard the roar of an engine. "We've got a chance. The van's leaving now, probably with the booze. Let's go. I can use the starlight scope to guide you. If you don't use your headlights, they'll never know we're behind them."

Grateful that her eyes had adjusted to the dark, Glenna stepped on the accelerator. The road was graveled, but filled with potholes and stretches of washerboard ripples deep enough to jar her teeth. Unfortunately there was no way to avoid the majority of them.

"The van's slowing down. They must believe they're safe," Joe said.

"I'll back off a bit. If we're still approaching too quickly, let me know, and I'll slow down some more."

They drove for nearly forty minutes, going to paved road and then back to dirt before the van arrived at his destination. It came to a stop in front of a hogan in an isolated area about twenty miles inside the Navajo reservation. "It looks like he's waiting for his contact," Joe said.

Glenna positioned the car so that she faced what was going on below, then took the starlight scope from Joe. Locking it onto the camera with a twist and click, she shot several frames of the scene below. Before long, another truck approached. "More players." She continued snapping photos. "I can't see them well enough to make out their faces, but the camera will record whatever we miss. I don't want to risk blowing the whole thing by trying to get closer."

A short time later the man who'd been driving the van unlocked the back. Catching a glimpse of the cartons of liquor hidden inside, Glenna took two more photos.

The passenger from the pickup checked the contents of the van, then finally handed over a large envelope. "The exchange has been completed," she told Joe. Glenna saw the man who'd driven the van there slip into the passenger's side of the pickup. The guy who'd been brought there by the pickup's driver took possession of the van. Within moments both vehicles were heading back to Ganado. "I'm going to follow the guys in the pickup. They're the ones who delivered the booze and the buyer."

Before long, they entered the small community of Ganado. Glenna followed them at a discreet distance, taking advantage of curves in the road to turn on her lights without being seen. She watched the driver of the pickup pull into a gas station and drop his passenger off. Observing from one of the side streets, she saw the man walk directly to a large, black Jeep and get inside. The moment he pulled out, Glenna eased out onto the road.

"That might be the same vehicle that was seen in the neighborhood of your brother's workshop around the time it was vandalized. I'm going to risk getting closer. I want to get that license plate number. It would also help if we could get a good look at the driver without getting his attention. I'll try passing just as soon as I have the plates, but you'll only have a few seconds to glance at his face." She accelerated slightly, got the number and sped past the Jeep.

"He's got a thin face and red hair, that much I'm sure of," Joseph said moments later. "I think we've located our man."

She called in the license plate to Hopi police headquarters, and gave them a quick rundown of events. "Let's see what they have on this guy." She didn't have long to wait.

"His name is Robert 'Bobby' Shaw. He's a local businessman," the dispatcher's voice came over the radio. "The captain said to tell you that he's suspected of conducting most of the illegal gambling operations in north central Arizona and south central Utah. He lives on two houseboats he owns on Lake Powell, going back and forth apparently at random."

Signing off, she placed the mike back on its hook. "Gilbert was supposed to have played poker on a boat on Lake Powell. Now we have the connection. What puzzles me is why Shaw is making the booze run himself. Is he low on personnel he can trust?"

"Maybe this is his own venture, one he's trying to keep his backers from knowing about."

"Then it's possible his backers were the ones watching him *and* us tonight," she said, weighing the information carefully. "Let's try to find out more about this guy. Where would we go if we wanted to link up with the game that's being run on the lake?"

"That's an illegal operation, so they're bound to be cagey about strangers. We could check the bars in Page. If I see someone I know, maybe I can find out how to get an invitation."

"Let's give it a try. Are you willing to go undercover with me tonight if we get the chance?"

"Yes, but I better warn you. I have enough cash on me to pay for a few pitchers of beer, but I certainly wouldn't have enough to buy into a game. Not unless they're playing penny ante," he added with a sheepish grin.

"I can stop by an automatic teller in Page and get some emergency funds."

"In that case, I'll do my best to get us to the right places."

"Any suggestions where to start?"

"I heard my brother mention a place called The Mirage a few times. It's a tavern that caters to a middle income crowd. But it can get rough there. My brother got himself into one heck of a fight with a local who made a comment about Indians. Then again, Gil was never very diplomatic in touchy situations."

"I have confidence in you. Besides, you'll have me as a backup if anything happens. What more could you possibly ask for?"

He grinned slowly. "Actually, I was thinking that you're the one who might need protection. You provoke confrontations, I'm the soul of equanimity."

"I'll let that pass, just to prove you wrong," she grinned smugly.

It was late at night by the time they arrived at Page, near Lake Powell. They made a brief stop at an automatic teller machine, then continued to The Mirage, located in the center of town.

Evaluating the site carefully, she parked down the block and started toward the entrance with Joe. "Keep your wits about you. A lot could happen to trash our plans."

As they walked down the sidewalk, Joe fought the urge to place his arm protectively around her shoulders. Glenna was small of stature, but she certainly didn't need his protection. She was a tempting combination of softness and steel.

As they entered the lounge, his eyes drifted over the other women there. Although a few were quite attractive, it quickly became clear to him why he'd never married. There was no one who could compare to Glenna. He'd wanted to believe that his love for her had vanished, but now as she slipped her hand in his, he knew that he'd been lying to himself all along.

She tugged at his arm, and he bent down as she spoke over the loud Western music from the sound system. "Let's get closer to the bar and sit down at one of those empty tables. From there, you'll be able to see the entire room."

Joseph ordered a beer, then looked at Glenna. Surprised, he heard her order one for herself. As the waitress left, he whispered into her ear. "I thought you couldn't drink on duty."

"When I'm undercover, different rules apply. We're supposed to blend in as much as possible. The beer isn't so much for drinking as for show."

Joseph allowed his gaze to drift from table to table. "Wait here," he said, his eyes fastening on a man in the far corner. "I'm going to talk to that Hopi man over there in the cowboy hat. Jerry and I went to school together. He's not a gambler, but he knows lots of people and lives off the reservation. Let me see if I can get any information."

Glenna watched Joe's back protectively as he approached his friend. She wasn't sure if he could pull it off. There was a basic core of honesty about Joe she suspected would make him a lousy undercover operative.

As he returned to where she sat, Joe's expression was guarded. "I didn't get very far. I don't think he trusts me."

"We'll try again," she said, wondering if perhaps they were wasting their time after all.

"He did suggest that we try the Midnight Roundup. It's a bar about a quarter mile from here. It's rougher, the kind of place where you have to share your pretzels with the cockroaches."

"After a recommendation like that, how can I possibly resist?"

They returned to the car and quickly got underway. As she maneuvered the next corner, she glanced in her rearview mirror. "Hmm."

He shifted in his seat, pretending to face her, but trying to steal a glimpse behind them. "Unless you want me to turn completely around, you better explain that."

"No, please don't try to look. I think we may have been followed. Could your friend have put someone on our tails?"

"I doubt it, but maybe someone saw me talking to him and didn't like the idea."

They were a few blocks from the Midnight Roundup when the car turned down a side street. Glenna exhaled softly. "You know, I think I'm getting paranoid. Sorry about the false alarm."

"No problem."

The Midnight Roundup had far more patrons that the previous tavern, and they were forced to park about two blocks away. "This place certainly does a brisk business."

"With this many people here, I'm sure to run into someone I know. I used to work at the Glen Canyon Dam, just west of here."

"Joe, you're basically very honest, and often show exactly what you're thinking. Do you think you can convince anyone you're looking for a game just so you can find some excitement?"

He gave her a hard look. "First of all, I'm not that transparent. There are things about me you'll never know. Don't make the mistake of believing you can read me completely because I choose to let you see inside me. I try to adhere to the philosophy of being predictable to your friends, and unpredictable to your enemies. As to the second part of your question, yes, I think people expect you to go a little crazy after someone you love passes on. Only you and I and the killers know what's going on behind the murder. The others will just figure I'm out to take my mind off things."

She'd struck a nerve, but there was no time to reply. As they entered the bar, the sounds of raucous laughter filled her ears. They maneuvered slowly through the crowd. After several minutes they finally managed to get a table near one of the exits, but only because someone else was leaving. Joseph's gaze wandered over the faces, as if searching for a waitress. He was still looking when an Anglo man approached and slid easily into the chair across the table from them.

"Joe, I haven't seen you in ages! What brings you into town?"

"A change of scenery," Joe answered, then shrugged. "Pete Mulder, this is Glenna, an old friend from college."

"Pleasure to meet you." He shook her hand. "I've never seen you around here before, I would have remembered. Are you new to the area, or just visiting?"

"I'll be here a little longer, I live in Flagstaff. I came to see Joe a few days ago, figuring it's a good time for him to be with a friend."

"Yeah," Pete acknowledged. "It's always tough when one of the family.... Well, you're doing the right thing, Joe. You've got to go on with your own life and not dwell on things."

Joe nodded absently. "I just wish I could be a better host. Glenna's finding it a bit tame around here. She's used to spending her paychecks in Las Vegas, but all Page has to offer is bars and loud country music," he gave her an apologetic shrug.

Glenna knew the tack he was taking. "Well, even in Flagstaff there are always one or two places you can go for some excitement if you have a little extra cash. Maybe we could ask around, not everybody goes to Las Vegas, you know."

Pete hesitated for a moment, then finally met their eyes. "Look, there is a place like that around here. I'm surprised you haven't heard of it," he said, glancing at Joe. "It's a floating game, literally. It's on a houseboat on Lake Powell and strictly by invitation only. But I can get you in. Just tell them you're a friend of mine and you'll be okay." He gave Glenna a condescending smile. "But, I better warn you. This is pretty high-stakes poker, blackjack and roulette. Bring several hundred dollars, at least, if you're really into it."

"By the time I was sixteen, I could out bluff my father and his old army buddies at their Friday night games. I bought a car and managed to keep up the payments just with the pots I won. They were really glad to see me move on to college," she smiled. "I'm into it, all right!"

He laughed. "Okay. A man everyone calls Bobby runs it. I don't know his last name, and it's probably better that way. Here's what you do. Go to the southernmost ramp at Wahweap Marina. There's activity going on all hours of the day or night. Wait for someone to approach you in a green boat. When they ask you if you had any luck with the walleye, tell them no, but you landed a three pound channel cat. Got that?"

Joe nodded. "Then what?"

"Put yourself in their hands, and they'll take you wherever the games are tonight. By the way, you will be checked with a metal detector, so if you're carrying any kind of weapon, even a pocketknife, get rid of it. They frown on things like that."

"I'll remember," Joe said, eyebrows raised.

"Have fun." He stood up and offered Joseph and Glenna his hand.

As he left, Glenna could barely conceal the excited edge in her voice. "This is it! I can feel it."

They made their way quickly to the car. "Glenna, you're carrying your handgun, right?"

"Of course I am. I always have a concealed weapon with me," she answered easily. "But I'll leave it behind before we meet the launch. To be honest, I don't like going in there unarmed, but we have no choice. There's no way I'll be able to fool a metal detector."

"Exactly what do you hope to accomplish tonight? Wouldn't it be easier to have Bobby Shaw hauled in and then confront him with what you know?"

"Easier, yes, but he'd have no reason to cooperate with us. We don't have the kind of physical evidence or eyewitness testimony that makes a good case for anything besides smuggling contraband onto the reservation. We need o link him to gambling first and then try to learn what, if anything, he had to do with your brother's murder."

"So what's your plan, providing we do get on the houseboat?"

"First, we'll establish ourselves as legitimate by gambling and having a good time. Going as a couple will help. People aren't quite as suspicious of a man and a woman out together for an evening of fun. While we're at the table, we can check out the other people there. Maybe we'll hear something that will help, or strike up a conversation with a disgruntled gambler."

"If Shaw employs any people from my tribe, I'll try to talk to them and see if they know anything that could help us."

"Good idea. When we're ready, we'll stir up some trouble and demand to talk to Shaw. I'll figure out how to work on him once I see him face to face. Just be sure to let me take the lead."

As they arrived at the lake, Glenna's training took over. Her senses became alert, and even small details in the nighttime shadows stood out sharply under her scrutinizing glance. When she turned to glance at Joe, she saw the tension of the moment mirrored on his face. "Try to relax. You look too much like a cop on his first field assignment." She handed him half the money she'd taken from the special account. Then, after stashing a few things under the seat, they left the car.

As they waited where Pete had instructed, Glenna glanced around. It was mid evening and most of the boats were in their slips for the night. "I expected someone to be on the lookout or just walking around, but no one's here."

Joseph stared at the water. "There's a green speedboat down about a hundred yards, just at the end of the marina. It's starting to head our way."

"They must watch the dock from there," she said, her voice low.

A few minutes later the speedboat nestled up beside the old tires that cushioned the dock, and a powerfully built man stepped out. He took a line and fastened it to a stanchion, then a second man joined him on the dock. This one moved with a definite air of authority. "Wonderful night," he said. "Have any luck with the walleye today?"

"No, but I landed a three pound channel cat," Joseph answered, and mentioned his friend's name.

The man eyed them carefully, then signaled his companion, who brought out a metal detector. "Pete told you this would be necessary?"

Glenna and Joseph both nodded.

The man checked out Joseph first, ensuring he wasn't carrying a weapon. But as he passed the sensor down Glenna, a sharp buzz sounded. "What's this?"

The man who'd stood back reached inside his windbreaker.

Chapter Eleven

Joseph stiffened. Had she locked away her pistol in the car but forgotten to remove ammunition or a knife?

Glenna smiled weakly, then reached down slowly and removed a shoe. Holding it to the sensor, she set off another, louder buzz. "Steel shank in the sole," she apologized. "It sets off metal detectors in airports, too. Sorry, I forgot I was wearing these."

The man held the sensor near her other foot, and it set off the detector, too. The boatman stood up and nodded to his partner, who had relaxed.

"Okay, you two are clean." He cocked his head toward the speedboat that would take them to the houseboat where the games were. "Climb in."

Joseph gave Glenna a hand stepping into the gently rolling boat, and struggled to keep his fear from showing. It wasn't going undercover that bothered him. He'd known the risks and had accepted them willingly from the start. But he hated water. Anything deeper than a bathtub made him nervous. He didn't have the remotest idea how to swim, and suspected that he'd sink without a trace if he tried.

"Hey man, I've seen that look before. You've never been out in a boat before, have you?"

Joseph was tempted to deny it, but knew that any attempt to disguise what he felt at this point was bound to arouse suspicion. "No, you're right. My parents didn't raise me to be a sailor."

"Put on a life jacket, if it'll help," the other man suggested.

Joseph took a deep breath, then let it out slowly. "I'm okay."

"Honey, you should have told me," Glenna said sweetly. "I wanted to have a little fun tonight, but not at your expense."

Joseph saw that the sweetness of her tone didn't quite reach her eyes. She probably wanted to strangle him for not telling her in advance. "I'm glad to do this for you, baby," he said in a tone he knew would set her teeth on edge. "You always know how to thank me for showing you a good time."

She blinked, but recovered fast. "We can play nurse and patient in the morning," she cooed. "You always love that."

One of the men choked, but covered up by clearing his throat. The other had turned around, his shoulders shaking in the moonlight.

Joseph stared at her. He'd meant to tease her, but she'd turned the tables on him. He had no idea what to say, particularly knowing that the men were listening eagerly. This was bound to be a story they'd retell for months.

Joseph saw Glenna's eyes twinkling mischievously. She was enjoying this too much. There was no telling what she'd say next. He acted on instinct the minute he saw her open her mouth.

Pulling her against him, he covered her lips with his own. He felt her stiffen with surprise, and knew that he'd taken her completely off guard. Then, just as abruptly, Glenna's reaction took away his illusion of having gained the upper hand.

She turned soft in his arms, and shifted to sit on his lap. Her lips parted, inviting him to take more. His heart began drumming so fast he thought it would burst out of his rib cage. He tried to keep the contact light, but his body was already beginning to swell and tighten. Then her tongue darted inside his mouth.

Flashes of pure fire ran down his body to his groin as she clamped her mouth to his and tasted him boldly. A feeling of submissiveness quickly gave way to an overwhelming desire to possess and conquer. She was making him crazy!

She pulled away a moment later, trying to even her breathing. "Oh my! I almost forgot we weren't alone!"

Joseph saw her eyes gleaming impishly, but the flush on her face and her swollen lips told him she hadn't escaped unscathed, either. She had not been spared the white-hot sensations that had stormed through him.

"You look like you've made a remarkable recovery," the boatman goaded.

Glenna chuckled softly and allowed her gaze to casually drift down him. "Yes, honey, you seem to be feeling much better."

He couldn't strangle her or toss her overboard. Too many questions would be asked. Besides, he needed her. As his thoughts turned to the business at hand, his smile faded.

"There they are," the man said a second later as they turned south down what had once been a narrow canyon. "You'll be aboard soon."

Glenna studied the brightly illuminated houseboat then smiled at Joe. "Well, the fun's really going to begin now!"

After they'd stepped across, the speedboat pulled away and headed back. Going in the first hatchway they came to, Glenna was surprised to see how large the houseboat really was. About two dozen people were inside a spacious room that had been divided into two sections by a high partition.

Selecting the least crowded side, she sat down at one of the blackjack tables. Joseph watched her for a moment, then went to a counter that served as the bar. After buying a drink for her, he returned to the bar and studied the room.

Glenna broke even in the first two hands. Not finding anyone of interest there, she moved to the next table. Draw poker wasn't one of her favorites, but she knew enough about it to do a creditable job. She won one hand out of four.

Realizing that Joseph was much too intent on the players and the employees, she stopped at the close of a hand and walked to the bar. He was talking to the bartender, although the man was obviously not saying much back.

"Honey, I bet you're just a natural at stud poker," she teased. "Why don't you sit at that table, and I'll bring you luck?"

As they moved across the room. "What on earth are you doing?" he whispered.

"Trying to do something—anything—that will make others think you're having a good time. So far you look as if you're enjoying this as much as a visit to the dentist," she answered softly.

After fifteen minutes at the table, Joseph had lost one hundred dollars. She led him to the next table, where he lost seventy-five dollars on the first two hands. "Honey, I think you and I need a break. Lady Luck's running out on us."

She started toward the bar with Joe. As the sliding panel leading to a tiny kitchen was pushed open, Joe caught a glimpse of a man he recognized as Navajo. "I'm going to talk to him," he said, explaining quickly.

"Be careful," she warned.

No one seemed very interested in the kitchen, so his entrance was easier than he expected. He nodded to the Navajo. "It seems you and I are the only Indians around here. Is that the way it usually is?"

The Navajo eyed him suspiciously, ignoring his question. "What are *you* doing here? You have no need to leave your village to play cards. This is a *bilagáana* place," he said, continuing to fill an hors d'oeuvres tray.

"I came here with a white woman who likes games like these. She finds it exciting," he said with a shrug. "It's much tamer than I expected."

"Get into a fight and you'll see how fast things change."

"Not me. Say, I have a cousin who's looking for night work. How did you get this job?"

"Shaw lets me square debts this way," he stopped speaking suddenly, then glanced at Joe. "That's not true with first timers though."

"No problem. My lady friend has plenty of money."

"That's a good thing. We don't need any more trouble around here."

"Something happen recently?"

"Enough to make me think of quitting," the man answered obliquely. "The boss takes it out on everyone if one of the customers makes a fuss."

"Who's the boss? That Bobby Shaw guy?"

He nodded. "When there's trouble, he makes sure it's solved quickly. He'll go the easy way first, but if that doesn't work he can come down *real* hard."

"What's holding you up?" one of the dealers, wearing a black tie and a white long-sleeved shirt, came inside the kitchen. "The trays are empty, Neskahi. Get moving." He glanced at Joe, his eyes wary. "What are you doing in here?"

"I came to see if I could get something a little more substantial, like a sandwich. My friend is drinking too much and I wanted her to have some food."

The man shook his head, then led Joseph back outside the kitchen. "Don't worry, partner. The night's young, and your lady friend's just having a good time."

Joe spotted Glenna walking to the blackjack table and quickly filled her in. As Glenna took the one available chair and was dealt in, he remained beside her.

Even though she tried to lose, Glenna ended up winning the next two hands and recovering what Joseph had lost earlier. It seemed the more risks she took, the more it paid off. She couldn't go on with the rest of her plan if she kept on winning.

Glenna left the table, handing her chips over to Joe to continue playing in her stead. Walking slowly, she went to the restroom, eavesdropping on the conversations she passed on the way. As two large men emerged from one of the cabins, she caught a glimpse of a red-haired man still inside.

She returned to the table a few minutes later, a plan firmly in mind. They'd been playing for two hours, and it was time to meet Bobby Shaw. If Joe had managed to lose most of what she'd won, her plan would work like a charm.

Joe didn't disappoint her. The stack of chips she'd left before him had dwindled to only a few.

She feigned wide-eyed shock. "Why, honey, they must have cheated you. I left you with a whole stack of twenty-dollar chips!" She glared accusingly at the dealer. "He doesn't know a thing about the game. Have you been taking advantage of him? Where's your boss? I left here a minute ago, now he's down three hundred dollars." She raised her voice so that everyone in the room could hear.

Before she could say another word, she felt a hand on her shoulder, and the place suddenly became very quiet. "If you'll come this way."

Joseph stood up quickly. "She doesn't go anywhere without me."

"That's okay, honey. I can handle this."

"No way." He stared at the man. "The lady and I go together."

Glenna wanted to kick him in the shins. This was no time for gallantry. If they wanted to see her, fine, she could handle it. Before she could say anything more, the man nodded curtly.

"Fine, he'll probably want to see you, too." Another employee appeared behind Joseph. Glenna had never seen a larger man in her life. He looked like a concrete wall, and his expressionless face certainly resembled one.

They were escorted through a small hatchway that eventually led to the upper deck. From up there, the entire lake stretched out before them, visible over the low slopes of the inlet. Silver rays of moonlight shimmered and danced on the surface of the water. It would have been the ideal spot for a romantic interlude. Only at the moment, that was marred by the distinct possibility that several of her favorite bones were about to be broken.

A tall, almost cadaverously thin, red-haired man came out a moment later and leaned casually against the rail. He faced the water, as if Joseph and Glenna were scarcely important enough to merit his attention. "I understand you have a problem. I don't like problems, so let's see what we can do to work this out quickly."

It was the way he said it, with the casual disinterest of someone who'd grown blasé about violence, that worried her most. She'd learned to gauge people well and this man was making her skin crawl.

He turned around slowly, his gaze drifting over Glenna. "I suggest you start talking. I resent it when people waste my time."

"I wanted to meet you, Shaw, I thought if I made a little noise, it would get your attention," Glenna answered.

There was a total lack of emotion behind the gray eyes that coldly studied her. As his gaze shifted to Joe, his eyes narrowed. She thought she saw something there, a tightening like a snake preparing to strike, but in the blink of an eye it was gone. He looked at Joseph.

"I believe I know you," he said in a detached sort of way.

"We haven't met. I would have remembered," Joe replied, his tone even more emotionless than Shaw's, if that were possible.

"Nonetheless, I know you." He paused half a second, then nodded. "You're Gilbert Payestewa's brother."

"Yes."

"Then why have you come? Gilbert told me you don't gamble. And why is this annoying woman with you?"

Glenna stared at him. "If you want to know something about me, ask me directly."

"I have no desire to speak to you at the moment," he clipped, then focused his attention back on Joseph. "What *are* you doing here?"

Joseph hesitated for a moment. Trying a lie now could end up getting them both killed. "It's true I don't gamble, but my brother's been murdered. I don't deny that Gilbert's fate was of his own making, but I want the Hopi items he took returned.''

"And you think I have them?"

"No, but I was hoping that you, or one of your customers, might be able to help me find out who did.''

Shaw considered the question. "If you think I know something about the theft, then you must also believe I know something about your brother's murder. Coming here under those circumstances shows me that you're either extremely brave or very, very stupid. Which is it?''

Joseph shrugged. "Make up your own mind.''

"I asked you a question," he insisted, not raising his voice. With a nearly imperceptible movement of his hand, the two men who'd remained close by came forward. They yanked Joseph's arms behind him tightly, but Joseph didn't flinch or struggle. The man smiled. "You know that you and the woman are outmatched. That's why you didn't try to put up a fight. Yet, you're not even close to surrendering. I can see it in your eyes." He met Joseph's gaze, then moved his hand again and the men released him.

Joseph stood still, arms resting by his sides as if nothing had happened.

Glenna inhaled quickly, realizing that she'd been holding her breath. She would have attempted to keep it from going any further if Shaw hadn't backed off. Since they obviously hadn't considered her much of a threat, she would have had the initial advantage and that's all she would have needed. Using a sleeper hold on Shaw, a move that would make him pass out or kill him, depending on the length of time it was applied, would have kept his men at bay. Yet despite her self-confidence, she was relieved to see that the situation had eased.

As her eyes strayed over Joseph, her admiration for him grew. She was a trained agent, but these guys made her very nervous. He appeared to have taken the entire incident in stride.

"I didn't like your brother," Shaw said pointedly. "I already like you a great deal more."

Joseph said nothing.

"But you came here to learn something and I don't want to send you away empty-handed. What can I tell you?"

Glenna recognized the tactic. It was a way of getting information. Through Joseph's questions, he'd gauge their progress. She wanted to warn Joseph, but there was no way to do that covertly.

She spoke before Joseph had the chance. "Look, all he's trying to do is find some things that were stolen from his tribe. If you know anything, then tell us. We've dropped quite a sum of money on your tables tonight just for the chance to see you. You're not exactly accessible, you know."

Shaw gave her a thoughtful look. "How exactly do you fit into this?"

"I'm a good friend of Joseph's," she said, averting her gaze as if she were embarrassed by the question.

"So my men tell me," Shaw replied with a knowing half smile.

For some strange reason everything this man said came out sounding sordid in one way or another. "That has nothing to do with why we're here. The question now is, will you help us?"

Shaw stared at the lake. "It's a peaceful night. Let's walk around the deck." Shaw insisted on keeping Glenna between Joseph and him while his two men flanked the group. "I can tell you what kind of work your brother did for me and why, if you think that might help."

"It could. I won't know until you tell me." Joseph loathed having to hear about his brother from this guy, but maybe it would help to get him talking.

"Gilbert loved card games, but he wasn't much of a gambler. You could guess his hand just by looking at him." He grinned at Joseph. "I've heard the same thing about you, I might add." He glanced at Glenna. "Though you seem to have a knack for it."

"Tell me about Gilbert and his job here," Joe said.

"Gil paid off his gambling debts doing whatever jobs I needed done. Most of the time, he ran errands for me. You see, I was one of the few people who could actually trust Gilbert with money. He would deliver it whenever I said without any problem. He knew that if he didn't he'd find himself short on relatives." Shaw turned to look at Joseph.

The muscles around Joseph's jaw bunched. "How much money did he owe you?"

"None. His debts to me were squared. I don't let people run up big tabs."

"You must have paid him extremely well for these errands, then, Gilbert never earned much money on his own. Tell me, was there any specific reason you chose a Hopi man as courier? Could the work have entailed pick-ups made inside our villages, for example?" he challenged.

Shaw stopped walking and faced him. His stance was casual, hands in his jacket pockets as if completely relaxed. "If I had forced your brother to steal the objects you're looking for, I wouldn't be likely to admit it to you, would I? Wise up! I'm just trying to give you a few leads. I know at least some of your brother's contacts in the white world. People who are very interested in the type of things you're searching for."

Hearing a speedboat approaching from the main channel, he turned to one of his bodyguards. "We may be having some late arrivals. If they pull up, make sure they're greeted properly."

"Tell me about the leads you mentioned," Joseph said, ignoring the craft, which was slowing down.

Without warning, three loud cracks sounded against the backdrop of the motor. Glenna pulled Joe down hard to the deck as bullets whizzed past them.

She yelled at Shaw who was still standing, but saw him clutch his chest, surprise etched on his face. Before his bodyguard could reach out, Shaw toppled over the rail and dropped into the lake.

Chapter Twelve

As the bodyguards fired back at the fleeing boat, Glenna kicked off her shoes and stepped to the rail. Ignoring the gunfire, she dove into the icy lake.

Glenna swam toward Shaw and grabbed his collar. He wasn't conscious, and his weight slowed her as she dragged him back to the houseboat. The minute she reached the side of it, Joseph pulled her out of the water while the two bodyguards hauled Shaw onto the deck.

"He's not breathing," one of the bodyguards said quickly.

Joseph crouched by Shaw's side. Applying pressure to the wound that had pierced Shaw's ribs, he administered CPR as best he could.

"We need blankets, he might be in shock," one of the bodyguards said, watching Joseph work. "Go get some, Charlie. And tell the others to keep the customers inside. Say we were scaring off some drunks with a few shots into the air, and the boss fell in."

Glenna moved toward Shaw, water dripping off her onto the boat's wooden deck. It was bitterly cold, and almost impossible to keep her teeth from chattering. The remaining bodyguard reloaded his pistol with a fresh clip. Then with his eyes toward the bow of the boat, he slipped his weapon inside the holster attached to his belt.

With catlike speed, Glenna reached around his back and grabbed the pistol. Before he could stop her, she had the gun.

"Face down on the deck! And keep quiet!" she ordered, shaking from the cold more than the excitement.

The man, complying slowly with her request, spoke. "We have to call a doctor."

"Shaw's dead," Joseph said, rising to his feet.

The second bodyguard returned with the blankets just as Joseph spoke. Hearing what Joe said, he stopped and began to back away. "I'm getting out of here."

"You're not going anywhere," Glenna said firmly. The man finally noticed the pistol pointing at him. "Take your gun out slowly with thumb and forefinger, then place it on the deck," Glenna ordered. "Slide it over to me, then lie face down."

The man complied. "Lady, I don't know what you think you're trying to do. You'll be in just as much trouble as the rest of us if the rangers show up."

"Somehow I doubt that," Glenna snapped back, signaling to Joe to retrieve the weapon. Never taking her eyes off the men, she leaned toward Joe and whispered in his ear. "Hold them here, I'm going to the cabin and radio shore for some help."

"What about the other employees?" he answered, matching her tone.

"Don't worry. I've got a plan," she said, grabbing a blanket and wrapping it around her.

With a clear purpose in mind, Glenna retrieved her purse from the deck then hurried to the main cabin. Stopping a few feet away from the door, she listened, her eyes taking in the room inside. The Navajo man was serving drinks, and the dealers were back at their games. Everyone seemed oblivious to what was going on outside, the staff obviously had been convinced nothing was wrong.

When she walked in, Glenna held the gun just out of sight inside her purse. Those who looked up only chuckled at the blanket and the dripping water, assuming she'd fallen overboard. Then they went back to their cards.

She crossed over to the Navajo waiter, the only one who was still watching her. Placing one finger to her lips, she showed the man the pistol in her hand, still out of sight to everyone else. Beside it was her FBI identification card, easily seen in the room light.

"You don't have to point that thing at me," the man muttered, shaking his head. "I was hired to serve food on this boat, not fight for Shaw."

"Then take me to the radio without attracting any attention," she clipped.

He complied, leading her into Shaw's tiny office. The radio was beside the control console that piloted the boat.

Glenna ordered the man to lean against the wall, then frisked him for weapons. Satisfied he wasn't armed, she moved away and quickly sent out a message to the rangers. "They'll be here shortly, so go back out and keep serving drinks. Don't even think of trying to alert the others. If you start trouble for me, I'll return the favor. With interest," she added coolly.

"I read you," he answered. "By the way, who really got shot out there?"

"Shaw. He's dead, and the killers got away in a speedboat. What can you tell me about that?"

"Nothing about the boat sounds familiar, but I guess it was just a matter of time before someone killed Shaw."

"What makes you say that?"

"His type of business generated enemies and problems. Also, things have been very strange around here lately. We're under new ownership. Shaw's just a manager for someone else now, and I don't think he cared much for the arrangement."

"Who's the new owner? Have you ever seen him?"

"No. All I know is that every time Shaw left for a meeting with him, he'd return in a foul mood."

The lake patrol with armed park rangers arrived fifteen minutes later in a large cabin cruiser. Without Shaw's bodyguards to act as lookout, few noticed the approach of the craft, they were too busy at the game tables.

Taking the Navajo waiter with her, Glenna joined Joseph, who was still outside with the prisoners. As the law enforcement team came on board, she quickly identified herself.

Glenna gave one of the men a fast summary of the events that had transpired while the rangers took possession of the craft. "We're going to need divers as soon as possible," she said. "Shaw fell into the lake and lost his jacket. It's possible there's some evidence down there."

"Did you get a look at the men who did the shooting, or their boat?" the patrol leader named Gonzales asked.

"It was too dark, sorry." She turned and looked at Joe, who shook his head. "Believe me, I wish we could be of more help."

Glenna assessed the special law enforcement officer. He was in his late forties and his eyes had the thickly lidded quality of someone who wanted to get some sleep. From his expression, she surmised she'd given him even more reason to hate the night shift.

"We've worked with the Bureau before and know you people don't like to give out much information," he said, "but there are some questions I need answered. For instance, what are you doing here? What kind of case are you working on, and why weren't we notified?"

She answered his questions as truthfully and succinctly as possible.

"Shaw has his fingers in several operations, and most of them are illegal," Gonzales conceded. "We raided him a few times, but all we got was slapped with a harassment suit. The evidence was always tossed overboard or into a hibachi by the time we got on deck."

"Do you know who his backers were?" she asked quickly. "I understand he'd just been forced out—demoted from owner to manager of the operation."

"We never were able to tie him to anyone specifically. He always covered his tracks well. Do you think it was just a coincidence that the hit happened when you were aboard?" Gonzales watched two of his men inspect the body.

"No, I don't, but that's just a gut feeling."

"Okay. We'll talk some more later."

She watched Gonzales join his men, adding a hand to their efforts.

Joseph came up and stood behind her. "They're questioning the bodyguards and the others now. I've already given my statement." He paused, then continued. "Remember when we were on our way to Midnight Roundup and you thought we were being followed?"

"Yeah," she answered, nodding thoughtfully at his implication. "I think someone was onto us almost from the start. They might have decided to take out Shaw, then, either as punishment for smuggling liquor, or to ensure that he couldn't give us any information."

"Unfortunately we made it easy for them by standing out on the deck. Obviously Shaw felt safe on his boat. He never saw the hit coming."

"That raises an interesting possibility. If we hadn't been standing on the deck, would they have tried to get on board to kill Shaw? That might have been difficult unless they had the cooperation of his lookouts." She glanced at the ranger who was talking to one of his men. "I better go fill him in, then see if I can find some dry clothes. I'm freezing."

It took most of the night before all the witnesses had been interviewed, transported back to the nearest holding facility on shore, and then processed. Hours later, dressed in oversized Forest Service coveralls, she was finally ready to go back to her hotel. Joe had spent most of the night in the lobby of the Page police station waiting around, yet his mood hadn't darkened as much as hers.

She glanced at the light shading of a beard that dusted his face. It could barely be termed five o'clock shadow, there just wasn't enough there to make that much of a difference. Yet there were lines around his eyes and a deep-set weariness that edged his expression.

"Did you learn anything new?" he asked, following her to the car.

"I participated in questioning all of Shaw's employees. Everyone insists they have no idea who shot at us earlier, or who might have killed their boss. I only learned one bit of useful information. Some customers were allowed to join the houseboat wherever it was on the lake without being escorted in like we were. The rule was, if a gambler known by the crew approached, he was to be allowed on board. The only thing that marked the arrival of the speedboat as unusual was the hour. Normally players didn't join them quite so late."

"What about the divers, did they ever report in?"

"Yes, but they didn't find anything. They'll look again in daylight, but no one's very optimistic." She stiffened her arms by bracing them against the steering wheel, trying to work out the kinks in her muscles. "I'll drop you off at your car, then I'm off to the motel. I'm too tired to even think straight anymore."

"Let me buy you something to eat first. It's been a while, and a few hors d'oeuvres scarcely qualify as a decent meal."

She smiled. It had been a long time since anyone actually expressed concern over her nutrition. "Thanks, but I'm too tired. If you're famished, I think there might be a candy bar in the glove compartment."

He shook his head. "No, I was worried about you."

Those simple words touched her. She wasn't exactly making stellar progress on the case. Yet instead of demanding that she be replaced, as many civilians personally involved might have, he was being supportive. "Joe, you're really terrific," she said softly.

"Damn straight. It's taken you long enough to see it."

She glanced at him quickly, then burst out laughing. "I think we both need sleep."

"I'm going to try and talk to the other *kikmongwis,* each village has one. Maybe one of the others remembers someone who visited their village and showed particular interest in our religious artifacts."

"Will you have trouble getting them to speak to you?"

"I don't think so. By now, word of what our village father, my uncle, has asked me to do has reached them. They'll cooperate."

As they approached the Cultural Center, Glenna glanced around and spotted his car near the entrance. "I'll catch up with you tomorrow sometime. First thing in the morning, I'm going to check back with the police and rangers in Page. There's still a few details we have to wrap up."

Glenna said good-night to Joseph, then drove to the motel in Keams Canyon. Carrying a bag holding her wet clothes, she went to her room. The impersonal setting seemed to really get to her tonight. Working for the Bureau had kept her too busy to dwell on what was missing in her life. Yet as she crawled between the cold sheets, she wished Joe could have been there with her. It wasn't just so she could have the comfort of being with someone. Something special was happening between them and it made her want to believe in things she'd long given up hope in. She didn't dare label it, but in a world filled with deception, it was wonderfully real.

JOE STARED INTO THE EMPTY void beyond his headlight beams. Being with Glenna was fast becoming habit forming. He'd hated leaving her tonight, even though he'd be seeing her again in a matter of hours. In the embrace of darkness, he thought of how he would have liked to have spent the hours until dawn. He pictured her in his arms, her alabaster skin against his bronzed chest. He would have pleasured her in ways he'd only done in his imagination.

The visions that flashed before his mind made his body burn. With effort he forced himself to dwell on the other questions. Why hadn't she remarried? She was beautiful and very desirable. Surely she must have had her pick of men. Was she still in love with Brad? The question haunted him, but the more he considered it, the less likely it seemed.

It was different than it had been so many years ago. Now, Glenna responded to him in both subtle and not-so-subtle ways. He was much too aware of her not to notice the signs. Then again, there was another possibility. He'd seen what he'd wanted to years ago instead of the truth. Perhaps he was making the same mistake again.

He took a deep breath and let it out again. No, this time it was happening. Yet as tempting as it was, he couldn't allow his feelings for her to overshadow the duty he had to fulfill. His life and his clan's future hung in the balance.

As he thought of the days ahead, he wondered what the gods held in store for him. He could end up with everything he'd ever wanted, or more alone than he'd ever been.

Joseph walked inside his home minutes later. Silence echoed back at him, haunting in its emptiness.

JOSEPH FINISHED his meeting with a village father on Third Mesa. For the first time he felt the same impatience with his people that *pahanas* often complained about. He desperately wanted to find answers, but no one seemed to have any to give. The most he'd been able to get was a promise that they'd search their memories.

There was only one village father he hadn't spoken to yet. Joseph had gone to see him earlier and found him making preparations for a kachina dance rehearsal. It would be held in his home kiva later that day. To his surprise, the *kikmongwi* had asked him to return later and join them in the ceremonial smoke. He was quick to accept. Perhaps the invitation had only been extended as a courtesy since Joe was also a member of their society, though his group was in another village. Yet the gesture was significant.

As he approached the kiva, set at one end of the village, he heard voices inside and the sound of men building up the fire. Normally he would have changed inside, but in deference to the others already there, he decided against it. Standing by the side and out of view, Joseph stripped down to a breechclout, as was customary, then descended the entrance ladder.

The village father greeted him, and offered him a pipe filled with native tobacco. Joseph puffed on it for a moment, then passed it to the person seated beside him. Despite the cold outside, the fire and the people inside the small, circular structure of the kiva made the temperature comfortably warm. He watched in silence as the men went through a portion of the dance.

Finally the elder approached him. "I have no information to give you yet, Joseph Payestewa. But if there's anything to be learned, I will find out. By having you come here today, I've in essence told the others in our village that I'm in agreement with the task your *kikmongwi* has given you. It might make things easier."

"I appreciate whatever you can do. My mother is growing weaker, and I'm not at all sure how much time she has." He exhaled softly. "I'm doing the best I know how, but I can't do it alone."

He placed a hand on Joseph's shoulder. "We will make a special *paho* for you. You'll have to work hard to keep your thinking clear of fear. Remember that anything you direct your thoughts to is made more powerful."

"Is there anything I can do for you?"

The elder shook his head. "We have other business that will keep us here for several more hours, but there's no need for you to stay. We realize you have your own duties to perform."

Joseph climbed up the ladder quickly and walked to where his clothes still lay. As he bent down to retrieve his sweater, he heard a soft gasp behind him. He turned around, more curious than anything else. The women in the village were used to seeing men in their native garb from time to time. Yet they normally stayed away from the kivas, unless specifically asked to come.

His gaze took in the area, then fastened on the intruder. Glenna stood beside a tall pine, less than five yards away. "What in the heck do you think you're doing?" he said in a harsh whisper. "You can't imagine how much trouble you'll be in if they find you here."

As he finished the sentence, he heard the sound of someone coming up the ladder. Grabbing his clothes, he reached for her hand and started running.

Chapter Thirteen

"What—"

He never slowed a step. "Quiet, Glenna. We've got to get out of here."

Even though she tried to match his pace, she remained half a step behind him. Her heart was pumping a mile a minute, but not because of the quick jog they were doing. He had a set of heart-stopping buns that the breechclout did nothing to hide. She forced her eyes away. "There's no one following us."

He stopped, scarcely winded, and turned to face her. "You better thank your lucky stars for that. Intruders aren't tolerated. The least that would have happened is that you would have been banned from the village."

Her gaze drifted over him, though she really hadn't meant to do that. His muscles were taut with exertion and sharply defined in contours of hard, bronzed flesh. The traditional garment enticed her, daring her to touch and release the wild fires that flickered behind his dark eyes.

She forced herself to look up at him, and suddenly realized that he was aware of what she was feeling. Her whole body tingled. "You look pretty darned good in that. Too bad you can't wear it more often," she managed with a shaky smile.

"I could," he said, his voice so deep it sent vibrations right through her. "For you."

She swallowed, but there was no moistness in her mouth. Everything around her seemed to shift into slow motion as he took her hand and pressed it to his chest. She caressed him gently and his muscles quivered beneath her palm.

"I like it when you look at me like that," he said, his voice raw. Animal instincts burned in his blood as he saw signs of arousal in her face. She wanted him, maybe as badly as he wanted her. Desire clawed at his gut. He wanted to sink so deep into her that he became a part of her soul.

She traced a line hesitantly above the cloth that covered him, scarcely hiding his arousal.

He groaned with need. "Glenna," he pleaded in a tortured voice.

Seeing his own passion mirrored in her face, he covered her mouth with his own.

His erection throbbed so painfully he thought he might burst. He tried to hold back the fire spreading through him, but the way she yielded to him made his kiss turn savage.

With a soft whimper, she pressed herself into him. Her need touched off a spark in him. His tongue delved into her mouth, taking more. Caught in a storm of blazing heat, he ground her against him.

The sound of men's voices rising in the familiar cadence of a song snapped him out of it. "We've got to leave."

"We're not close to the kiva anymore. No one can see us here," she said in a shaky voice.

"We're not safe, believe me." He picked up the clothes he'd dropped on the ground. Working quickly, he slipped into his sweater and jeans. "By the way, how did you find me?"

"I asked around." She heard the soft rasp of the zipper as he fastened his jeans and her gaze drifted downward. "It wasn't hard . . . er . . . I mean, difficult," she corrected. "It wasn't difficult."

He smiled and shook his head. "You better count yourself lucky that they started the song. I'm not sure I could have stopped otherwise."

"I'm not sure I would have let you," she answered.

Heat slithered through him as he heard her words. He stared at her for one long, breathless second. "We have to go," he said finally. "Where did you leave your car? Not near the kiva?" he added, alarmed.

"No, it's about a quarter mile down the hill. I decided to walk around." She glanced at him now that he was clothed. "You must have been freezing," she commented.

"No, it was much too hot for that," he answered, holding her gaze.

"Joseph, tell me one thing," she asked as they started back to her car. "What would have happened had they discovered us trying to get away from there?"

"My penalty would have been much more severe than yours," he answered obliquely.

"A curse?"

"That, perhaps, but there would have been other harsher physical measures involved, too. I can't say more."

"You took quite a risk for me."

"You would have done the same on my behalf had the situations been reversed," he said quietly. "The feelings between us are too strong for either of us to do anything else." He saw her start to protest and shook his head. "Don't bother to deny that you care for me."

"Yes, I care," she admitted in a barely audible whisper. As she saw his gaze soften, anguish made her throat tighten. For all the good it would do them. She could never be what he wanted, nor give him what any man would have a right to expect.

He walked with her to the car, his gaze wary as he noticed they were being watched from a villager's doorway. He wanted her safely out of the village as soon as possible. "I'll meet you at the coffee shop near the Cultural Center."

With a nod, she got into her car, started it and drove off. She needed time to get her thoughts together. She was heading straight for heartache, and she couldn't see any way of stopping it. Joseph had finally begun to trust her, only he'd yet to learn about her personal reason for coming. When he did, would he think she'd set him up? Uncertainty and apprehension circled the edges of her mind like a hungry wolf.

Ten minutes later she met Joe at the entrance to the coffee shop. "I need to update you on a few things. Then I'd like your help tracking down an Anglo man who lives on Navajo land adjacent to the Joint Use area. He's married to a Navajo woman, I'm told."

They sat down at one of the booths. "The Navajo police now have the film we took of the liquor smuggling operation. I wrote out a report for them. While I was at the station, I checked up on a few other things. It turns out that the pieces of paper we found near Gilbert's body were I.O.U.'s signed by Gilbert, probably for gambling debts. This morning the lab guys were also able to establish that one of the tire prints at the scene of the murder matches up with Shaw's vehicle, the black Jeep. This links him to the crime physically, and strongly suggests he was the one who broke into Gilbert's workshop. Also, traces of rabbit fur were vacuumed out of his Jeep. This isn't conclusive, but it's a distinct possibility that the *Masau'u* robe was in his possession for a time."

"Shaw's dead, so even if he had the ceremonial robe and mask, there's little chance of us being able to track it down. Our only hope is if one of his people is able to provide us with a lead."

"We already spoke to both of his bodyguards. The men claim they don't know anything about the items. One of them said that Shaw had a real good friend, Mac Johnson, who often drove the liquor trucks for him. Mac knew all the other drivers, and in fact, whenever Shaw couldn't oversee an operation, he was the one who took over. They said Johnson's the only person Shaw would have confided in."

"And this is the Anglo you need to find?"

"Yes, the problem is that I went to the location they gave me, but all I found was an abandoned hogan. A death must have occurred there because a hole was punched through one of the walls."

Joseph nodded. "Did you try the wife's relatives?"

"That list is endless," she said. "I was wondering if you could ask the elderly Hopi couple who graze their cows there if they know where Johnson went. I was told that the two women were friends. But the Hopi woman doesn't speak English."

He smiled. "You're speaking about Frances Sekaquaptewa. She speaks English, only she chose not to speak to you. She doesn't particularly like strangers."

"Will she talk to you?"

"Yes. She's been close to our family for years. I don't know if you realize this, but the ones who give me the most trouble are the people who don't know me or my clan. Friends who are friends stick by you no matter what happens."

Half an hour later they were heading to Mac Johnson's new hogan. The Hopi woman's face had practically lit up when Joseph had gone to visit her. She'd even given him some healing herbs to take to his mother. Although all Glenna had merited were a few suspicious glances, she was more than willing to speak to Joseph in their native tongue.

"She knew that our *kikmongwi* had asked that we work together," Joseph explained. "When she saw you around here alone, she figured you were just another white woman who shouldn't be trusted."

"I thought it would be okay since I'd gone there looking for a Navajo couple. Besides, it *was* on my way back to town."

After leaving the Hopi woman, they pulled up beside an isolated hogan and waited in the vehicle until an Anglo man came to the door. Glenna studied the man as she walked to meet him. He was shorter than she was, about five foot one, and very rotund, reminding her of one of the

Botticelli cherubs. "He looks as lethal as a teddy bear, but don't underestimate him," she warned Joseph quietly.

The man nodded when she flashed her ID. "I've been expecting you to show up. I heard about Bobby's murder, and I figured it was only a matter of time before you people tracked me down." He appeared completely calm, almost resigned. He waved her to the center of the room, and offered her a seat on some cushions that had been dispersed on the floor. "As you can see, I'm not exactly in Shaw's economic class. Bobby and I were just friends. He let me do jobs for him every once in a while so I could pick up some extra money. I don't know anything about his gambling operations. When you have to watch every dime, you don't give your money away."

He glanced at Joe curiously. "You look like someone I used to know." His eyes narrowed slightly. "Are you related to Gilbert Payestewa?"

"I'm his brother, and that's the reason I'm here."

Although he answered Glenna's questions, Mac Johnson either didn't know much or he was determined to cover himself. "Tell me what you know about Gilbert's connection to Shaw," she insisted.

"I'm not sure you're going to want to hear this," Johnson said, looking at Joe.

"There's very little I don't already know. Whatever you say won't come as a shock."

"Gilbert was in hock to Bobby all the time, so Bobby used him as a convenient slave. He was Bobby's cheapest source of labor. Gilbert was also Bobby's favorite source of entertainment. Gilbert was a fighter, and I think Bobby enjoyed goading him. There was nothing Gilbert could do against Bobby's two paid goons, although he tried more than once."

"Were you ever there when Gilbert got roughed up?"

"Only one time, and there was nothing I could have done to stop it. Bobby had just finished polishing his nickel-plated, .32 semi-auto, and Gilbert picked it up from the desk to admire it. That was a big mistake. That pistol was Bobby's pride and joy. He had it customized with silver and turquoise inlay on the grips. He told me that he'd purchased it using exactly one half of the profits he'd made the first week his boating casino opened. To him, it was a symbol of his success. He practiced with it often, and I'm told he was a good shot."

Glenna tried to remember any mention of the pistol in the police reports, but couldn't. Yet they'd searched every inch of Shaw's boats, even with an explosives-sniffing dog, and found only gambling paraphernalia and the body-guards' known weapons. "Where did he normally keep this gun?"

"Either on him, or within reach at his home. You *do* know most of the time he lived on the *Chipper*, not the *Lucky*, where the casino was."

"I thought he went back and forth," Glenna countered.

Mac shook his head. "Not as much as he wanted to make people believe. It was his way of throwing off an angry loser who might come looking for him. That's also one of the reasons why he was always armed. He carried a weapon everywhere, and I *do* mean everywhere. He'd even have one with him when he went in to take a shower. Having a gun close by was his security."

"Did you notice if he'd grown even more cautious and wary recently?"

Mac nodded. "These past four months have been especially tough on him. First, someone muscled in on his business. Bobby told me that he still owed the man who'd originally financed his operation, and that the guy had sold him out. Bobby wanted to walk away from the entire thing, but they wouldn't let him. They told him that if he played by their rules, which included no booze smuggling, they'd turn the entire operation back over to him in a few months."

"How come? What were they after?"

"Beats me. Bobby couldn't figure it out, either. That's what worried him the most. He just couldn't get a handle on these men."

"How large a percentage did they take from his operation?"

"Nothing outrageous, or Bobby would have squealed like a wounded pig. But they wanted something, count on it. Bobby was scared to death of those guys. He even had one of his part-time helpers, a Hopi by the name of Secakuku steal some explosives for him. He said he needed an equalizer when dealing with certain people. One of those guys showed up at Bobby's one day, and found out about the stolen dynamite. The man really got steamed. He took all he could find, leaving Bobby just enough to do some kind of 'job' that they wanted done. Bobby did manage to hold onto a few extra sticks he had stashed someplace. He never told me where."

"Do you think Shaw suspected that his days were numbered?"

"Sure. That's why he kept smuggling the booze. He wanted a large cash reserve in case he had to make a run for it. His biggest problem was that he needed time to amass the money. Since he knew he'd be vulnerable until then, he became incredibly careful. These last few months, he even started moving his personal houseboat from one docking slip to the next. He told me that it probably wouldn't deter his enemies, but if someone came looking for him, the least he could do was make it difficult for them."

"So the *Chipper* wasn't always docked where it is now?"

"Bobby rented several slips, and even worked out deals with other people around the marina from time to time."

"Thanks," Glenna said, standing up. "You've been a great help. The police will probably want to talk to you, also, when they get the chance."

"Why would they come now? Do you think I'm keeping something back?"

She shook her head. "I'm not working the case from the same angle they are. They'll have different questions and concerns."

Glenna drove away from the hogan, lost in thought. "We have two nine-millimeter semi-autos accounted for, but not the thirty-two he mentioned."

"Is that the same caliber that killed my brother?"

She nodded. "It is, but that doesn't mean it's the same weapon. I'm going to go to the houseboat where he lived and search it myself. Maybe there's a secret compartment the crime unit missed. If not, I'm going to find out where that houseboat was tied up the night your brother was killed. If that gun's around, or he has any of those explosives, I'm going to make sure we find them."

Joe was unusually silent as they drove back to Lake Powell.

"What's on your mind?" she asked, sensing he was troubled.

"Finding out Shaw was my brother's killer is important to you, and I can understand that. But to me it's just another broken trail that could have taken me to the missing objects."

It wasn't until that moment that she realized just how unimportant revenge was to him. "I wish I had as much nobility in me as you have. I would have found lots of satisfaction in knowing that the man who'd killed my brother had also paid with his life."

"I don't have superhuman control, nor am I exceptionally noble. A part of me is glad he paid for the death he caused, but I'm not particularly proud of that."

He might not think himself special, but he was. She'd spent too much of her time these past few years dealing with criminals. Joseph's total honesty disarmed her. With a man like him to share her life, she'd never have to worry that the ugliness underlying her work would eventually destroy her own humanity. His love would shine so brightly she'd always find her way back.

She shook her head, dismissing the thought. It was ridiculous, of course. Fantasies, nothing more. His entire life, the focus of his tribal beliefs, all centered around continuity. And that was the one thing she could never guarantee him, neither as a woman nor as an agent.

"You're very quiet. Have I burst your bubble?" he asked sadly. "For someone in a fact-based profession, you sure can be a romantic."

"Maybe it's because of my profession that I *am* an incredible romantic. You need to believe in the good more than the bad, otherwise it'll pull you down."

By the time they arrived at the lake, Glenna was eager to get back to work. She picked up the radio handset and contacted the police, requesting that Shaw's employees be questioned again. They needed to find out where his houseboat had been docked the night of his murder. Also, divers would have to be sent out once that location was determined.

Glenna left the car near the docking slip and ducked beneath the yellow tape line. "We'll have to work together, Joe, otherwise it'll invalidate any evidence we find." Seeing him nod, she led him inside the houseboat. "Now, if you wanted to hide a gun in a place like this, where would you stash it?"

After an exhaustive forty-minute search, Joe sat down in one of the leather chairs inside Shaw's living quarters. "He was much too smart to keep the gun. I don't think we have any chance of finding it."

"If it was so special to him, he may not have discarded it completely. He could have dumped it into the lake someplace where he'd be able to retrieve it later. He wouldn't have even had to risk it being damaged by the water. He could have sealed it in plastic."

"This is a large lake."

"Yes, but remember, it would have to be a place he could find again." A small piece of yellow paper that had been wedged underneath a table leg to level it caught her eye. She picked up the paper and unfolded it. "Have you ever heard of a Murray White?"

"No, is it important?"

She shrugged. "Probably not, but this paper has his name and some dates scrawled on it." Hearing the sound of men's voices approaching, Glenna went out onto the deck to meet them. The divers were busy checking their gear as she approached. "I gather you were able to find out the information we needed."

"Yeah, apparently he spent the night in slip 10-B at Antelope Point. Nice sheltered spot. It's not going to be difficult to search."

Glenna rode in the forest service's boat to the small peninsula below Antelope Island. While the aquatic team worked, she waited on board. Her thoughts automatically drifted back to Joe, who'd stayed behind at the marina. She stared at the flat-topped bluffs that surrounded the lake. It was so peaceful here, it seemed like a giant breach in the natural order to be searching for a murder weapon. How it must have hurt Joseph to have the chaos she dealt with touch his carefully structured world!

She watched the bubbles from the air tanks burst on the surface of the cold, blue-green waters. Leaning over the side, she tried to catch a glimpse of the men below, hoping that this time they'd have something to show for their efforts. Tying Shaw to the murder with some physical evidence would help her open new avenues of investigation at the same time she closed that part of the case.

A moment later one of the divers surfaced. Inside the mesh basket in his hand was a clear plastic bag. As he drew near, she could make out the nickel-plated pistol it contained. The diver removed the mouthpiece and gave her a triumphant smile. "Is this what you were looking for?"

"You bet it is." She took the mesh basket from him and immediately tagged and labeled their find. Placing the pistol and bag inside an evidence pouch, she glanced up. "So far so good. Let's see if you guys can turn up anything interesting where the *Chipper* is docked now."

They returned to the marina at the southwestern end of the lake, and the divers began searching beneath Shaw's personal houseboat. This time Glenna waited on shore with Joe. "We're starting to uncover many things," she said slowly, "and that's bound to make Shaw's backers nervous. You better start watching yourself and your family very carefully. If they were willing to kill Bobby

Shaw to punish him or keep him from telling us anything, they might try to play hardball in other ways, too."

"My parents won't leave the reservation, particularly now that my mother's so ill. No one can get to them there. Sara is very progressive, but she's with her clan, and neither she nor Juanita will be left alone, either. And as for me, I've always been good at looking after myself. I'll be just fine."

She started to say more when one of the divers popped up. Removing his mouthpiece and pushing up his mask, he climbed out of the water. "I found only one thing of interest. I went as far from the boat as I figured anyone could pitch something from the deck, and spotted this." He held up the mesh basket, giving her a look at its contents. "It's a jackknife."

As the light hit it, Joe's eyes fastened on the inexpensive knife. "That's Gil's pocketknife, the one I gave him."

"We'll return it to your family as soon as we can," Glenna assured him quietly, "but we'll need it as evidence first." Giving his arm a squeeze, she walked to the water's edge and took the basket from the diver. "Where's your partner?"

"Roger's on his way back, making a pass under the hull. There was nothing else left to check."

A moment later a second head popped out of the water. "Get your gear back on, Ted. We've got a large waterproof bag attached to the bottom of the hull. It's tied in place so it'll stay put. I'm going to need help to make sure I don't damage any of the evidence."

Chapter Fourteen

Glenna watched both men disappear beneath the surface of the water. "The way I figure it, Shaw must have had one of his men take the knife from Gilbert before he shot him. Later on, when he realized he still had it, Shaw pitched it into the lake."

"Yes, that sounds logical."

When the men finally surfaced, Glenna saw that one of them was holding the mesh basket with great care. She went toward them quickly, eager to see what they'd found. "Dynamite," she observed, seeing the contents of the plastic bag. "Good, it's still dry. The lot numbers could make it easier to trace."

"There are blasting caps and fuse cords in there, too. Handle it carefully."

With a nod, she took the basket from them. While she labeled the evidence pouch, Joseph stared at the other bag that contained Gil's newly rusted pocketknife. Like his brother's life, it had been discarded and rendered useless. Sorrow lay like a heavy weight upon his shoulders. Without Shaw in the picture, however, he didn't have the remotest idea of where to go next. Of course, there was the possibility that Shaw's backers would come after *him*. He'd welcome that if it would give him the chance to find the items.

"Joe, are you okay?" Glenna approached and sat down next to him on the rock.

"Yeah, but I'm going to have to tell my parents that Gil's murderer is dead and I have no idea how I'm going to answer all the other questions they're bound to ask. How long will it be before you learn anything on the explosives?"

"A couple of days, maybe less," she said, walking back with him to the car.

As they returned to the reservation, Joseph's gaze drifted over the red- and orange-colored rocks, rich with iron ores, that dotted the landscape. "Would you come to my mother's home with me? It might help if they heard about the progress we've made so far—such as it is—directly from you."

"Of course I'll come. But Joe, if you don't mind my saying so, it sounds like you're losing hope. If you are, then I think it's time you took a closer look at all you've managed to learn. We *are* getting someplace, even if it isn't very fast."

"I'm not losing hope," he countered evenly. "If anything, I'm more determined to keep stirring things up. I intend to become a major headache to Shaw's backers."

"Be careful, Joe. You're not trained to handle it if they turn on you."

"For you, fighting seems invariably linked to the use of force. But that's not always the best weapon. There's much to be said for persistence and intelligence. Men like the ones we're facing rely on violence and intimidation when dealing with their enemies. They don't understand those who fight in other ways. Because I'll resort to violence only as a defense, our opponents will see that as a weakness and underestimate me. Ultimately that's going to give me the advantage."

He had a point. "It makes me nervous to fight your way. I've grown up with the idea that the best defense is a good offense. Yet deep down, your way feels right. Violence feeds on itself and instead of challenging it, perhaps I should start concentrating more on diffusing it."

"That philosophy is the heart of the Hopi way. That's why our tribe has survived throughout the years. *Hopi* means 'the peaceful people.'" He glanced at her. "The problem is that you've always preferred men who are just like you, the ones who charge into life aggressively."

His answer touched her. Certain brands of courage had more dazzle and flash. She couldn't deny that there had been a time in her life when she'd never even known other types existed. "That was true once," she admitted, "but most of us grow up sooner or later." She gave him a quirky half smile.

"So I *am* the type of man that attracts you," he said, expecting a flood of fast protests. "That's nice to know."

"Really? Why?"

Her response threw him. "Don't ask questions like that, unless you're very prepared to hear an honest answer," he whispered.

She tried to suppress the shiver that ran up her spine, but didn't quite manage it. His voice felt like silk caressing her bare skin. She glanced furtively at him out of the corner of her eye and saw him smiling. "You do make car trips interesting," she mumbled.

He grinned roguishly. "I can make all sorts of things interesting when the situation is right."

As they approached his village, the lighthearted feelings they'd shared disappeared almost as if they'd never been. Glenna sensed his growing tension as she parked in front of his mother's home.

"Let's do what has to be done," he said, leaving the car.

She walked with Joseph inside the home, then followed him to his parents' bedroom. Wilma Payestewa's face looked ashen. She seemed to have aged a dozen years in a matter of days. Deep lines accentuated the hollows on her face. Her eyes blazed sharply like a woman in the throes of a fever. "What have you learned?" she asked, her gaze fastened on Joseph.

Joe glanced at Glenna, asking without words that she give his mother the news. Her heart lodged in her throat. She felt as if by not producing the ceremonial items, she'd failed to comply with a last request. She took a deep breath, afraid that the shock of seeing Wilma Payestewa's condition would show on her face. "We know who killed your son," she said softly. "That man is also dead now. We believe that his bosses are behind the theft and we're working very hard to identify who they might be."

Wilma's eyes searched hers. "But you still don't know where the robe and the mask are," she observed, her voice dropping almost imperceptibly.

"We have leads, but it'll take a while longer to follow them up."

Glenna spoke to Joseph's parents for a while longer, then left for the Hopi police station. As she walked through the front doors of the station, the captain came out to meet her. "Glad you stopped by, I have something for you." He led the way to his office. "The Bureau sent you a fax, and told my department to make copies for ourselves, so I've already read it. Your request that ballistics put a priority on the gun was honored, and you've got a match. The nickel-plated .32 pistol, legally registered to Bobby Shaw, *was* the weapon used to murder Gilbert Payestewa. The rounds taken from Gilbert's body match the rifling on the gun."

She followed Captain Kywanwytewa to his desk, and took the papers he was handing her. "Okay, here's what we have," she said, thinking out loud. "The dynamite and detonators were easy to track down since they were stolen, possibly by Secakuku, from a mining operation in the area. Now we have to worry about the several sticks and detonators that are still missing."

"There is some good news," he said, thumbing through the files. "Here. This arrived before the fax. Justin Nakai brought it with him on his way back from the Phoenix office."

She read through the report quickly. "So we were right. The objects burnt in that fire were definitely *not* authentic. This is interesting," she added, reading on. "The explosives were set off using a blasting cap and kerosene, so those sticks of dynamite are still unaccounted for." She sat down and placed the papers on her lap. "So tell me, who could have provided quality reproductions of the artifacts? They wanted us to find pieces of them, but there's no way they could have guaranteed how much would actually survive. That's why I think they would have made sure those replicas were as authentic as possible hoping to fool even the experts."

The captain stared across the room, lost in thought. "There's an Anglo man in Keams Canyon. He markets copies, some of them are quite good. I don't have any way of proving what I'm about to tell you, so I'd rather it stays between us." Seeing her nod, he continued. "For several months we've suspected that he's been stealing original art, using the pieces or paintings as models to make copies, then selling the phony work to dealers all across the country. We checked him out, but found nothing unusual."

"Why do you suspect him then?"

"One of the Navajo traders reported spotting a signed, numbered lithograph by a well known artist. It looked authentic, but had to have been a copy."

"Why is the trader so certain it's not the real thing? Lithographs of the same work can number in the hundreds, can't they?"

"Yes, but the man knew it was phony because he owns that lithograph himself, right down to the same number."

"Where can I find this artist?"

The captain walked to the file cabinet, retrieved a folder, then scribbled down an address on a sheet of paper. "He keeps late hours at his business studio, then opens up around noon."

She nodded. In other words, if she wanted to have a good chance of catching him at work, tonight would be the time. "Strange hours for an artist," she said. "I thought they needed the daylight."

"His business is well lit, take it from me. He's got enough floodlights on the outside alone to rival Phoenix." The captain walked with her to the hall, then stopped. "On another note, we still haven't located Secakuku, but I'm certain he's going to turn up soon. Meanwhile, good hunting tonight. If you need any help, call. I'll have my deputies stick close to that area just in case."

"Thanks, Captain." She started to walk out, then stopped and fished out the paper she'd found in Shaw's houseboat. "Would you check out this name for me? If you need to, call the Bureau offices and have them help. It may be a dead end, but I'd like to make sure."

As she started to pull out of the parking lot, she saw Joseph's car approach. He lowered his window and pulled up beside her. "I thought I'd pass by on my way home. Is there anything new?"

"Some," she answered filling him in. "I'm on my way to Keams Canyon to interview the man. I'll catch you tomorrow and tell you what I can."

"Do you need an interpreter?"

"Not this time, he's not Hopi or Navajo. Go home and get some rest. If I could, believe me, that's exactly what I'd be doing."

"I might still be able to help. It's possible I know him."

"His name is James Morris."

"I *do* know who he is," Joseph said slowly. "Gil and I met for lunch one time and he came up to our booth. Gil walked off with him for a few minutes, then returned. He told me that the guy kept pressuring him to find art pieces by local artists. He wanted to copy their work, then sell the copies out of the area as originals. He made quite a bit of money, and was known to pay top dollar to anyone who helped him."

"Do you think he might have been interested in the mask and the robe?"

Joe shook his head. "I can't remember the conversation exactly, but somehow I have the impression he was interested in painting and sculpture. I remember Gilbert saying that it was too bad he wasn't looking for a card shark—*then* he could have helped him." He gave her a wry smile. "I didn't see the humor in that, then, and it's even less funny now."

"So it turns out the captain's suspicions were right," she mused. "What I'd like to know is whether Morris ever worked on commission. What we found of the artifacts that Secakuku burned in the fire might have passed for originals if we hadn't raised some questions. The experts had to inspect them very closely."

"How do you plan on getting Morris to talk to you?"

"It'll probably take a few threats of jail, so I'll be playing 'bad cop' tonight."

"If I'm there, it might go easier. He'll assume that Gil told me what he's up to and that you're not going to be taken in by evasions."

"Okay. Get in, we'll go in my car. Just remember you're there to worry him, nothing else."

Driving through Keams Canyon at that hour didn't take long. By the time they reached the road where James Morris' studio was located, she was alert and ready for action. As the captain had told her, the area was brightly illuminated. It would have been difficult for anyone to approach unnoticed. "It's like a Hollywood studio out here."

"Maybe he's worried about thieves. Like they say, it takes one to know one." Joe pointed to the van parked next to a loading dock. "It looks like he's getting ready to leave. Or maybe he's moving out. He's even got boxes in the front seat."

"I'm going up to see what's going on. Hang back, just in case," she said, parking her car.

Glenna walked to the side of the van. No one seemed to be around. She called out, staying well behind cover, but only silence echoed back at her. One of the van's back doors was open. As she came around by the taillights, she could see it was filled with crates and supplies.

Resting her right hand on the butt of her pistol, she edged in closer for a better look. Just then the other rear door flew open, slamming against her! She threw up her forearm, protecting her face, but the impact sent her sprawling onto the asphalt.

Before she could recover, a man leaped down from the van, crowbar in hand. Glenna rolled to one side, evading his attack. The steel fork struck the pavement inches away with a hammering thud that sent sparks and bits of tar and gravel flying.

Diving away from his next blow, Glenna scrambled to the balls of her feet. As she reached down for her pistol, she saw him bearing down on her, his arm arcing backward, ready to strike.

Chapter Fifteen

With a wild squeal of tires, her car appeared out of nowhere on a collision course with the man. Shock registered on her assailant's face, but he recovered instantly. With amazing speed, he shot toward the loading dock steps, scrambling out of the path of the vehicle aimed at him.

Grateful for Joseph's fast thinking, Glenna darted after the man. She was determined to stop him before he could leap from the dock onto the back of his van and make an escape. As he hurtled the gap, she lunged forward. Glenna caught his foot in midair and held on long enough to throw him off his mark. The man hit the back door of the van and crashed down to the pavement.

She scrambled to his side and was there, pistol ready, when he started to struggle to his feet. "FBI," she informed him. "Get up! Hands against the van, feet spread out. You know the position." She frisked him quickly and efficiently, then cuffed him to the door of the van. "Is there anyone else inside the building?"

"Find out for yourself," the man spat out.

"You're already headed for jail, mister. Don't make it harder on yourself. Do you always assault strangers?"

"I didn't know you were an FBI agent. I still don't. Show me a badge."

"So you only assault citizens," she countered, bringing out her ID. "Nice touch."

"I thought you came here to rob me. I was perfectly justified in doing what I did."

"Nope, wrong again. I called out. For all you knew I could have been a stranded motorist looking for help." She quickly informed him of his rights.

"I know that speech. Save it. Just tell me what you're doing here and what you want," he growled.

Glenna noticed him avoiding having to look at the merchandise inside the van. "Well, let's see what we have here."

His eyes grew wide as he suddenly saw Joseph standing by the car. "I know you!" he said miserably. "Your brother put you on to me."

"Hello, Morris," Joe said, then glanced over at Glenna. "The Hopi police will be here soon. I called them."

Glenna left Morris cuffed to the van. Keeping an eye on the warehouse entrance, she glanced inside the cargo space. "Nice lithographs. I recognize the artist's name, too. Why do I feel that we're going to find lots of hot merchandise here? I'm going to need two arrest forms just to record the counts against you, my friend." She smiled slowly. "We've got you, Morris, so how about a little cooperation? For starters, you could tell me if anyone else is hiding inside."

"No one," he replied sourly. "I work alone in my studio. If you want to know anything else then cut me a deal."

"The only thing I can promise is that things should go a lot easier for you if you don't hold out on me. I can testify that you offered to cooperate and judges have a way of looking kindly on that."

"Fine, so cut to the chase. You want to know who my Navajo contacts were? Get some paper and I'll give you their names."

"I'd rather you start with your Hopi contacts."

"I don't have any Hopi contacts. I tried a couple of times, but I couldn't get close to any of them. I wanted to put Gilbert on the payroll, but the man didn't have the connections I needed. I assured him I didn't care how he got the pieces I wanted, but he spouted some phony excuse about not stealing from his tribe."

"What makes you think it was phony?" Glenna countered.

"After what he did? Hell, at least I wasn't after ceremonial stuff. I just wanted art."

"There's a little matter I want to discuss with you, Morris," she prodded. "There was a fire set not too long ago in one of the villages. In the debris, we found what remained of the stolen ceremonial objects. Only once we examined the evidence, we discovered they weren't genuine. Someone planted fakes to mislead us. The police and I did some digging and learned that you've got quite a gift for making quick replicas. Why don't you tell me more about that?"

His eyes grew wide. "I want my lawyer."

"What a surprise! Well, I'm sorry you don't want to cooperate, after all. With the evidence we already have, we'll be able to prove it was your handiwork anyway. Of course, if we find the slightest link between your replicas and Gilbert Payestewa's murder, we'll also have you for conspiracy. That'll really add some years to your time behind bars. Think of all the new friends you'll have time to make."

"Hey, wait a minute," he protested. "I had nothing to do with anyone's murder."

"Convince me."

"Someone contacted me through the mail," he admitted. "I was sent specs for a Hopi mask and belt and asked to duplicate it within seven days. They quoted me a very generous fee. There was also a second, smaller envelope in the packet. In it was a photograph of my son, which had disappeared from my home a few days earlier. It was torn in two. I didn't need much more of an explanation."

"Did anyone else see that note?"

"No way. They instructed me to burn it and flush the ashes and that's exactly what I did. I wasn't taking any chances with my kid's life. I studied the specs they'd sent and finished the job. The items were simple to make since I already had access to most of the materials I needed. Two days later, I left the mask and belt in the trunk of my car like they'd ordered. I was worried they might not consider the job acceptable since I had to leave the shells off the belt. That's why I decided to leave a note explaining that I hadn't been able to get the right type."

"Did you stick around to see who made the pickup?"

"I wanted to, but I lost my nerve. It's one thing when someone threatens me personally, but I don't take chances with my kid. Later that afternoon when I went back to my car, someone had retrieved the merchandise. They left an envelope stuffed with money for me, so I figured that they were satisfied."

"Are you just getting ready to close down your operation here?"

He nodded. "When I attract the attention of people who are willing to go after my family, it's time to pack it in."

By the time she turned Morris over to the Hopi police, Glenna was exhausted. "It was a good thing for me that you came along tonight, Joe. By pulling that stunt with the car, you bought me the few seconds I needed. I knew I wouldn't have time to finish drawing my weapon before he struck." She paused and smiled shakily. "You know, despite everything that was going on, I was certain you'd find a way to help me."

"We've learned to trust in each other," he admitted.

"You're right. It didn't come easy to either of us, but I think it was even more difficult for you because of our past." She drove back toward the station where he'd left his car.

"I needed to hold onto that anger, Glenna," he said. "Haven't you guessed by now? I was in love with you."

She stared at him in shock for a second. "Why didn't you ever *say* anything? I waited and waited, then finally decided that *you* weren't interested in *me*." She exhaled softly. "So when Brad came along, I started going out with him."

He didn't answer for several seconds. "What are you saying?"

"I was crazy about you, but besides a little flirting and kidding, I could never get much of a response. After a long while, I figured it was time to give up."

His mouth dropped open slightly. "I never said anything because I didn't have much to offer you. I knew I had to return here where I was needed, yet life on the reservation could be very tough on an outsider. Resentments and prejudices run both ways. It would be difficult for any *pahana* to be accepted fully. I also had no idea how my family would react to you. Since you aren't Hopi, any children we would have had wouldn't have been considered part of our tribe."

The revelation left a bitter taste in her mouth. Knowing what she did now, that concern was moot. "Our past is said and done. The feelings that we had belong to that time, not the present." Glenna pulled into the Hopi police's parking lot and parked next to his car.

"Are the feelings really gone, Glenna?" Placing his palm against her cheek, he tenderly guided her face around to face him. "What I feel for you, what I see in your eyes when you look at me, tells me a different story."

She drew away slowly, then shook her head. "The only thing I can offer you is my friendship, and you already have that."

He watched her pull back into herself, then nodded. "Maybe that's for the best," he said at last. "But you know, I don't think you realize just how much your friendship means to me. It's nice to be able to talk to someone who knows my culture as well as the white world's and isn't judgmental about either."

His humanity touched her deeply. "I think we both need friendship right now, Joe. Being here is the best thing we can do for one another."

"Look, I know it's late, but neither of us have eaten in quite a few hours. Why don't you come over to my home and let me fix us something? It's been ages since I had someone over for dinner, and I've always liked to cook. You can tell me all about your job, and I'll tell you about mine. We'll catch up on all that's happened to us since college."

"You're on," she said, "but you better lead the way in your car. I could miss the turnoff in the dark."

The drive failed to relax her as much as she'd hoped. Was it really possible for them to remain just friends? She wished she could have been sure.

Joe waited for her at the front door, then led her inside to the kitchen. "Have a seat. I'll see what I can fix." He opened the refrigerator, then glanced back at her. "If you want to eat right away, I can fix a green chili omelette. We can have something more substantial like enchiladas if you don't mind waiting."

"The omelette sounds fine. I realized I was starving as soon as you mentioned food." She took off her jacket. Seeing his eyes stray to her gun, she smiled with understanding. "I can take it off if it makes you uncomfortable."

He nodded. "It does, because I'd like to think you're here tonight as a friend, not as an agent."

She went to his living room and returned unarmed a moment later.

"All I've got to drink is water or milk," he said. "The chili I used is very hot, so you might prefer the milk. That'll help cut its spiciness better than water."

"Milk it is, then. I'll pour for us."

She retrieved the carton from the refrigerator, but for some reason she couldn't quite unstick the cardboard spout. The plastic-coated paper seemed to have been fused together. Unwilling to admit defeat, she tugged at it, then in desperation tried to pry it apart with a fork. All she eventually managed to do was puncture a small hole right beneath what would have been the spout.

With all the finesse she could muster, she brought the carton to the table and slowly filled the two glasses. The process took a while and required squeezing the container like an udder to get at the milk. "If you say *one* word," she warned, never looking at him, "I'll arrest you. And do remember my handcuffs are nearby."

He sat down, face impassive, as she returned and sampled the chili and cheddar cheese omelette.

"It's quite good," she said, then looked up. The moment their eyes met, they burst out laughing.

A few minutes later he leaned back in his chair. "That felt good. I don't know how long it's been since I've laughed."

"Same here," she answered. "Sorry about your milk carton, but I think they glue it like that on purpose. I started buying the plastic jugs because of it."

She walked to the window, and looked out at the dim outline of sandstone and sagebrush. "It's so isolated out here. Do you get lonely?"

"Sometimes, but that's the price I pay for the peace and quiet, which I love. You spend most of your time in a city. Does that keep you from getting lonely?"

"I suppose not," she admitted, "although I never thought much about it until Brad and I split up. You learn to think of yourself as a couple, so when you suddenly find yourself alone again, you're very aware of it."

"You couldn't work things out?" He had come to stand behind her at the window, his lips close to her ear.

She shook her head slowly. "No, and staying together would have been even worse. We were tearing each other's hearts out," her voice dropped to a barely audible whisper. "It was a very difficult time."

She chose not to elaborate and he didn't pressure her. He wasn't quite sure what had happened, but it was obvious that some of those scars had never healed. He turned Glenna around and pulled her gently into his arms and stroked her hair. "You have the rest of your life ahead of you. Don't look back anymore, that's over and done with."

"Yes, the marriage is, but some aches will never go away," she sighed.

He tightened his hold, letting the quiet in him talk to her. Slowly she began to respond. A sharp throb of excitement made his body swell as she wriggled in his arms and pressed herself into him.

Joseph tilted her head upward, then bent down to taste her lips. When she threw her head back, urging him to take more, his control vanished. He locked her body hard against his and claimed her mouth in a deep and possessive kiss. He loved her wordlessly, his tongue surging forward to meet hers, then drawing back in a provocatively sensual rhythm.

Glenna yielded to him as if it were the most natural thing in the world. Her mouth was clamped against his with a hunger that matched his own. Her wildness sparked every male instinct within him.

"Woman, unless you're sure you want me," he groaned, "you better leave *now*."

She captured his gaze. "I'm not going anywhere, Joe."

"Then it's decided," he answered, his voice raw. Lifting her into his arms, he carried her into the living room and set her down near the picture windows that faced the mesa.

"You brought me here just so I could see the desert?" Her eyes were bright, her grin gently goading him.

"Think again." Joe hauled her against him and kissed her with savage purpose. His hands moved over her, undressing her quickly and surely.

Discarding the cloth barriers, he drew the dark circles of her nipples into his mouth and was rewarded by the soft gasp that escaped her lips. Until the sun rose they'd belong to each other, and the tenderness that filled him would spill over into all the ways he'd make love to her tonight.

He moved away from her, and quickly stripped off his clothing. As he did, he could feel Glenna's eyes searing over him hungrily. His body threatened to explode under the boldness of that look.

Glenna watched him, breathless with anticipation. His body was as spectacular as she'd dreamed. It was a heart-stopping combination of bronzed silk and steel. His muscular skin gleamed in the half light as he came toward her.

He turned her in his arms until she faced away from him, then guided her to her knees on the floor. Staying behind her, he continued to caress her until she writhed under the thoroughness of his fingers. When she tried to turn around, his hand tightened around her waist. "No, baby, like this. I can touch all of you this way as I feel you against me."

His words burned through to her soul. She whimpered as she felt his hardness pressing intimately against her. "Now," she managed.

"No, we're going to do this slowly. Then when you're slick and moist with wanting, I'll enter you and finish what we've started."

Her breathing was ragged. He would not be hurried, and there was nothing to do but let him set his own pace. She leaned against him, barely able to hold her body upright.

Suddenly a flash of light seemed to engulf the room, and the house trembled as an explosion shattered the living-room window.

Chapter Sixteen

Acting on instinct, Glenna bolted from the floor and dove for her gun. She trained the barrel on the door with one hand and reached for her clothes with the other.

Joseph scrambled into his jeans as he moved to the window, staying low. He peered outside cautiously, then turned to her in alarm. "Run!"

She dashed toward the door. "What did you see?"

"The explosion dislodged one of those giant boulders at the top of the mesa. It's coming down in line with the house!"

As they rushed out the door, both glanced up at the moonlit hill.

"Faster," he urged. Grasping her hand firmly, he ran to the right, eyes on the high ground to their left.

The boulder's thundering descent was erratic. It bounced from one side to the other as it continued to gather speed. Trying to anticipate its path, Joe moved in a zigzag pattern. A split second later, much to Glenna's surprise, he turned and began to head straight toward the boulder.

"No! We've got to move laterally," she said, trying to pull away. "We'll get killed." By now she could even *feel* the boulder approaching. Its size appeared to increase with each passing second as it heaved itself toward them. Yet Joe's course remained set as he rushed seemingly right into its path.

Frantically she tried to pull him to the side, but he was too strong for her to fight. "Joe, what are you doing?"

In horror, she watched the massive juggernaut that was hurtling down in a collision course with them. It was only yards away when Joseph yanked them headlong into a narrow, rocky arroyo. His momentum carried her forward and she landed in a few inches of icy water next to him. It was then that she finally understood his plan. Pulling her underneath a sandstone overhang, he pressed her against the hillside.

Glenna looked up feeling the enormous shudder as tons of rock bounced over the ditch. A moment later she heard the sickening crunch of metal, and then silence.

Joe pulled her against him, brushing the spots of muddy water away from her face. "I thought we were both goners. Are you okay?"

She nodded, not trusting her voice.

"I couldn't explain my plan. There wasn't time!"

"I thought you'd gone crazy!" She pulled away. "Joe, we can't ever let our guard down again. It's too dangerous, and for more than one reason. Tonight, it nearly cost us our lives. That explosion was man-made. Someone tried to kill both of us."

He crawled out of the ditch, then gave her a hand up. "I know."

As she glanced around her eyes focused on what was left of the Bureau car. The boulder missed the house by ten feet, but it had rolled across the hood of the vehicle like a giant bowling ball on its way downhill. The massive rock lay fifty yards further down the slope. It was lodged within another bend of the same arroyo that had saved their lives.

She walked to the car and studied the flattened mess. "I hope you have a telephone, because there's no way the radio in there is going to do us much good."

"I don't have a telephone, but I do have a shortwave radio. When you live this far away from everyone, you need at least that."

"See if you can raise the Hopi police. There's a lot of work that needs to be done here tonight. Then let's both get into some dry clothes. The trunk of my car wasn't damaged so I should be able to get a dry pair of jeans, socks and boots from there.''

Hours later, after a futile search for signs of the would-be murderer, Joseph and Glenna met with the Hopi police captain in front of Joseph's home. Discouragement and frustration gnawed at all of them.

Joe's gaze strayed over Glenna. ''Would you like me to take you back to your motel? I'd let you borrow my car, but that'll leave me stranded.''

''Take my Jeep. You can keep it for a while,'' the captain offered. ''It's unmarked and there's a radio in it.''

''I'd really appreciate that. I'll need something to use until the Bureau can replace my car.''

The captain handed her a set of keys. ''By the way, one of my men has special training in demolition and explosives. He said that from the physical evidence, the perpetrator used a blasting cap and safety fuse to trigger the explosion. From the residue and traces of paper, he thinks it was a permissible form of dynamite used for mining because of its reduced fire hazard. Tomorrow we might be able to get the lab people to try and trace the source. I hope we found enough to run tests.''

She smiled wryly. ''Don't worry. Once this guy learns his plan didn't work, he'll probably try again and we'll have more evidence.''

''You may be right,'' the captain conceded. ''I'd start watching my back very carefully, if I were you.'' He glanced at the men, then refocused his attention on her. ''Your office faxed a report to you today. I glanced at it as it came off the machine. It appears to be a detailed accounting of Shaw's bank records. I brought it with me. It's in a folder on the passenger's seat. I've also got the information you asked for on Murray White, the man whose name was written on that piece of paper you found in the houseboat. It turns out he's Shaw's attorney. He specializes in collections.''

''Thanks, Captain. I'll study everything carefully and let you know what I turn up.'' She opened the trunk of her car and transferred its contents to the back of his Jeep. "Shall I drop you off?"

"No thanks. One of my men has to go past where I live. I'll hitch a ride with him."

Joseph, who'd been talking with the other officers on the scene, came to join her. "I'll meet you at the motel early tomorrow. I have an idea that I want to discuss with you. It may or may not turn up a lead, but it's worth a try."

"All right. We'll talk then," she said slipping inside the Jeep.

Joseph watched her drive away. The others soon followed. As silence settled in around him, he walked inside his home. Wind was gusting through the broken windows so he took some plywood from the garage and boarded them up. The chill dissipated slowly.

As he walked to his room and undressed, Glenna was on his mind. Her softness, the sound of her voice, her sighs, all replayed themselves in endless scenarios that made his heart race like fire across a dry prairie. He didn't get much sleep. When morning finally came, he was eager for the chance to get busy.

Joe tossed the covers aside, the quiet in the house grating on his nerves. At a time when everything he valued was being challenged, his love for her had surfaced with the intensity of a need long denied. Age hadn't given him wisdom. He was more a fool now than he'd ever been.

He took a shower, letting the ice cold water assault him. Maybe that would put an end to the restlessness gnawing at him. By the time he stepped out, he was freezing and shaking, but that inner fire still remained.

Thirty minutes later he was on his way to her motel. Throughout the drive, he concentrated on what he wanted to discuss. Eager to speak to her, he walked quickly to her room and knocked.

She looked tired when she opened the door. "Come in." While he took a seat, Glenna attached her holstered pistol to her belt, then reached for her blazer. "Tell me about the plan you wanted to try out today."

"A thought occurred to me," he said. "One of the Navajo police officers mentioned that the broken transistor radio found in the motorcycle saddlebags had Gil's shop tag on it. But it doesn't make sense that Gil would have carried along a radio that didn't work. I'm certain he took it with him for a reason."

"That's a good point. I think we need to find a technician who can take a look at the radio and tell us if there's anything unusual about it."

After telephoning ahead, they drove to the Navajo police station. Glenna was certain that Joseph was on to something. As she signed the papers required to release the radio into her custody, the Navajo police chief came toward them. "Here's the name of a man we use to repair our equipment. He'll take a look at the radio, but he wants to know what you expect to find."

She shrugged. "I'm really not sure. At the moment all I want to know is if there's anything special about it."

"That's straightforward enough," the police chief said, and handed her the address. "I'll tell him you're on your way."

They arrived at a busy looking repair shop half an hour later. A short Navajo man with angular features regarded her with wariness. "The police chief said you needed some help. I'll do what I can, but I make no promises."

"Fair enough." Glenna stayed by the man's side as he worked. Legally, she couldn't let the evidence out of her sight. The man seemed to go over every component with great interest. Finally he glanced up. "The reason it doesn't work is simple. This radio's been modified to pick up a certain frequency signal only, one not in the band of commercial radio stations. It's a highly specific receiver. It's similar to the tracking systems used in wild animal research. Where's the sending device?"

"Would you know it if you saw it?" Glenna asked.

"Sure, once I got the chance to examine it. Having the receiver close by would make it easy to find, providing the signal's been activated."

"What's the signal's radius?"

"I'd say only about a mile, depending on the terrain and strength of the transmitter's battery."

"I'd like you to come to a workshop with us and check to see if the transmitter is there. Can you do that?"

"No problem."

They spent the next few hours helping the repairman sort through Gilbert's tools and equipment. The receiver hadn't picked up any signals, so they were forced to take the lengthier route to narrow down the possibilities. It was close to two o'clock by the time the man took a seat inside the office. "Look, I've searched everything I can think of. The sending device isn't here. I really have to be getting back to my shop. This has been interesting, but I've got my own work to do."

"Thanks for coming. You've helped us more than you know," Glenna said, seeing him out.

Joseph leaned against the doorframe, more at peace now than he had been in a long time. "I always knew my brother must have had some kind of plan in mind. He wouldn't have turned over those items without some chance of getting them back. He bugged the mask, robe, or both. That's why he brought them here."

"The people he went to meet obviously didn't know about the transmitter. They overlooked the radio completely."

"I'm certain now that Gil intended to follow them in the motorcycle. The device would have helped him track the objects to wherever they were being taken and the cycle would have enabled him get through almost any kind of terrain. Of course, the transmitter is useless to us until we can get a closer fix on the location of the mask and robe."

"And keep in mind that the transmitter could have been discovered by now or just quit working," Glenna added. "My next step is to pay a visit to Shaw's attorney. At least that's one lead I can follow up on right away."

"While you're doing that, I'll see if I can go back and get the Navajo technician to make us a duplicate of the receiver since the original has to be returned. Maybe we'll get lucky and pick up the signal somewhere."

Glenna dropped Joseph off near his car. As she watched him go, her mind flashed forward to the day when they'd have to say their final goodbye. Halfway propositions would hurt too much, but the thought of leaving him made her heart shrivel up inside her.

In a dark mood, she returned to the motel to study the evidence and to make a few telephone calls. She wanted more information on White before she approached him.

Glenna spent the next hour amassing information. A list of meeting dates taken from Shaw's desk calendar and computerized for access and comparisons revealed an interesting fact. Shaw's meetings with White coincided with sizable additions to Shaw's bank account. Acting on a hunch, she telephoned an IRS agent she'd worked with in the past. It paid off. She learned that the IRS had discovered a few discrepancies in his returns, but he'd paid the fines and no charges had ever been brought against him. IRS agents, however, still suspected that the attorney continued to earn unreported income.

Glenna set out on the drive to Holbrook, the small Arizona city where the attorney conducted his business. She had a feeling she'd be spending a very interesting afternoon.

She entered the modern frontier town of Holbrook shortly after three. As she drove to the attorney's office, she prepared herself for the encounter. It was bound to be tough questioning a lawyer, but she needed the answers he could give her.

Murray White's office was in a recently renovated building across from the courthouse. As she walked down the halls she noticed security cameras had been strategically placed around the corridors. A moment later she stepped inside the suite. The plush surroundings surprised her. She'd expected something smaller and less ostentatious in a town this size. It certainly made her wonder how lucrative the collections business was.

The man's young secretary looked up from a computer terminal. A small wooden plaque on her desk gave her name as Kitty Graham. With a pleasant smile, she informed Glenna that her boss would be tied up for another thirty minutes. Graciously, Kitty offered her something to drink.

Glenna accepted, hoping for a chance to take a quick look around.

The woman pushed a button to blank the screen, then excused herself. In a second Glenna was at the computer. The secretary had simply turned off the monitor to clear the screen, and the program was still active.

Glenna hadn't been able to subpoena the lawyer's records, but from the software manuals beside a computer terminal, it appeared the attorney did his books in-house. Familiar with that accounting software, Glenna entered a command for the computer to list any files with Shaw's name. The machine was fast and efficient, and by the time the secretary returned, Glenna was leafing through yesterday's issue of a Wall Street business newspaper.

When she was finally shown inside the man's office, Glenna had gained one piece of information that would serve her well. The attorney had made a large number of moderately sized withdrawals from his own accounts the day Shaw had come to visit him.

Cordial yet professional, Glenna identified herself and sat down in the chair across from his desk. Murray White was in his late fifties, and looked as if he was used to living a very comfortable life. His hands were well manicured and he sported the deep tan of a man used to leisure time outdoors. "As I told your secretary, I'm contacting everyone who's been associated with the late Bobby Shaw. I need to know the nature of the business Shaw transacted with you and your firm."

"I'm sorry, but that's privileged information."

"Mr. White, your client has been murdered. Your assistance could now help us find his killer. Don't you think you'd be serving his interests by cooperating?"

"All I can tell you is that I was Robert Shaw's attorney."

"What type of business did Shaw contract you to do for him?"

"My specialty is collections. I'm also able to advise businessmen on legal matters. Shaw chartered his houseboats around Lake Powell at night and ran a small nightclub," he answered, carefully wording his statement.

"What he had was an illegal gambling operation that's been shut down," she said pointedly. "State and federal authorities are working on that case as we speak."

"I wouldn't know about that."

Glenna matched stares with the attorney. It was obvious that he was going to stonewall it to the last. She had to play her trump card. "You look like you're doing quite well in your business. Surely a practice in a town this size can't be all that lucrative."

"It's sufficient, and I know how to invest the money I do make."

"How good are your business records?" She leaned back and regarded him speculatively. "More to the point, do you think they would survive a very close audit by the IRS? I know you provided substantial funds that were funneled into Shaw's illegal gambling activities. With a tip like that, it shouldn't be too hard for the IRS to find evidence against you."

"Look, I handle business matters for different clients, but I haven't broken the law."

"I'll pass that along to my contacts at the IRS."

The lawyer steepled his fingers beneath his chin, challenging her with a cold glare. "Okay, so exactly what do you want to know?"

"Was Shaw working for you?"

"No, not in any way, shape or form."

"Did Shaw hire you, or were you working for someone else through him?"

Her question threw him momentarily, but he recovered quickly. "Both," he answered at last. "I guess you could say that I was an intermediary."

"Who was the other party?"

He hesitated for a moment, then met her gaze. "I want my name kept out of this, or I stop talking." Seeing her nod in agreement, he started to say more when his intercom buzzer went off. Irately he answered the call. "Kitty, I told you I am never to be disturbed when I'm in a meeting."

"The man said it's an emergency, and that I was to put him through."

"What man, and what kind of emergency?" he insisted.

"I don't know, he wouldn't say. He only told me to tell you he had to talk to you *right now.*"

"All right," he replied, somewhat mollified. He glanced at Glenna. "Let me see what this is all about, then we'll continue."

"Would you like me to step outside?"

He shook his head. "No, just give me a minute." He picked up the receiver and identified himself.

Several seconds went by. Murray White never said a word, only listened. Glenna noticed a pallor begin to develop over his face. By the time he placed the receiver down, his hands were trembling.

He met her eyes. "This interview has just ended. I have nothing further to say to you."

Chapter Seventeen

Glenna went back to her car. There was no doubt in her mind that White had received a threatening phone call. It had been perfectly timed, too, which strongly suggested that White's office had been bugged. That's why she hadn't said anything to the lawyer when he'd asked her to leave. She wasn't about to give those listening something else they might be able to use.

She fully intended to contact the attorney's secretary later, once the woman was away from the office. Judging from White's reaction, she doubted that she'd get anywhere asking him. It would have taken one heck of an actor to duplicate the pallor that had blanched his face during that telephone conversation.

Glenna drove through the Navajo Nation to Hopi land. Those behind the crime were beginning to feel the heat, and that was good. If she made them nervous, they'd start making mistakes and she'd be right there to take advantage of it. What worried her most was that time was running low for Joseph's mother.

As her radio came alive, she picked up the mike. It was the captain. "We've something here that I think you'll be interested in," he said. "How soon can you make it in to the station?"

"Twenty minutes."

"Good. I think you'll want to get moving on this as soon as possible."

"Can you give me any more information?"

"I prefer you get it firsthand."

Glenna stepped on the accelerator, and made the twenty minute drive in fifteen. As she strode inside the Hopi police station, the captain came down the hall to meet her.

"I saw you pull up," he said. "Come into my office. There's someone I want you to talk to. If you have problems understanding him, let me know. He's a medicine man from Second Mesa. His name is Ned Siemptewa, and he's extremely upset. He lapses into our native language often."

As Glenna stepped through the doorway, she saw the elderly Hopi man straighten his five-foot-five frame. His gray-white hair was held in place by a red bandanna tied across his forehead in the old-fashioned style.

Siemptewa's eyes blazed as they went from Glenna to the captain. "It's an insult. Now you bring another *pahana* to compound the problem?"

"Ned Siemptewa, this is Special Agent Glenna Day of the FBI. We need her help. These men are out of our jurisdiction."

The medicine man's anxiety slowly seemed to turn into weary acceptance, and he reluctantly told his story. "A young man with an English accent came to see me at my home today. He placed several hundred dollar bills on the table, then told me that he had a friend who needed my services. He wanted me to go with him right away. I told him I'd have to know what was wrong with his friend before I could figure out what to take along. He assured me that everything I needed would be provided, but refused to tell me anything else. I started to say no because things didn't seem right to me. That's when he placed a set of keys on the table. He told me that they were to a brand new, three-quarter-ton pickup. It would haul much water up the steep sides of the mesa for both myself and the village."

"Did you accept, Mr. Siemptewa?" Glenna asked.

"No. There's something very wrong about his offer. Why would he resort to a bribe so quickly, and why wouldn't he tell me what was wrong with his friend, or what ceremony he expected me to do for him?'' Siemptewa lapsed into a thoughtful silence. ''I don't trust him. I gave him back his money and keys and told him that I needed to prepare spiritually first. I told him that if he was still interested, he should see me later. At first, my only plan was to make sure I wasn't there when he came, but then I got worried. If he couldn't find me, he might go looking for another medicine man and my actions would endanger someone else. That's when I decided to come here and ask the police to help me. I don't think this *pahana* is going to take no for an answer.''

''Would you allow us to watch your home until he returns?'' she asked.

''That's what I hoped you would do,'' he answered patiently.

''I'd also like to place a listening device inside your home.'' She saw his expression harden and quickly added, ''Just until he leaves. It'll give us an opportunity to hear what he says to you.''

The old man shook his head. ''No microphone. There are many others who come for my help, and for me to do that, I must know what they're thinking as well as what they're feeling. I won't place anything in my home that might betray the trust they have in me. My *wuye* would not approve.''

The captain glanced at her and explained. ''A *wuye* is a non-human partner that gives him and his clan protection.''

She nodded, remembering, and tried to come up with an alternate plan. ''We can't arrest him for attempting to hire you to perform a ceremony,'' she told Siemptewa. ''What we *can* do is use him to lead us to others who may have committed a crime against the Hopi people.''

The medicine man gave her a long look. ''You're thinking of the mask and robe,'' he observed. ''I also wondered if there was a connection.''

''Can you give us a description of the man who came to see you?''

"His hair is brown like yours," Siemptewa answered. "His eyes were the color of piñon nuts, dark brown without being black. He was taller than the captain's deputy, say five foot ten or eleven. He had a well-trimmed beard and a mustache."

It was too general a description, and the beard and mustache could have been a disguise. Still, it would have to do. "We'll take positions around your home and watch," she said, glancing at the medicine man then at the captain. "We'll also photograph every white man who comes in. Once the man you've told us about arrives, step to the front door. That'll be our signal that you've made a positive ID and we'll follow him as soon as he leaves."

They were in position less than a half hour later. From her vantage point in a storage hut, she had a clear view of the medicine man's home. Standing near the back of the hut to avoid being seen, she watched the people who came into the medicine man's small home.

"He seems to have quite a few patients," she commented.

"Ned Siemptewa is our best *túhikya*, one who knows by touching. He's quite gifted."

The hours went by slowly. Just as she was about to turn over the watch to the captain, Glenna saw an elderly woman approach the medicine man's door, then go inside. Something about the woman didn't seem quite right, but she couldn't say why.

"Captain, did you recognize her?"

"No, but I don't know everyone around here. Why do you ask?"

"To me, she seemed very limber, even though she's stooped over. I'll have a closer look at her when she comes out, just in case." Glenna turned away from the window and zipped up her jacket.

"She's taking off!" the captain yelled from the window. "She's running like a cougar's after her."

Glenna leaped for the door and ran out into the street, but the woman had already disappeared into a crowd of people. As Glenna spun around trying to spot her, Siemptewa appeared at his door. "That was him! He was wearing a disguise."

"We'll find him. Search north, I'll check south," she told the captain and his deputy, then hurried on ahead.

They searched the village, but found no traces of either a Navajo Indian woman or the tall British stranger the medicine man had described.

Glenna met the captain near the plaza at the center of the village. "It looks like the other side scored a point on this one." Her disappointment turned even more bitter as she saw Joseph approach.

Joseph looked at the captain, then at her. "I heard what happened, and I've got some news from my father that might help. It seems a British anthropology professor named Michael Newton has been spending a great deal of time in our villages."

"I'll contact our man at the Cultural Center," the captain said, walking to his car. "They've got a radio there. Let's see if he knows about Newton."

After getting the information he needed, the captain reported to Glenna. "Professor Newton has been thoroughly checked out and it appears that the man's legitimate. Despite that, the Cultural Center has had him followed ever since he started asking too many questions about our practices."

"Let's find out if Michael Newton is the man who contacted Siemptewa."

They met Ned outside his home. The medicine man's silent gaze left little doubt that he was completely disillusioned with their abilities.

"Have you ever met Michael Newton?" Glenna asked.

"The Professor?" Ned shrugged. "It isn't the same person, if that's what you're thinking. All the medicine men know Professor Newton by now. He's been trying to learn about our tribe and asks questions constantly. He's irritating, but nothing more."

Glenna's heart plummeted. Casting a quick, furtive glance at Joseph, she wondered how he managed to bear the disappointments. They must be twice as difficult for him to take. Thanking the medicine man, she walked back with Joe to where they'd left their cars.

"There's got to be a connection," Joseph said. "Reason it out. We know that the person who approached Gil knew a great deal about our culture. Now we're faced with one man who's a professor and another from the same country who's trying to buy a medicine man's services. If they'd both been Hispanic, I would have said they weren't necessarily connected. But there aren't that many British people in this part of the country."

"No, but there are actors," Glenna said slowly. "Has it occurred to you that this might have been setup to purposely throw us off the trail?" The surprise mirrored on his face answered her. "I'm going to go back to my original lead," she continued. "I've got to find out what part Shaw's attorney plays in all this and the best way is going through his secretary. I'm going to do a quick background search, then go have a talk with her."

Joseph nodded. "I'll see if I can find Professor Newton. I'm still not ready to give up on him."

Her heart went out to him. He must have been desperate to find something concrete to pursue. "How's your mother?" she asked.

"Not good. I saw her briefly this morning." Joseph glanced at an indeterminate point on the horizon, then added, "I can't let my brother's actions cause another death. I have to find that ceremonial costume and get it back here soon."

After saying goodbye to Glenna, Joseph drove to Second Mesa. Tracking the professor didn't take long. He was at one of the villages there, studying an impromptu game of shinny, a kind of hockey game.

Joe watched the professor for a while in the fading light of the cool winter day. Finally he went to stand beside him. The man gave him a broad smile. "It does look like fun, doesn't it?"

"It is," Joe agreed. "Kids have played it for generations."

"I beg your pardon, but aren't you Joseph Payestewa? Someone pointed you out to me a few days ago. You're in a bit of a jam, aren't you?"

"You could say that," Joe agreed.

"Have you any leads on the *Masau'u* costume? I understand the FBI is making inquiries concerning the stolen artifacts."

"Yes, they are. In time, I believe they'll be successful."

"I still can't fathom what makes that mask and robe so important to the tribe. What exactly are their powers."

"It's all tied in to the functions each society serves," Joe answered, deliberately being vague.

The man nodded. "Indeed, but I don't suppose you'd care to be more specific." He gave Joe a hopeful look, then shrugged when he didn't get the response he wanted.

"What brings you to our villages?" Joe asked casually.

"I've had an interest in your culture for years. I'm here in the States on a mentorship program from England. There's much I've yet to learn about the Hopi, but it's been absolutely fascinating."

Joe saw an elderly woman he recognized from his youth watching Professor Newton from her front yard. Curious, he said goodbye to the professor and went to meet her. Jane Lehongva must have been in her late eighties, but it was hard to tell. Hopis didn't believe in counting the passage of years. Thinking about old age and the infirmities that came with it was considered extremely foolish, considering the power of thought.

Her gaze drifted over to him as he approached. "You're on the trail of what was taken from your mother," she observed.

It wasn't a question, so Joe merely acknowledged it with a nod. "I'm making some progress," he added.

"That's good," she said.

"Forgive me if I pry, but why are you watching the *pahana?*"

"I don't trust him," Jane answered flatly. "He asks too many questions about our ways and never gives up."

"No telling what he might do to get answers?" he finished her train of thought.

"Exactly, and that includes the students he sometimes brings with him." She gestured toward the other side of the village, calling his attention to another white man emerging from a small shop. "They help him spy more than learn from him, I think."

Joe watched the young student then, saying goodbye to Jane, strolled up to him. "Hello," he said pleasantly.

The young man smiled at Joseph, and continued studying a man weaving an intricate rug.

"Are you trying to learn?" Joe asked, hoping to start a conversation.

"I'd be lousy at weaving, I haven't got the patience. But I am trying to learn about your culture. I'm just a beginner, though, so try to forgive me if I stick my foot in my mouth, okay?" he added with a sheepish smile. "The professor's the expert. He's studied your culture for years. I wish you could see his collection of Hopi ritual objects."

Joe heard soft footsteps behind him and turned his head. The professor's smile seemed drawn too tightly to pass as natural. "Let me clarify that what I own are replicas," Newton said, glaring at the young man. "I'd let you see my collection, but I'm afraid most of it is back in England."

"I'd be interested in seeing photos," Joseph said.

"I'd love to show them to you, but I'm afraid I've temporarily misplaced the lot of them. One of my students must have carried them off by mistake."

"We have some skilled artisans who'd be glad to help you if you're still building your collection," Joe said casually. "Have you had an opportunity to work with any of our people?"

"Yes, I have. I've purchased some magnificent *tiponis*, and have a replica of a doll of Calakomana that is my most prized possession." He glanced around the village. "How can I convince the village father to let me inside one of the kivas?" he asked Joseph. "I've tried, but I just haven't been able to get permission. I know it's been done. Others before me have even taken photographs of your ceremonies."

"That's precisely why we no longer allow anyone in there."

"Perhaps if your religion was rendered less mysterious, the curiosity about it would stop. Then you probably wouldn't have to worry so much about thefts," he suggested sympathetically.

"Archaeological sites have been robbed for years. It has nothing to do with mystery, only greed."

"You may have a point. Well, I must be leaving, I'm scheduled to meet with the village father. Maybe he can tell me more about *tihus,* the small effigies the warriors are supposed to carry into the ceremonies. Do you think I could get a replica of one of those made?"

Joseph shrugged. "You can always ask."

"Well, yes, I suppose I can."

As he moved off, Joseph's eyes stayed on Newton. That's when he saw John Chapella, who he'd known since high school, discreetly following the professor. If the professor was up to something, John would find out.

Still, there was one thing Glenna could do that neither Clyde nor any of their own people could legally attempt. It might be a good idea to surprise the professor at both his home and office and search the premises for stolen artifacts. Perhaps that would prove fruitless, but at least Glenna might be able to take a look at the photos, which he knew were not lost.

The next morning, Joseph tried to catch Glenna at her motel, but she had already gone. Taking a chance, he drove to the Hopi police station. As he started to walk inside, she came out, practically colliding with him.

In that unguarded moment, he saw the special light that sparked in her eyes and knew she was glad to see him. The knowledge pleased him. Even if they never had more than what they'd already shared, a part of their souls had bonded. He was as certain of that as he was of his own name.

"I was just on my way to try and find you," she said with a quick half smile.

"I must have read your mind and decided to save you the trouble," he answered with a grin.

She held his eyes for one breathless moment, then finally averted her gaze. "It seems Kitty Graham, the attorney's secretary, has left town for a few days. At first, I was more suspicious than ever, but the neighbor who's watering her plants said that she'd planned this for months. She's cross-country skiing somewhere in Utah. I'm afraid the only good news I have is that I have transportation of my own again. The Bureau sent down another car for me."

"Well, I've got some leads you might want to pursue," he said, then recounted what he'd learned from the professor and his student.

"I don't have sufficient cause to get a warrant to search his home or office, but let me go talk to him. Maybe I can rattle him a bit and learn something useful. I'll also request the Bureau do a background check on him. It might take a while since he's a foreign national."

They arrived fifteen minutes later at the village. "Any idea where to begin looking for him?" Glenna asked.

"Let me ask around." Joe walked up to an older woman stacking kindling. "She doesn't know where the professor is," he translated, "but she remembers seeing John Chapella hurrying to the south end of the village. We should go there, too, John won't be far behind Newton."

They'd only gone a few hundred yards when Joe spotted Chapella searching in the vicinity of a kiva. "Something's wrong. The professor shouldn't have gone anywhere near there."

As they approached, John glanced up. "I've lost him," he told Joe quickly. "I saw him getting into a truck the student was driving, but as they rounded a corner he must have ducked out. The kid left the village alone, so the professor must still be around here someplace."

"Surveillance is tedious," Glenna sympathized. "It's easy to lower your guard, and a minute is all it takes to blow hours of work."

"I was not lax," John defended, shaking his head adamantly. "Today of all days, I was especially careful."

"What do you mean? What's special about today?" she asked.

"The Tao society is rehearsing in that kiva today," he said, gesturing to his right. "The *na'atsi*, their standard, has been erected at the hatch. I figured that Newton might have been around there, but I couldn't find him. Of course, I can't go inside since I'm not a member of that society. I was already in enough danger getting that close. If the *pahana* has chosen to disregard the sanctions, he'll soon learn that the gods exact harsh penalties." John shook his head, amazed by the man's folly. "I started searching other nearby kivas, ones on higher ground where he might be tempted to photograph from, but I haven't had any luck."

"We'll help you look," Joe said quickly. "I'm a member of the *Tao* at my village, so I'll go in closer."

Glenna followed him while John searched further south. "I won't get near the building, I promise, but let me help you search the surrounding area. If we work together, we're less likely to miss him."

He nodded, meeting her gaze. "Just be *very* sure you don't walk next to the kiva. It can be extremely dangerous."

They approached cautiously, moving quietly across the hard-packed, sandy soil. Fifteen feet from the kiva, Joe signaled her to veer off. He then moved to the right, circling the building while she remained further behind.

Glenna studied the area. The circular structure was off by itself several hundred yards from the main village, but someone who wanted to photograph it would find any of the piñons tempting. She gazed at the tree limbs, searching, then the surrounding brush. The birds were perched calmly and nothing seemed to be disturbing them. She glanced back as singing erupted from inside the kiva and saw Joseph leaning over some object on the ground.

A moment later he came toward her. A dark rage simmered behind the twin black pools of his eyes. "Look what

I found," he said, producing a small tape recorder. "Newton must be close by. I'm sure he intended to pick this up before the men came out."

They stepped quickly back into the shadows and waited. Ten minutes later, the professor appeared from behind a low adobe wall, camera in hand. As Joe stepped forward, the professor's attention shifted to him.

Newton took a step back when he noticed Joe had the recorder, then turned toward the trees.

Suddenly John appeared from out of the brush and placed a hand on the man's shoulder, his grip firm. The professor spun around, bringing his forearm up and breaking John's hold. In an instant he dashed past him, but before he could take more than a few steps, Joe moved in to cut him off.

Glenna stood her ground about five feet to his left. "It's three against one, professor. Give it up now. You'll have a few charges to face, but if you press this, you might end up with a few broken bones in addition to that."

The man looked at her, then at Joseph. Finally he relinquished his camera to John. "Okay, okay," he answered. "You people don't understand. By permitting qualified ethnologists to chronicle your ceremonies, you'd be providing yourself with a record. Your culture is slowly being lost because you won't allow this. Secrecy is working against you."

"And the only reason you're here is to help the noble but ignorant savages, right?" John countered cynically as he handcuffed Newton. "Spare me. No one here is that stupid."

"A paper on some of your lesser known rituals would help establish me as a leading authority on your culture, I don't deny that. But it would help your tribe, too. You'd have written accounts that you can go back and refer to. Word of mouth isn't always reliable, particularly when so many younger members of your tribe are leaving to find jobs elsewhere."

Joe shot him an icy look. "You're stealing our culture for your own profit. Don't try to couch it in sanctimonious drivel. It's the influences people like you bring into our culture that create the problems my brother faced."

"From where I stand, I'd say it sounds like you're busy finding your own excuses. At least what I did could have had some constructive use, and didn't take anything away from you."

"What you've done is desecrate something you know nothing about and respect even less." Joe watched as Chapella guided Newton into the rear seat of his four-wheel-drive vehicle.

John shut the door on his passenger, then glanced at them. "I would appreciate it if you'd follow me to the station. You'll have to sign some forms."

Glenna and Joseph rejoined the two men at the station. The captain supervised as statements were taken and signed and Newton was assessed a stiff fine. With barely disguised contempt, the captain led Newton to the lobby.

"You'll be escorted out of Hopi land, professor, and you will not be welcome here again."

"My vehicle is back at the village."

"One of my men is bringing it here now. Our patrol car will see you safely off the reservation."

As the captain took Glenna aside, the professor came up beside Joseph. "If it wasn't for your meddling, none of this would have happened."

"You've brought this trouble down upon yourself. Don't look for someone else to blame."

Newton grinned slowly. "It doesn't matter. My work here is done. I've already gathered what I needed from your tribe. That recording would have only been a backup." He raised one eyebrow. "What is that I see in your eyes, Payestewa? Temper? I thought you didn't allow yourself that." He chuckled softly.

As they escorted the professor outside, Joe's eyes remained on the man, his fists unclenching as he regained control. As soon as Glenna returned, he told her what Newton had said. "Now do you have sufficient cause to search his home?"

"No. What you've given me isn't enough to sway a judge," she said, wishing she could have offered more tangible help. "Besides, Joe, if he goaded you like that, chances are we'd never find anything there anyway." His sadness touched her so deeply it stopped being something that was exclusively his. "I'll tell you what. We can have an officer go by Newton's with Gil's receiver. If he gets a signal, we'll get a warrant. In the meantime, we'll go back to my motel, check for messages, and do a little brainstorming over a late lunch. Maybe together, we'll be able to think of something we've missed, or come up with a new direction to take."

By the time they arrived at the motel lobby, it was three in the afternoon. The weather had turned decidedly cold, and she found her blazer was not enough to offset the chill. She crossed her arms across her chest. "I wish I'd worn something warmer."

"The sun's disappeared behind the clouds. From the looks of it, it'll stay that way for a while." He started to unfasten his leather jacket. "Here, take this."

"No, that's okay. If you freeze it'll make me feel guilty," she teased, fishing a set of keys out of her purse. "While I get my messages, will you stop by my room and get my sweater coat from the closet?"

"No problem. I'll be back in a minute."

Glenna went to the desk. With a smile, she read the name pinned on the young desk clerk's blouse. "Are there any messages for room 114, Maria?"

She went to the box and came back holding two slips of paper. "These are the only telephone messages, but someone was looking for you earlier. Did he ever find you?"

"No, did he leave his name?"

She shook her head. "He never said, but we only spoke for a second."

Instinct and intuition combined, sending the first spidery touches of fear through her. "What did he look like?"

She shrugged. "He was tall, with a heavy mustache. He didn't say much, and seemed to have one of those eastern accents, maybe New Englandish. He had a large briefcase and was well dressed, so I assumed it was one of your own people from the city. Why don't you go look in your room? He might have slipped a message under the door.''

Or left a deadly calling card. She felt her body go cold. Spinning around, she raced down the hall faster than she'd ever run in her life. Joe was about to enter her room!

Chapter Eighteen

As Glenna turned the corner, she saw Joseph down the hall casually pulling the key from his pocket. "Stop!" she yelled at the top of her lungs.

Startled, Joseph jumped and turned in her direction, almost dropping the key. "What are you trying to do? Scare me into a heart attack?"

"Don't touch anything! Stand away from the door," she added quickly. As she reached his side, she paused to catch her breath. "Give me a minute, and I'll explain." Struggling to even her breathing, she told him what she'd learned from the woman at the desk.

She stepped closer and crouched by the bottom right of the door. "My mark is gone. I placed a small piece of transparent tape right across here. The housekeeping staff probably isn't responsible since I gave specific orders for them not to go into my room unless I was there. After that attempt at your home, I've been extra careful."

"Do you think someone's inside? If he is, he certainly knows we're here now."

"I don't think the person who went into my room planned to hang around. My guess is that he left a trap for us." She stared at the door for a minute, then called his attention to obvious scratch marks near the lock. "I'm going around the side of the building. My window is accessible from the inner courtyard, providing you don't mind some rather prickly pyracanthas in your behind. Let's take a look into the room from out there."

Joseph stayed close, matching her strides. "Shouldn't we call the police?"

"Let's see what we're up against first," she said. "There's a chance this is only a false alarm." As they reached the courtyard, she picked her way through the thorny bushes beneath her window. Watching the ground carefully, she spotted a large footprint in the sand. "This is how he climbed out," she said. "You can see the path he took. I'm going to crawl in. The screen's off the window, and it's unlatched. It should be safe since he's already used it." She reached up to slide the window open, then stopped when the heel of her hand brushed up against something thin and slippery. Her first instinct was to jerk her hand away immediately, but her training said otherwise. Nerves tingling, she stood on tiptoes and looked where her hand was resting. A piece of monofilament fishing line was just below her palm, pulled taut by the pressure she'd inadvertently exerted on it.

"Joseph." Her voice sounded strangely detached as she tried to keep calm and steady.

"What is it?" he asked, immediately aware something was wrong. Following her gaze, he looked at her hand.

"I think I've touched some sort of trip wire. Can you take a careful look from my left side? I don't think this is a good time for me to move around."

Standing beside her, Joseph peered inside. "Whatever you do, don't pull on that line. It's attached to the window and to a small piece of wood that's holding the jaws of a clothespin apart. The jaws are wrapped with wire and connected to what looks to be a bomb. Pulling the wood out by opening the window or moving your hand would close the clothespin and allow the wires to touch. If that happens . . ."

"Evacuate the building and have someone call the Hopi police department," she said instantly. "Tell them what's happened. I'm going to need some trained techs out here."

An eternity passed with each minute that ticked by. Earlier she'd been cold and had wanted a coat, but now beads of perspiration rolled down her body. She watched the people stream out of the building, noting that the motel hadn't been very crowded. Soon afterward, she heard sirens and saw the police officers arrive. Three men kept everyone else back while a young Hopi officer approached. He was wearing an armored vest and carrying a second one. "We'll put this on you just as soon as I check the situation out."

"Are you the bomb squad?" she asked with a shaky laugh.

"No, there's another guy, too, but he's on vacation," he answered with a half grin. "Not much by city standards, but we're well trained."

"I'll keep that in mind."

After verifying what Joseph had seen, he placed the vest on her, careful not to jar her hand. Last of all, he positioned a blanket over her, covering her head. "I'm going to the front door. It looks like that's clear, but I want you to keep the protective blanket over you. If we trigger anything, you're going to have less than two seconds to drop to the ground before the battery sets off the dynamite we know about."

Joseph, wearing a vest, came back to join her. "Let me help her."

"Are you nuts? Get out of here!" Glenna protested loudly.

The officer waved a hand at him. "She's right, man. We have enough problems without increasing the danger to someone else."

"You're going to be busy with the front door, right? If her hand shifts even slightly, you'll need to have someone in a position to see that clothespin and warn you." He turned and looked at Glenna. "And how well can you hear from beneath that blanket?"

Glenna hesitated. Joseph was right, but she didn't want him risking his neck, too. "With incentive like I'm going to have, I won't budge until it's time. And don't worry, I intend to break land speed records diving to the ground."

"He could be helpful. If he's willing to do this, I think you should accept it," the officer advised. "I better get started. I'll shout 'now' when I'm ready to open the door. I'd give you a radio, but that could set off a remote control device elsewhere." He took a deep breath. "If something goes wrong and I need you to move fast, I'll yell 'duck'. When you hear me, don't hesitate, act immediately and get that blanket over the both of you!"

"You got it." She felt her muscles tense and her mouth suddenly became very dry.

With rocklike surety, Joseph stood beside her. Only the slight narrowing of his eyes attested to his fear. "We better get ready," he said.

"There's still time, Joe. Get out of here as fast as you can."

"No. We'll see it through together." Joseph looped one arm around her shoulders tightly, the other gripped her forearm. "If we have to move fast I'll pull you from the window, then duck under the blanket with you."

A few seconds later the officer shouted "Now." Joseph could see him enter the room, glance around hurriedly, then walk closer to the window. "We were right. There were no surprises near the door. You can breathe again. That is, until I start trying to disarm the bomb."

"Does it look like a professional or amateur job? It would be great if you could take a photo of it."

"Nope, that'll just take more time, and I'm not willing to risk it. I'll diagram it for you later. I've seen this type before. It's simple, but extremely effective. The dynamite charge itself is enough to blow the contents of this room halfway across the mesa."

"How long before I can move my hand?" she asked.

"A few minutes, so hold steady until then. If you jar anything, we'll become a hot lunch for the buzzards."

"What a wonderful way you have with words, officer," she answered cynically.

"Hey, I didn't hire on as a public relations consultant."

He crouched by the bomb and studied the wiring. "Okay, I'm going to cut the wires from the detonator to the battery. After that you can move your hand if you have to, but the detonator itself is sensitive, so stay put. We don't want it set off by static electricity."

A pang of anxiety quivered through her as she watched the man work, but she kept her hand steady.

"Okay, the first part's done," the officer said.

Glenna lifted her hand slowly, then wiggled her fingers.

"Okay, now get ready again. I'm going to disconnect the detonator from the rest of the bomb."

She had to clench her jaw to keep her teeth from chattering. She'd never been more scared in her life. Out of the corner of her eye, she glanced at Joe. Shadows from the nearby bushes played across his face accentuating the steely intent that kept him beside her. She knew then that nothing short of the blast, and maybe not even that, would have moved him from her side.

"Okay, I'm finished here. It's safe now."

Joe took a deep breath then let it out again. The wind that had begun sweeping across the mesa was frigid, but it couldn't compare to the icy grip of fear that had held him until now. They could have both died, but the thought of having survived without her made his stomach clench into a painful knot.

"Glad that's over with!" Glenna said, taking her first full breath. She waited a few moments before speaking again, hoping her voice would sound more normal. "Make sure you check the dynamite against the lot numbers that were reported stolen."

"I'll have the information passed to you as soon as possible."

"Hey, and . . ." She grinned. "Thanks."

"Don't mention it." He grinned back. "But the one you should really thank is your friend. He didn't have to stay here, you know. His job was strictly volunteer."

Glenna waited until the officer walked away. "To both that officer and I, this was part of the job, but what you did . . ."

"Was my choice," he finished for her. "Maybe it was good that this happened, Glenna. It's a very effective reminder of how treacherous our enemies are."

"You've got that right," she muttered. "You realize that we were meant to discover the tampering at the door, then be killed at the window when we tried to go in that way."

"We can never again underestimate how devious the person behind this is."

"I've got to talk to the desk clerk, Maria. She saw the man who came to my room and I'm going to need an accurate description." Glenna walked to the hotel lobby, now filled with employees on the way back to their posts. After a few minutes she discovered that the young woman had left during the commotion. No one else had seen the visitor she'd mentioned.

"Maria was afraid that she'd get blamed," the young man behind the counter answered. "I don't think she's going to come back."

"Do you know her address?"

"Yeah, but she won't be there." He paused. "*Are* you going to get her fired?"

"No, but we need to talk to her right away. She saw the guy who came to my room, and from what I've heard so far, she's the only one who did. That means she could be in a great deal of danger because she can identify him."

"He'll never find her. Maria has too many friends and this is a big desert," he shot back defensively.

"She can't hide out forever. Even if she's way out on the reservation, she'll have to replenish her supplies sooner or later," Joe pointed out. "The people who planted that bomb are clever, and they probably have Hopi contacts."

The boy looked him in the eyes. "Your brother is dead. Why do you think they have other friends among our people?"

"Are you willing to gamble her life on the chance that they don't?"

The boy hesitated, then finally shook his head. "Maria will know I told you. Tell her not to be angry."

"We'll explain it to her, I promise," Glenna assured.

The directions they got to her uncle's hogan on the Navajo reservation were complicated and extraordinarily vague. "I suppose I shouldn't worry about finding this place," she said. "All we have to do is make sure we turn left past the fenced-in pasture with the white cows, but not go as far as where the horses are."

An hour later, they still didn't seem to be anywhere near their destination point. The single dirt track they were on wandered aimlessly through the desert. "I think we're lost," she said finally. "We left the road, or what could have passed for one, a good half hour ago. There were three brown cows there at the turnoff, but no white ones. We were also supposed to reach a wooden bridge that crosses a small arroyo. There are dozens of arroyos out here, but nothing large enough to merit even a gangplank. And my map is hopelessly out of date."

"Keep going. Maybe it's closer to one of the mesas."

They continued for another five miles until Glenna slowed the car. "There's something up ahead that might have been a bridge once. See those wooden beams that extend out into midair?"

"I think you're right," he answered. "From the looks of it, I'd say a flash flood damaged it and no one bothered to make any repairs. But there must be another way to the hogan or Maria couldn't have made it in."

"Instead of driving around, I think it'll be faster for us to leave the vehicle and go on foot. From the description the boy gave us, the hogan should be about three miles from here."

They'd gone about a mile when Glenna heard the thumplike slap of helicopter blades getting closer. She looked around, but saw nothing. "Does the tribe do range checks often out here?" she asked.

"They fly the fence line separating Hopi and Navajo holdings to make sure the Navajos don't graze their sheep on Hopi land. But we're too far in on the Navajo side. Maybe it's a medical helicopter going to or from Keams Canyon."

As the helicopter drew closer, it lost altitude. They could see it skimming the ground around the area where they'd left the car.

"They're searching for something or someone. You think there's an emergency at the hogan we're going to?" Joe suggested.

Glenna stared at the distant aircraft for a minute. The markings suggested it was a private helicopter, not a rescue craft. It was slowly moving their way and she was beginning to get a really bad feeling about it. "Listen, start heading for the rocks at the base of that small mesa."

She watched the helicopter swoop up, then hover a few hundred yards away. Someone was leaning out. "You don't think—" Well-aimed, rapid-fire rifle bullets whined overhead and struck a few feet in front of them. "Run!" she snapped.

They zigzagged toward the rocky mesa a hundred yards away. "They've got some incredible firepower," she managed. Her voice shook from exertion as they ran full speed. "But I'm armed, too, and I'm a damned good shot. Once we're behind cover, I'm going to give them something to think about."

A rapid burst of semiautomatic rifle fire impacted just where they'd been two seconds earlier, pelting them with pieces of brush and gravel. Finally they ducked behind one of the massive boulders that formed the ring of debris, called talus, that had rolled down from above.

"They can't get us here," he said, "at least not easily."

The helicopter banked and swooped down like a mechanical bird of prey searching for them in the rocks. Glenna removed her pistol from the holster then, bracing both hands, waited until the craft was within range. Ignoring the burst of slugs ricocheting all around her, she began squeezing off her shots at the hovering craft.

Glenna saw the hooded sniper jerk back. The barrel of his rifle went up and the helicopter suddenly veered away. She slipped out the empty clip and replaced it with one containing armor-piercing rounds.

"I think you hit him," Joe said. "I saw the guy flinch."

"Yeah, but obviously it wasn't bad enough to keep him from coming back."

Her eyes were glued on the helicopter as it came in for a second pass. She had only two more clips left so she'd have to use them sparingly and wisely. Changing her tactic, she concentrated on disabling the helicopter. She aimed at the engine compartment and squeezed off five rounds as it pulled up and passed overhead.

Glenna heard a change in the downwash sound. Seconds later the helicopter became visible again, moving away from their position. She waited, never relaxing her position, but the sound of the aircraft slowly faded away.

"We have to move while we have the chance," she said. "We can either go on to the hogan and hope they have a rifle, or we can try to make it back to my car."

"The hogan is just around the mesa. I caught a glimpse of it as we were running for cover. It's closer."

"Then let's go there," she said. Pistol in hand, she jogged around the rocky base of the mesa with Joe. It wasn't long before she saw the hogan. A pickup was parked beside it, but no one was outside.

"Stay sharp," she warned. "Whoever is inside may not exactly greet us with open arms. They must have heard the gunshots and are bound to be scared."

"We can't stand on convention and wait for them to come out to us. If those guys in the chopper come back, we don't want to be caught in the open." He crossed in front of her. "This isn't a macho stunt, so relax. I'm Indian and I belong out here much more than you do. They may not hesitate to shoot an armed white stranger, but they'll at least think about shooting another Indian, especially one who's not carrying a weapon."

"What makes you think I was going to stop you? It's a good idea."

He spun his head around, surprised, and saw the partial smile on her face. "It wouldn't have hurt to argue the point with me," he protested. Walking up to the hogan, he kept his hands out where they could see them, and his steps measured. "You might consider putting away your gun."

"I already have," she answered. "What I don't understand is why no one's appeared."

Joe approached the entrance, then stopped. "Hello?" No one answered, so he touched the small door. It swung open on its own, not latched. He suddenly turned, his face ashen. "Don't look in there."

"Joe, I'm a federal cop, remember?" she said softly, and stepped in front of him.

Standing to one side of the doorframe, she peered inside. Two figures were lying on the floor. The elderly man had been shot once in the back of the head. The young woman had a large hole in the side of her skull. The disfigurement, however, was not enough to obscure her identity. Glenna swallowed hard.

"Was that your eyewitness?"

She nodded. "Obviously they followed Maria. Otherwise they would never have traced her." She braced herself for what she had to do. "We're going to have to go inside and see if they have any rifles and ammo. It would also help if we could find the keys to that truck parked outside. The guys who shot at us are temporarily out of sight, but I don't trust the quiet. They may have landed and are now approaching on foot."

"As we were coming up here, I figured out how the woman managed to bypass the bridge. She just went straight up the hillside behind here. The arroyo really narrows a few miles ahead. You could drive in and out of it without any problem."

"We'll use their truck to go across and back to my car as soon as we can. I have to radio this in."

Glenna walked inside first. She had to force her hands to remain calm as she glanced around the blood-splattered hogan. She'd never get used to the violence she came in close contact with through her job. Yet even though she felt like screaming, professional demeanor prevailed.

"Try to find the keys," she said. "I'll look for weapons."

Joseph rummaged through the man's pockets. "I've got the keys," he said.

Glenna finished searching around the darkened interior. "They left no guns behind," she said at last.

Joe listened near the door. "It's quiet outside. I'll go check out the truck."

"No, I'm armed. I'll go." Without giving him a chance to protest, she grabbed the keys from his hand and stepped past him. She returned two minutes later. "The distributor's smashed and half the wiring has been yanked out."

He glanced at the sun. "We could wait until nightfall, and then go."

"It's only a bit after four, that'll take too long. I think we should take off now. The last thing I want is to be forced to make a stand out here with less than two clips of ammo and no transportation."

They jogged back, staying among the rocks whenever possible in case the helicopter returned. It wasn't until they'd reached her vehicle and completely searched it for tampering, that Glenna allowed herself to relax.

"These guys are starting to take some big chances. We must be getting close or they wouldn't be coming after us. They must know that if I'm killed, the Bureau will send in even more reinforcements. Their goal must be to temporarily slow down the investigation. Maybe they need more time to sell or deliver the objects."

She opened the trunk and brought out the hard plastic case that held her rifle and its ammunition, along with extra clips for her pistol. Placing the rifle case on the back seat where she could get to it quickly if necessary, she started the drive back. As soon as they were under way, she picked up her radio and tried to contact the Navajo police. The signal kept breaking up, but eventually she managed to establish intermittent contact. She explained what happened as briefly as possible. Then, detailing the markings she'd seen on the helicopter, Glenna asked for the location of the closest airstrip that could have housed the aircraft.

The Navajo police chief's gravelly voice came over the receiver, but the transmission kept fading. "Emergency landing . . . mesa west of you . . . Could be . . . Check and report."

"Chief, I can't read you. Say again."

She waited, but the only sounds she heard were static. Glenna looked around, noting that they'd reached a low spot in the terrain. "How in the heck am I supposed to check anything out here without specific directions?"

"I did catch 'west' of us, but there's a lot of 'west' out here." He glanced out the window, seeing nothing but earth and sky.

"Forget that, I'm not hunting for it. If the helicopter made an emergency landing, I want backup before approaching. I have my handgun and a bolt-action rifle in the back seat, but that's not going to give us a sufficient advantage against their rapid-fire weapon. We're going for help first."

He didn't say anything for a few moments. He knew she was right, but he still wanted to get a look at their attackers, if possible. "We could try to drive up to a high spot and take a look around."

"The only high spot I'm going to is on the road up ahead. If we see something, I'll call it back in."

"You told the police chief what happened. He wouldn't have asked you to go into a situation he knew was hopeless. He must know something we don't."

"Maybe my signal was breaking up, too. In either case, without more information, I'm not risking it." They were about to clear the rise when a man staggered out into the road only yards from her front bumper.

Chapter Nineteen

Glenna slammed on the brakes and veered sharply to the left. The car skidded to a stop by a sandy hillock of rabbitbrush. Dust and the smell of burning brakes filtered into the car. "Are you okay?" she asked, quickly retrieving her pistol.

"Yes." Joe glanced back at the road as he unbuckled his seat belt, and reached for the door handle. The man outside had collapsed onto the ground and was now struggling to his knees. "You're not going to need your weapon. He's not in much shape to fight."

"Come out my side and keep the car between you and him. He might be a decoy," she warned.

Glenna crouched behind the engine block and glanced around. A few junipers and dozens of clumps of brush were all she could see for hundreds of yards.

Joe remained beside her. "There's no one around here, at least not now. We'd see them."

She nodded, but didn't put her gun away. "I'm going to check him out. I don't think he's armed, but you never know." She glanced at Joseph. "Get the rifle out. It's loaded, so all you have to do is feed a shell into the chamber."

Glenna watched the man stagger closer, then sag to the ground again, breathing heavily. She moved forward cautiously, not willing to trust yet. "I'm Agent Day of the

FBI," she said. "I'm going to help you, but I want you to keep both your hands where I can see them at all times."

"I wasn't part of it," the man gasped, apparently out of breath.

Yeah, and all the men in jail are innocent, she thought to herself. "Just keep your hands out and we'll talk."

The man watched her approach. His brown hair had a streak of blood staining the area around his left temple, but his eyes were alert. Still struggling to catch his breath, he began, "I'm the helicopter pilot, Frank Wilson. I grabbed the mike and radioed an S.O.S. while making a forced landing on the road west of here. You shot the helicopter full of holes, and I was losing hydraulic fluid."

"Where are the others?"

"They were trying to help the man who was wounded when I jumped out. I took off running and never stopped. I know they were planning to use the helicopter radio to call for someone to pick them up."

"How did you get involved with these men and what can you tell me about them?" Glenna helped Wilson to his feet. His breathing was more even now and the blood from the cut on his head seemed to be clotting.

"I work for Sage Realty in Flagstaff. We use the chopper to take clients out to development projects. These three guys came up to me on the helicopter pad and forced me to fly them out here. I don't know anything about them except for that."

Glenna walked half a step behind Wilson as they returned to her car. "Okay. Lean against the door. This is just a precaution, but I've got to frisk you." She searched him thoroughly while Joseph kept the rifle ready. Finally she relaxed. "Joe, why don't you sit in the back with him in case he needs help. Just put the rifle and case up front with me." She saw him nod and knew he'd understood that she wanted him to keep an eye on the man while she drove.

Glenna tried again, unsuccessfully, to raise someone on the radio. That was no surprise, since places on the reservation where the signal was blocked abounded. "Mr. Wilson, we're going to need a description of the men who hijacked you.''

''I wish I had one, but they were all wearing ski masks and gloves.'' Wilson held a handkerchief gingerly up to his head. ''I listened to them, hoping to find out something that would help, but they didn't say much to each other. I do have one clue, though. The man who actually ordered the others sounded like he was British, or Scottish. Maybe Irish. One of those.''

She tried the radio again and this time she was able to make out a voice through the static. ''This is Agent Day. I've recovered the pilot of the helicopter.''

''We read you,'' the voice said, more clearly this time.

Glenna gave them particulars, then signed off. ''We're going to take you to Navajo police headquarters in Window Rock. They'll have a medical team there.''

''I don't need a doctor. I just cut my head when we made the landing. What I need is to call my boss and family to tell them I'm okay.''

''They can arrange that for you.''

Glenna pressed on the accelerator slightly, but didn't dare risk going over thirty-five. The gravel road had potholes the size of wells. By the time they arrived, the Navajo police chief came out to greet them. While the medical team checked the pilot over, the Navajo officer invited her into his office. ''The Hopi police have left a message here for you. The explosives and detonator in your room were from the same stolen batch found at Shaw's place. It's likely that the person who planted them originally obtained them from Shaw, or the other way around. In any case, you've got a connection there.''

Lost in thought, she fingered a groove on her forehead. ''At least that's some progress.''

''You've really stirred up a hornet's nest,'' the Navajo officer observed. ''I hope you find answers soon. Otherwise, the Bureau is going to send an army of people into the reservation. If you don't mind my saying so, that's going to create more problems than it would solve.''

"Probably so," she muttered, "but I don't think it'll happen, at least not yet. I *am* making progress, and I've handled it so far. They won't do anything to jeopardize my work." She stood up slowly. "Chief, I'm calling it a day. If you need me, I'll be back in my room at Keams Canyon."

The chief walked her to the door. "If we find out anything important from the pilot, we'll give you a call."

Glenna met Joseph by her car. "Come on. I'll give you a ride."

Joseph had little to say on the return trip. He stared pensively out the window into the gathering darkness. Glenna knew he had something on his mind, but decided to wait for him to sort his thoughts. By the time they arrived at the motel, he still hadn't spoken. She pulled in beside his pickup and parked. "You're too quiet, Joe. What's bothering you?"

He chose his words carefully. "I think it's time we view the motive for the theft from a different perspective. You suggested earlier that maybe we became targets for a killer because the criminals needed to play for more time. That started me thinking. Let's say that the person the objects were meant for *can't* travel easily. One reason for that could be that he's ill."

"Yeah, that's a possibility, but what made you think of that?"

"Up to now, we've been assuming that someone wanted the stolen objects because of greed or revenge. But there are other more Hopilike reasons for wanting these things." He took a deep breath and let it out again as if trying to bolster his courage. "Our villages have many ceremonial societies. Each one claims the power to control certain types of diseases. This is what's termed as their 'whip'. The robe, mask, and other items that were stolen belong to the *Kwan,* and are of *Masau'u,* who plays a very important part in many of our rituals. The *Kwan* happens to control diseases that waste the body away."

"You mean they can cure them?"

"Or cause them," he answered. "The society's whip is extremely powerful. It can afflict not only those who trespass on its rites, but also its own members unless they discharm themselves properly. I'm wondering if perhaps the person who stole the objects believes that the power of ritual can be acquired by possessing the items involved in it."

Glenna considered what he'd said, intrigued by the idea. "That's certainly an angle worth taking into account. Of course, that would also make the mask and robe even more irresistible to serious collectors."

"Keep in mind that what I've told you isn't information generally available to a non-Hopi. If this theory is correct, we're looking for someone with extensive knowledge of the Way, but who doesn't place much stock on the theology behind it. You can't steal power from the gods."

Minutes ago, she couldn't wait to get to bed. Now the prospect of having to wait until morning made her feel restless and impatient. "Our next step should be to question the village fathers. Let's see if any of them remember an actual trespasser on a healing ceremony. That would have been one way to learn of the healing powers attributed to the objects. If the thief had seen something that particularly impressed him, that could have fueled his desire to steal the mask and the other items. You've opened all kinds of possibilities for us."

"We'll ask the village fathers to remember as far back as they can. I believe more than ever that it's got to be someone with an extensive background in anthropology."

"Let's get an early start tomorrow. Meet me here at seven-thirty."

GLENNA SPENT ONE of the most restless nights she could remember. By the time the sun rose the next morning, she couldn't wait to get started. Joe was at her door carrying doughnuts and a thermos of coffee just as she slipped her blazer on. "I figured you wouldn't stop for breakfast," he said, "but thought you should have something to eat anyway."

"Thanks, I am hungry."

As they got under way, Joseph's mood grew somber. "I better warn you. What we're trying to do is going to be very difficult. This is not something they're going to want to think about. The village fathers feel that the damage has already been done. The gods will punish the intruders, so to them, the incident is best put out of mind."

That morning tested their patience sorely, but slowly they began to make progress. Finally they managed to compile a small and incomplete list of names, some dating back over forty years.

Glenna drove to the Hopi police station. "I'm going to fax this to my office, then have the names run through other data bases and N.C.I.C.—the National Criminal Information Center. We'll see what turns up."

Twenty minutes later they sat in one of the rooms at the station waiting for the fax to finish transmitting. Glenna searched through a report the office in Washington had sent a few hours prior to their arrival. "This background check I requested on Newton is as comprehensive as I expected. The photo they sent is a match, so we have a positive ID, but then again I never doubted he was who he said. He does have quite a reputation as a collector, which supports his story. He owns replicas he uses in his classrooms from time to time. Unfortunately the only noteworthy thing I can see here is that his financial situation is very weak. In fact, he's overextended himself considerably buying the additions he wants for his collection. His assets are nothing in comparison to his debts, but then you can't jail a man for that. Three-quarters of the population is probably in the same boat."

"So until we can get feedback on the names we were given, there's nothing we can do?" Joe asked.

"The village fathers gave us the names of some local residents. There were a few Navajos they suspected, as well as a woman who resides in Keams Canyon. You could try to track them down while I see if Shaw's secretary is back."

"All right."

"We'll rendezvous later," she said, and wished him luck.

The drive through the desert on the way to Holbrook was monotonous and gave her plenty of time to think. Her first order of business as soon as she reached town was to find a way of checking on White's client list. That was the easiest way she knew to tie him in with Shaw or his people. She remembered seeing a video camera in the lobby of the building where White's office was located. Perhaps the security systems people would be able to provide her with the answers White was determined to withhold.

After obtaining the name of the company from the label on the video camera, Glenna drove to their offices. Flashing her badge evoked instant cooperation.

The owner came out to talk to her. "We're ready to assist the FBI in any way we can, Agent Day, but we don't record during regular office hours. Our cameras just serve as a monitor for a security guard at the front office. You're welcome to look at our records."

She spent the next thirty minutes studying the security guard's logbook. Satisfied she'd been told the truth, she stood. "Thanks for your cooperation."

She sat in the car for several minutes considering how to best implement her next step. If White's secretary was back in town, maybe she could invite the woman out for lunch and question her informally. Glenna drove back to White's office building.

Kitty Graham glanced up and gave her a tentative smile. "Mr. White isn't in," she said slowly. "Would you like to leave him a message?"

Glenna shook her head, and then gave Kitty her best smile. "Actually, I was hoping to talk to you." Glenna made a show of looking at the clock on the wall. "Hey, it's almost lunchtime, and I had a small breakfast. Why don't we go out together?"

"Sure. Just let me lock up first. It's been really crazy around here. We had some security people come in and they removed a hidden microphone—a 'bug'—from Mr. White's office phone. Boy was he *angry!*"

Glenna smiled, glad that the attorney had done at least that much to fight his adversaries. Maybe the man had more backbone than she'd given him credit for.

"There's a little restaurant about a block from here that serves great green chili stew and homemade tortillas. We can walk, and that way I won't have to worry about the calories."

"That's fine," Glenna replied, though her idea of an invigorating walk was not one held during thirty-five-degree weather. She wrapped her coat tightly around her as they strode down the sidewalk. "Kitty, I think your boss is in a great deal of trouble."

"I've known something was wrong ever since the day you came to see him."

"Will you help me and him by providing answers to a few questions?"

She nodded. "But I don't know how much help I can be. After you left that day, Mr. White kept asking me about the call he'd received while you were in his office. Did I know the man, recognize his voice, and so on."

"Did you?"

She shook her head. "No, it wasn't any of the clients I normally deal with. And if it was any of the others, I really doubt I'd have been able to tell. See, Mr. White has other people who come to see him but never tell me their names. When they arrive, I just usher them inside his office. Mr. White did the bookkeeping on those accounts himself, too. I always thought there was something strange about the whole thing, but figured Mr. White knew what he was doing."

They entered the restaurant minutes later. Soon bowls of hot, spicy stew warmed them.

"Do you have any idea who those men are, or what their business with White was?"

"Not until recently," she answered honestly. "I was sitting at home, having breakfast, when I unfolded the newspaper. Right there on the front page was one of the men that had come to see him. His name was Shaw, and I remembered his name from our computerized client directory."

"Can you describe the others who came in by special arrangement?"

"Most were pretty ordinary-looking guys in their forties. To be honest, I didn't pay much attention to them, just showed them in to Mr. White's office. All but one, that is." She smiled. "Boy, was he great looking. He was tall, with light brown hair and a mustache. He had the nicest silver-blue eyes you've ever seen. He was so distinguished—old money—if you know what I mean." They finished their lunch, paid, and then walked back to the office.

"If my hunch is right, Kitty, someone has been threatening your boss. But before I can do anything to put a stop to it, I'll need to know if he's made any large expenditures lately. For instance, has White transferred any funds for clients or authorized large checks to be paid out? Think back, this is crucial."

"A few weeks, or maybe it was a month ago, Mr. White authorized a grant to a foreign professor who's doing some research here in the state. His name was Michael Newton." She settled in behind her desk. "What struck me as strange was that it was in cash, and that he insisted on hand delivering it himself. Also, that was the first time I know of that he did something like that. Allocating funds for research grants is not his usual way of investing money."

Hard, running steps came toward them. As Glenna spun around defensively to face the potential danger, her hand crept down toward the pistol at her waist.

Chapter Twenty

Murray White's eyes were filled with fury. "How dare you come here and question my secretary? I'm going to sue you for this. You have no right to pry into my personal business without a court order."

"I have all the legal authority I need, Mr. White. I'm investigating a murder."

"Which does not involve me. So why were you interrogating my secretary?"

"I was merely asking a few questions, with her permission."

He glared at Kitty. "You can start cleaning out your desk. You don't deserve the trust I placed in you."

The last few words struck a cord in Glenna. She could see them cut Kitty as deeply as they had when Joe had hurled a similar accusation at her. "Ms. Graham was trying to help you. We both know that you're being coerced."

"If you know that, then get out, and for God's sake, leave me alone."

"I can't do that," Glenna answered, "but I can offer you protection in exchange for whatever you tell me."

"I can take care of myself. Just get out."

Deciding he wasn't going to say any more, Glenna gave her card to Kitty Graham, placed one on White's desk, and left. Despite what had just happened, she'd finally made some progress. Professor Newton must have been hired by someone to record the ceremonies, and was paid through the attorney, Murray White. What she had to do now was learn who'd financed the operation.

As an idea formed in her mind, Glenna drove to the banks that were closest to Murray White's office. She was fairly certain that the cash that had gone to Shaw and Newton would not have been wired to the attorney through regular banking channels. Nor would it have been left in the attorney's own accounts for very long. Her one chance of finding the person bankrolling White was to identify the couriers who'd brought the money in. All she needed was a little luck.

She went from bank to bank and requested video tapes or photos taken at local automatic bank tellers on or around the dates coinciding with Shaw's deposits. If the men who'd brought the cash had conducted any personal banking business while in town, she'd have them. The only problem was that she'd have to go through hundreds of faces looking for a known criminal, or someone she recognized. Of course the process would be considerably easier if she could get Kitty Graham to help her.

It took hours to gather all the tapes and photos. It was close to five-thirty when she appeared at Kitty's home, an old, wooden-frame bungalow that had been well maintained.

Kitty's face fell when she saw Glenna. "Hey, you've made enough trouble for me already, so just go, okay?"

"Kitty, believe me, Mr. White needs your help."

"I know he's frightened, I spoke to him after you left. He apologized and gave me my job back, then pleaded with me not to talk to you again unless he was present."

"The only way Murray White is ever going to be safe is to fight the men who are threatening him. I don't want to scare you, but if you know something, you're impeding a felony investigation involving multiple murders and other crimes."

"I don't know what to do. I like Mr. White, and I don't want to add to his problems. I know he's not guilty of anything, and neither am I."

"What I need to ask you isn't intended to implicate him. We'll be talking about other people, not what Mr. White may or may not have done. If I can find out who the men who visited him were, then maybe I can identify the one who's behind the threats. You can be sure of one thing. If Shaw's any indication of what his special clients are like, that's where his problems are coming from."

Glenna explained what was inside the large manila envelopes she was holding. "Will you look at these and tell me if you recognize anyone?" Seeing her nod, Glenna went out to retrieve the small viewer she'd rented.

Hours passed slowly, but finally as they reached the second to the last roll of film, Kitty suddenly sat upright. "Wait, run that back."

Glenna reversed the filmstrip viewer that she was using to enlarge the images the bank security people had given her.

"That's not a very good photo, but I believe he's the well-dressed man I told you about," Kitty said. "I just can't swear to it because the face isn't clear enough."

Glenna studied the man on the screen before her. It looked a bit like Professor Newton with a mustache. She went to her car, retrieved her briefcase, then showed Kitty a copy of the Newton photo the Bureau had sent her. "Is this the man?"

"There's a resemblance, but I really don't think it's him. Of course, the guy in this photo has no mustache, but even so, I don't think it's the same person."

Glenna penciled a mustache on Newton's photo, then showed it to Kitty again. The woman shook her head. "No, it's close, but not a match."

Shaking her disappointment, Glenna returned most of the film to the security people who'd loaned it to her. She borrowed the one roll that contained the photograph of the man in question, and took it back with her to the reservation. The Hopi police would have someone who could make a print from the film.

Glad to have made some progress, she looked forward to telling Joseph. She knew it would help ease his concern for his family.

As her thoughts centered around him, she found herself envying the woman he'd one day choose as his wife. She'd have a companion who'd remain at her side through thick and thin.

With sadness, she compared that to her marriage to Brad. She'd never really blamed him for wanting out. Her body had betrayed her in a way vital to her own femininity, and destroyed his desire to share a future with her. Yet that failing had done far more than bring her marriage to an end. It had touched her soul, leaving a hole where her heart had been. And even though the wound had eventually mended, the ache from the scars remained, throbbing when the memories and the reality intruded into her thoughts.

JOSEPH STOOD at his mother's bedside. Her face had a deathly pallor, and her body was still. Only the slight moving of the covers indicated life. "I'm here," he said, touching the elderly woman's hand. The coldness of it made a shudder run through him. Automatically, he reached for another blanket and spread it over his mother.

Wilma Payestewa opened her eyes slowly. "I am glad you came. There's something you have to know." Her words seemed labored.

"Don't talk, Mother, just rest. I'll be here as long as you want."

"No, this is something you *must* know." She took a long unsteady breath. "My *dumalaitaka* appeared to me in a dream last night ... I now know that you will be successful in your search for the missing robe and mask."

"Mother, that's wonderful. You hold onto that. Both Glenna and I are working as quickly as we can."

"There's more, Joseph ..." she said slowly. "Someone with wolf-colored eyes will die. This person keeps a secret that eats at them from inside."

Joseph's heart froze. Her mother's predictions were usually right on target, and Glenna's eyes were a distinctive hazel. His gut clenched as an icy fear clawed deep into him.

"Yes, I see it in your face. You do love the white woman... Protect her any way you can, but be careful not to tell her what I've said. I'm not sure my *dumalaitaka* meant her...though it seems probable...and there's danger that the warning could influence her thinking."

"I'll do what I can to keep an eye on her, but she's not the type of woman who'll accept a man's protection easily. She's independent and prides herself on being able to survive quite well on her own."

"And that, my son, is probably why you love her. You need a woman who'll challenge you... She'll probably never surrender to you completely, except in one way...and that will make those times that much sweeter."

Joseph's mouth dropped open for a moment, then he closed it. He didn't have any idea what to say.

The elderly woman closed her eyes. "Go now. You have much to do for us."

Joseph said goodbye to his father, who sat silently near the bed repairing his old pair of *tochi*. He seemed worn out from lack of sleep. He'd kept a steady vigil day and night beside his wife, and refused any help except from her sister, who brought food for them at mealtimes. "Work quickly, Joseph," he said softly.

With a nod, Joe left the small house. Once outside, he took a deep breath, allowing the cold winter's night air to fill his lungs. He shifted the weight of sadness in his heart so he could bear it, and returned to his car.

It was late and Orion was low in the sky as he waited for Glenna in the motel's coffee shop. He had a clear view of the parking lot and knew he'd see her arrive. He'd been there for an hour when he finally saw her car pull in. As she left the vehicle, he could see from the look on her face that she was on the trail of something.

He went to meet her. "I didn't have much luck tracking down the people the elders suggested. I found only two, and either they weren't telling the truth or they've lost interest in learning the secrets of my culture.''

She filled him in quickly on what she'd done, and accompanied him inside to the coffee shop. "I've got the photos with me. There's a man at the Hopi police station that was able to make prints for me. I want to get your thoughts on this, then we'll compare notes."

Sitting at the booth, she opened her briefcase and took out the two photos. "Look at them carefully, comparing Professor Newton with the other man."

Joseph studied the photos. He put both down, then picked up the stranger's photo again. The face was familiar, yet not. In all fairness, however, the photo taken from the bank monitors was not a very clear one. "There's a similarity between the two, but you can say the same about lots of people. I don't think it's Newton, even though the man definitely resembles the professor."

"That's my consensus, too," she said, and leaned back in her seat. She wanted to go to her room and soak in a tub filled with steaming water. As her eyes drifted to Joe, she felt a familiar twinge. That tub would look even more appealing if he was in it with her.

She rubbed her eyes, forcing her thoughts to stop drifting like that. Hearing Joseph mutter something unintelligible, she glanced up.

He had his eyes glued on a television set in the lounge side of the room. The news was on. "Look at that guy. That's our man in the photo."

Glenna bolted out of her chair, not taking her eyes off the screen. "What channel is that on?" she asked, reaching the waitress behind the counter.

"It's the cable news," the woman answered disinterestedly.

As Glenna hurried out the door, Joseph dropped a few bills on the counter and followed her. "Where are you going?"

"To my room," she answered, rushing down the corridor. "I'm going to call the cable network. I want to know who that man was."

It took more time than she'd expected to track someone who could give her the information. She paced nervously around the room, phone in hand, as she waited. Finally, twenty minutes later, she had her answer.

Joseph, who'd sat still in one of the easy chairs, looked at her curiously. "So, who is he?" he prodded.

"He's Charles Murphy, personal assistant to international financier, Nigel Penhalligon."

"He must be acting on his own, then. Nigel Penhalligon is a millionaire businessman. Why would he have his people involved in the affairs of our tribe?"

"Penhalligon is in his early sixties, and from what I recall reading about him in the news magazines, he's always been interested in Indian mysticism. It's probably even more so nowadays. Rumor has it that he's got cancer and he's dying."

"Then let's see if he's on our list. Do you have yours with you?"

Glenna took out a copy of the names they'd gathered from the village fathers. "Here's a possibility," Glenna said, pointing to the sixteenth entry on the paper.

"Pennington." Joseph read. "It could be. It's certainly close enough to his name for a recollection that goes back decades and involved a foreigner."

"I'll see if I can learn when he was here and where he is now."

"You think he's hoping our objects can cure him?"

"I don't know, but it's an interesting speculation, especially because the medicine pouch was taken, as well. I'll make a call tonight to begin a high-priority search for the whereabouts of both Murphy and Penhalligon. I also want to find out if either of them have any archaeological background."

Joseph watched her walk to the motel room window. A light dusting of snow was beginning to fall. A young Indian man met his wife and children who were waiting for him in the courtyard. The parents watched for a moment while the two young children tried to catch snowflakes with their tongues.

Hearing the laughter, Joe stood behind Glenna and chuckled softly as the father lifted the little girl high in the air and spun her around. "That's the way it should be, you know. Life and duties intrude into the little time we have, and it becomes easy to lose track of what's really important. When you have love and people to share it with, then you have it all."

She watched for a moment longer, her heart threatening to break. "I wanted children and a family of my own more than anything. Still do, but there's nothing I can do about it. I can't have kids." She met his gaze, wanting him to understand her pain and realize the cost even speaking of this exacted from her. "When I took this case, I meant to do everything I could to find you. I've never forgotten what you told me about your mother's cure, and how the Hopi were able to restore her ability to have children. I'd hoped it was due to something I could use or do, also. As a non-Hopi I know I can't take part in your rituals, but you were my last hope."

"Honey, I'd do anything for you, but this is a very complicated matter. I don't know if I can help." He started to reach out to her, but she moved farther away.

"I don't want your pity," she said quietly.

"What I feel for you has nothing to do with pity. You should know that by now," he answered firmly.

She nodded slowly. "I'm sorry, but there's been so much hurt."

"Is that what came between you and Brad?" he asked.

She nodded. "We tried for a long time to have children. Finally he and I both got tested. We found out that I had fibroid tumors within the uterine wall. They weren't malignant, but they made pregnancy extremely difficult to achieve. I had them removed once, but they came back. The doctors said that if I had another operation, the scarring alone would pose a problem. There was nothing I could do without making things even worse."

"And Brad wanted a family." He saw the lines of anguish on her face sharpen and flash as she struggled to keep her tears in check.

"Very badly," she answered, her voice trembling slightly. "He wanted children of his own while he was still young and saw little chance of that with me. When he asked me for a divorce, I didn't contest it." She'd wrapped her arms around herself, and the gesture made her seem heartbreakingly vulnerable.

"And since then you've avoided relationships?"

"You can't imagine what that kind of rejection can do to a woman," she said, moving away from the window. "It's like a shadow over your heart that never goes away."

Joseph gathered her into his arms and held her tightly. Her pain was unbearable to him. He wanted to tell her that having her love would be enough for him; she filled his heart to bursting.

He eased his hold and tilted her head to meet her eyes. In them, he saw her strength and all the sadness loving had brought her. "I'll do whatever I can to help you, but my mother's healing involved some very complex rituals. My mother asked the *Tao*, who petition the goddess of childbirth, to cure her by using the power of their whip. According to our ways, I was then inducted into the *Tao* as soon as I was old enough. As a member, I have certain rights. I still can't take you to our ceremonies, but I can make a special *paho* for you and deliver it to our society's shrine. The *paho's* essence will be inhaled by a kachina and taken to the goddess as a gift."

Seeing the sorrow in her eyes made his chest feel as if it were being squeezed by a thousand steel bands. "Keep in mind that to us prayer isn't a supplication. It's willing something to happen with the aid of the gods. We're taught that when your motives are good, you have a right to expect results, so don't lose heart."

She sighed softly and rested her head against his shoulder. "I've always believed that there's a spiritual presence that watches over us. I think the time has come for me to yield to it," she said. "I have to find the child within me, the one who could trust with all the power of innocence, and believe that I will be given something in answer to my needs."

Joseph tightened his hold on her. "You're the most beautiful woman I've ever known, both inside and out." His love for her was stronger than anything he'd ever felt before. He wanted—needed—to show her what was in his heart.

When she looked up at him, her mouth parted and the invitation ripped through him like a million lightning bolts. Struggling to hold back, he kissed her lightly then nuzzled her neck, tasting the softness there. "Hold onto me, honey, hold me tighter," he whispered.

Glenna wrapped her arms around him and pressed herself against him. His chest felt hard and warm. He was offering her his strength and love, and she needed the comfort of both too badly now to turn away.

Joseph led her gently to the bed and continued to kiss her, smoothing away the hair that framed her face. He loved the feel of her and the way she leaned into his palm, asking wordlessly for his caress.

Her soft cries made him throb with the need to have her. Pulling away her sweater, he bared her breasts and nursed on the sweetness of her. Glenna's fingers entwined in his hair, pulling him to her and encouraging him with soft words that drove him crazy. Driven by an impatience he could scarcely control, Joseph pushed away and stripped off his clothing. As Glenna's eyes burned over him, he stood before her, encouraging her to see him and know him.

Still on the bed, Glenna started to wriggle out of her jeans, but he came up to her and stopped her. "Let me take over. You don't have to do anything except open yourself to my love." He knelt on the edge of the bed and slipped her clothing off. With barely controlled hunger, he kissed the flesh he bared, loving the way she twisted against him, seeking more.

He was so hard, he wasn't sure how much longer he could hold out. Joe lowered himself onto the mattress, then shifted until his shoulders rested against the headboard. Lifting her easily, he pulled Glenna on top of him.

He stroked and caressed her, but prevented her from joining him.

Fires raced through her, but he wouldn't allow her to finish what they'd started. As her fingers brushed his manhood, he inhaled sharply and tried to push her hands away.

She smiled slowly. "You want me wild, but you still want to be in control?" she whispered. "That's not fair, is it?" She refused to stop caressing him.

Shudders ripped through him. He could overpower her physically, but emotionally she consumed him, matching passion for passion. Grasping her buttocks in his hands, he lowered her onto himself. The tip of his shaft found her opening and for one breathless second, he held her there. Then with a groan, he brought her down the rest of the way. "Feel me," he groaned. "I'm a part of your body now and a part of your soul."

Glenna gasped at the sweet intrusion, her body alive with sensations that were almost too much to bear. Emotions came flowing up from someplace deep within until she almost cried with the intensity of it.

He felt her responding and it drove him beyond reason. He thrusted inside her fast and deep. She matched his aggression, yet at the final moment, yielded magically with a sigh. Past any conscious thought, he exploded inside her.

She held on to him tightly until the last shudder traveled through them. "Keep me in your arms like this for a while," she said, her voice unsteady. "I don't want to let go yet."

"You don't have to. As long as you want and need me, I'll stay with you," he answered quietly. He loved having her so close, and wondered how he'd ever slept without her in his arms. There was peace here, and though he knew that it would end all too soon, they had each other now.

She woke up shortly after dawn and felt him still next to her. For a long while, she basked in the glow of what they'd shared. She'd never regret a moment of it. Yet even though many loving promises had been whispered in the night, she'd never bind him to those. Joe needed stability and continuity, the kind he'd find with a Hopi wife and children of his own. She gazed down at his sleeping face, feeling her heart swell with a rush of love. It would break her heart, but when it came time for her to go, she'd step out of his life forever. She loved him too much not to let go.

By the time she came out of the shower, he was gone. She saw his hastily scribbled note. He'd left to prepare a *paho*. His promises would be kept. She took a deep breath, ignoring the way her heart twisted inside her. She would not fail herself by clinging to wishes and wants. Joe would never be hers. It was time to look to the future with eyes open to whatever dreams she could forge alone.

It was shortly after eight when he caught up to her at the motel desk. Glenna was busy circulating the photo of Charles Murphy, hoping someone would remember seeing him, but no one did.

With a quick smile, she turned her attention to Joseph. "I'm glad you came by. I wanted to let you know I'm driving back to Holbrook. Kitty Graham, White's secretary, suspects her boss's wife may have been kidnapped and that's why he's been afraid to talk to me. I'm going to have to go pay him a visit and see what's going on. What are your plans?"

"I'm going to my mother's house. After I finish there, I could circulate those photos for you. If Murphy ever visited any of our villages, someone's bound to remember."

"That would be great," she said, handing the copies over to him. "Tell your parents that my thoughts are with them."

Glenna drove to Holbrook as quickly as she could. Apparently, Kitty had overheard one of White's telephone conversations and had come up with the kidnapping theory. If what Kitty suspected was true, then the attorney's wife didn't have a chance unless he allowed the FBI to step in.

She walked inside the attorney's office an hour and a half later. White, standing by his secretary's desk, saw her come in. Kitty Graham looked up, but tried not to make eye contact.

"I still have nothing to say to you," White maintained, looking at Glenna. Fear sparked in his eyes. "Please leave."

"You're a very intelligent man, Mr. White, but you're in over your head. I did a little checking with your neighbors and around town," she said, keeping Kitty's name out of it. "I know your wife's disappeared. I realize that's probably why you're afraid to cooperate. Only what makes you think you can trust people who'd resort to tactics of that kind?"

"They swore they'd kill her if you interfered."

She followed him into his office, closing the door behind him. "Mr. White, they'll kill her if I don't. Even if they've kept her blindfolded, they can't be sure of what she might have overheard. These men aren't the kind who take chances just to play fair."

He crumpled into his chair like a rag doll. "I just don't want anything to happen to Regina."

"Then trust me. The Bureau has people who're experts in dealing with this type of crime."

"If I agree, then no one else but you gets involved. Period. I don't want half a dozen new faces popping up here. This isn't that large of a town, in case you hadn't noticed."

"All right, then talk to me. Tell me what they've said and done."

"I got a call the day you were here in my office. They told me that they'd taken Regina, and unless I kept my mouth shut, they'd send her back to me through the mail."

She could see from the taut lines around his eyes that the message had achieved its desired results. "I need to have you recall everything you can about that phone call. Were there any background sounds that might give us a clue?"

"After what they said, my mind just froze. I couldn't remember anything useful if I tried. But I record all incoming calls until the caller and business are identified. It's routine. In this particular case, I never did turn the tape off.''

Glenna's hopes soared. "I'd like to hear the tape right now."

White reached into a file cabinet and pulled it out. Placing a small recorder on the desk, he played the cassette for her. Glenna tried to shut out the voice, which was obviously disguised, and just listen to the background. A train whistle was blowing and cars were honking.

"We can't do much with that," the attorney said, guessing what she was thinking. "The Santa Fe Railroad has tracks all over this state."

Glenna leaned back in her seat and stared across the room, lost in thought. "May I use your telephone?" She looked up the number and dialed the regional office of the Santa Fe Railroad. Using the time of the call as a reference point, she asked the clerk to try and pinpoint where the trains traveling across their area were at that time. Finally she placed the receiver in its cradle. They'd be getting back to her as soon as possible.

"When the call came in, how long had it been since you'd seen your wife?" she asked.

"A few hours, that's all."

"That gives us some hope. Did you try to contact her after I left?"

"Yes, and when she didn't answer the telephone, I went home. She was gone."

"They must have taken her between the time you left for work and the time of the call. My guess is that my coming didn't trigger the kidnapping, it was already planned. They meant to get some leverage to make sure they could control you," Glenna concluded.

White nodded, unable to look her in the eye.

"Can I see the bug that was found in here?" Glenna asked hopefully. "Maybe it can be traced."

"I did a dumb thing. I threw it in the incinerator. But the man who removed it from the phone said the person listening in could be a hundred miles or more away. It used the phone lines somehow. Does that help?"

"It tells us that the people we're dealing with are very competent professionals. But we knew that already." Glenna glanced around the office. "It's time for me to start looking for your wife, and to do that I'm going to need a photo of her."

White picked up one he'd kept on his desk, took it out of the frame, and handed it to her. "This was taken last Thanksgiving."

While the Santa Fe Railroad official made the difficult queries she'd asked for, Glenna drove to the small Holbrook airfield. She circulated the photo of the woman, as well as Murphy's and Newton's. No one had seen any of them around. After checking the log, the airfield manager assured her that no flights had taken off during the morning in question except for instructors and student pilots.

The news buoyed her spirits. That meant that she could still pursue the train lead. Since they hadn't flown Mrs. White out, it was possible the kidnappers had remained in the general area. And even if they'd driven her out of state, she stood at least a slim chance of finding someone who'd seen the victim with the kidnapper at the time the call was made. A lead could develop at that point. Now she needed to pinpoint where the call had been made from. She drove quickly to the railroad office and met the manager she'd spoken to on the telephone.

"Around the particular time you gave us, there are three intersections that are usually filled with cars waiting for our trains to pass. One engineer said he always blows the train whistle at a certain curve near Gallup, New Mexico, because he has to travel past a bend and frontage road crossing the tracks. He wants to give everyone, particularly motorists who're in a rush to get to work, a clear signal that the train is close by."

Glenna jotted down the address. It was about two hours away. On her way to Gallup, she had a call relayed to the police there. A quick check revealed that there was a run-down motel called the Night Owl near the bend the engineer had mentioned. It catered mostly to those looking for a few hours' lodging. Glenna officially requested local assistance in executing a clandestine search of the area. It was possible Mrs. White was being held in the vicinity, but she didn't want to tip off her captors yet. If her guess was right, they might need to conduct a hostage rescue operation.

Making arrangements for White to be notified, Glenna placed the red light on top of her car and pressed on the accelerator. She intended to make the normal two-hour or so drive in as short a time as possible.

Chapter Twenty-One

Joseph decided to contact the *túhikya* from Second Mesa, Ned Siemptewa, first. There was a chance he'd recognize Murphy's photograph. When Joe showed him the photo, the man grew agitated. "The man I saw had a beard, but the eyes look the same. I think that's him. Why don't you ask Tom Loloma? He might be able to confirm it for you. He's a healer on Third Mesa and this morning I learned the *pahana* went to see him before he came here."

Joe drove quickly to Third Mesa. Excitement and new-found hope made his spirits soar. Thirty minutes later, he met with the medicine man.

The Hopi healer had his gray hair tied in a ponytail fastened at the base of his neck. Turquoise of a deep Persian blue decorated the intricate squash-blossom necklace he wore around his neck. "Yes, I believe that's him," he said, pointing to Murphy's photo. "The cut of his hair and the shape of his nose is right." He gave the photo back to Joseph. "He was a strange one, but very knowledgeable about our ways. Some of the things he knew haven't been spoken about for generations. They date back to Voth, that missionary who never learned that some trusts are not to be broken."

Joseph nodded. Many anthropologists had betrayed the Hopi people until the tribe had finally become wise to the false promises of the *pahanas*. "Did he ever ask to buy ceremonial items?"

"He wanted me to make a special *paho* for him, for the well-being of a friend. I saw no harm in that. He claimed it would be used in a reverent way."

Joseph exhaled softly. He had no doubts now that Murphy was indeed working on behalf of his boss. "Did he ask for anything else?"

"No, just that. I told the *kikmongwi* before I did anything, and he gave his approval."

Joseph drove to his mother's house, his thoughts occupied with what he'd just learned. Proving that Murphy was involved did not mean that Murphy also had the stolen items. Yet a clear trail was beginning to emerge and he was profoundly glad to see it. His mother's condition had further deteriorated in the past few days.

A short time later he arrived at his mother's home. All the normal kitchen sounds and smells he'd come to expect were gone. It was as if the house itself felt the approach of death.

Shaking the mood, he went to his mother's room. His father looked up and stood as he approached. "Would you stay with her for a while? I have some things to take care of, but I didn't want to leave her with anyone else except you."

Joseph nodded, knowing his father wanted to visit one of the clan shrines. "I'll be here as long as necessary," he said, sitting by his mother's bedside.

Wilma Payestewa opened her eyes slowly. "You have much on your mind today," she said.

"I'm worried about you," Joe answered honestly.

"Yes, but it's more than that. You were never good hiding your thoughts from me, Joseph. Something else is disturbing you. It's there in the way you're sitting, and the way you keep looking at my *Marau-vaho*. I was presented with that special *paho* when I was received into the women's religious society... That was long before you were born."

Joseph nodded, remembering the story. "This has a connection to that time in your life. Glenna's asked for my help. There's very little I wouldn't do for her, but this is out of my hands," he said, explaining about her inability to bear children.

"Falling in love with a woman outside our tribe carries certain problems. But giving up the right to ever have children of your own...." She exhaled softly. "Perhaps there is another way, even though Glenna can't be brought into the kiva... My word still counts for much among our tribe. I will petition the *Kwan*. The purpose of many of their ceremonies is to ensure a continued blessing on the physical aspects of fertility and the normal functioning of the reproductive organs... Your uncle is the head of that group and will benefit as much as us when the objects are returned... I'm sure I can persuade him to hold a healing ceremony for your woman."

Joseph felt a pleasant stirring, hearing Glenna referred to as "his woman." But she belonged to no one except herself. As it had been so long ago, he had nothing to offer that would hold her at the villages. He walked to the window and stared at the barren countryside. It took love and a special eye to see the beauty that was there.

"Yet even if she could have children, they would not be considered Hopi by our tribe."

"There is another way, though it isn't common. I could adopt them according to our Way, and they would become part of our clan."

Hearing his father come into the room, he turned around. His father gave him a wan smile. "Our neighbor has made some stew for us. I'd like you to go get it, but before you do, would you haul water for them? Johnny makes the four-mile walk every day, but it's getting very difficult for him."

"I'll see to it right away." Joe grabbed his jacket and fastened it tightly. It was the hardest of all work, and he was surprised a man as advanced in years as their neighbor was, still managed it.

The task took him almost ninety minutes. The walk, however, helped him unwind and think. His mother's condition, though grave, had apparently stabilized. He clung to that fact, determined to see it as a sign of hope.

As he walked back into the small home, his father came to him. "She fell asleep after you left. I thought all was well, so I went and chopped some wood. When I returned, she was awake and insisting on talking to you right away."

Joe placed the pot of mutton stew on the stove to warm, and hurried into the bedroom.

His mother's eyes were feverish as they came to rest on him. "You've come. I've had a very disturbing dream."

"About whom?" Joseph asked, trying hard to keep his tone calm. Very few things could unnerve him as much as his mother's visions.

"Let me tell you what I saw, then you can judge for yourself," she answered. "In my dream, I was inside a small, dirty room where a young woman was tied to a chair. I could sense that she was in danger, and that she thought she was about to die. I tried to find out more, but then I was outside and saw a white owl standing watch over the building... It was as if death was watching and waiting for the time to make itself known." She shuddered. "The woman—I couldn't see her face—had light brown hair draped to her shoulders."

Fear stabbed through Joseph, clutching at his insides. "Do you believe it was Glenna?" he asked, his voice strangled.

"It could have been, but I'm not sure. My dreams aren't as clear as I'd like them to be."

Joseph nodded. "Do you know when this is going to happen?"

"I feel it will be very soon," she answered slowly. "Find her, Joseph. She's a good woman. In many ways she needs you just as much as you need her."

The elderly woman's intuition never failed to surprise him. "You've done your part by telling me. Now it's my turn. Don't worry about either of us," he said.

Joe hurried to the Hopi police station. He wasn't exactly welcome there, but he didn't know how else to go about finding her. As he stepped inside, the officer at the desk glanced up. His cool gaze remained professional, but didn't quite disguise his distrust. "What can we do for you, Payestewa?"

"I need to find Agent Day. I have some information for her."

"Tell us, and we'll relay it to her."

"I have to convey the message myself," he replied, refusing to be put off.

The captain stepped out of his office and motioned for Joseph to join him. "If it's really that important, then you should tell me. She's going to be gone the rest of the day. I received word just minutes ago that she's looking for a hostage in Gallup."

Joseph stood up. "It's all right. I'll wait until she gets back."

The captain moved to one side, blocking his exit. "If you're thinking of going to Gallup and trying to find her, I'd strongly advise against it. There'll be cops everywhere, and all you can do is get in the way."

"I have no intention of interfering with her job, so don't give it another thought."

Joseph walked out of the station and started east on the shortest route to Gallup. He'd only traveled a few miles when he spotted a patrol car behind him. With a frown, he adjusted his rearview mirror and kept an eye on the vehicle. They couldn't detain him, they had no grounds to do so. This was probably Captain Kywanwytewa's way of gauging his intentions. Glenna would be warned that he was coming; the captain was obviously trying to help Glenna out. It was too bad that he didn't believe Joe was doing the same thing.

The drive seemed interminable. He tried to push his mother's vision out of his thoughts, but her words echoed in his mind. Fear sank deep into him, permeating every facet of his being.

He arrived in Gallup in less than two hours. Immediately he drove around the area of the police station until he located a coffee shop where several police cars were parked. He went inside, finding exactly the kind of environment that would best serve him. Hand-held radios were alive, their crackling calls coming in at random intervals. He ordered a cup of coffee then waited, listening.

Two cops sitting in the corner booth monitored reports that came over the air. "That Fed's a great one for stirring up trouble," one said. "She went with two of our detectives to check out a lead, and they had to fight their way out of a place called Sal's Bar. It's right next to the Night Owl motel. The woman went right back in, though, and managed to find somebody who would talk. Now she's asked for the S.W.A.T. team, so who knows what's going on."

Joseph realized he was shaking as he listened to the almost casual discussion. Forcing himself to stay calm, he placed a dollar bill on the table for the coffee and hurried out the door.

He'd seen the sign for the Night Owl as he'd driven into town. He headed for it now. By the time he arrived, a heavily armed team of men with bulletproof vests were advancing on a room at the far end.

Joseph left his car parked along the curb and started toward the motel, but an officer soon blocked his way. "Sorry, buddy, but this is as far as you go."

The sound of a window breaking made him flinch. Joe struggled to see around the enormous Anglo police officer who stood in his way like a tractor trailer. Two loud pops followed, and a stream of smoke came out the shattered window. There was the loud crash as a door was kicked in, then yelling.

Before he could make out what was going on, he saw the police emerge. Two of the black-clothed officers wearing gas masks dragged a coughing man out by the collar, then held him down on the ground while they handcuffed him.

Another officer came out a second later, carrying a woman in his arms. She lay still, her light brown hair stained with what looked like blood.

Instinctively Joseph pushed the officer aside and rushed forward. He heard the sound of running steps behind him, and suddenly two officers tackled him to the ground. The side of his face was pressed against the gravel, tiny stones cutting into his skin.

From that vantage point, he saw someone approach. It was a woman, gauging from her legs and shoes. He tried to turn and look up, a spark of hope burning in him, but the cop behind him pushed his face back down and handcuffed him.

"Don't move, buddy."

As the woman crouched down, he shifted his gaze upward. An overwhelming feeling of relief spread through him the moment he saw Glenna's face. "You're all right," he breathed.

"Yes, *I* am," she answered coolly, "but you seem to be having definite problems."

"I thought you were the woman they carried out," he managed. Despite the uncomfortable position he was forced to maintain, he felt a rush of warmth just having her close by and safe. He tried to catch her eye, and with effort, succeeded. "Are you going to help me?"

"I didn't cross the police line—you did." She shrugged. "You'll have to convince the officer."

"Are you enjoying this?"

"As a matter of fact, I am. It serves you right for rushing in here like you did. They could have shot you."

"I came to protect—" He corrected himself quickly. "Help you, and I thought I'd arrived too late."

"Protect or help," she commented off-handedly. "It looks like you're the one who needs rescuing."

"Fine, so will you?"

She signaled the officer, who undid the cuffs. "You better have a *very good* reason for being here, Joe. If you don't, I'll turn you right back to him." She gestured toward the cop.

Joe stared at the six-foot-four redhead who was glowering at him. He looked as if he wouldn't need much encouragement to complete the arrest he'd started. In fact, Joe had the distinct impression there was nothing he would have liked more than to shove his face right back down on the gravel. "I do have a good reason, but you've got work to do here and what I have to say will take some time."

She glanced at the officers guarding the man who'd held Mrs. White prisoner. "You're right. There are a few things I've got to take care of now, so I'll meet you later tonight at the coffee shop. We'll discuss this then."

He knew she was furious with him, but knowing she was okay was more than enough to make him happy. He watched as the woman they'd rescued sat up. A man he judged to be her husband held her tightly. The resemblance between the woman and Glenna was unquestionable. He exhaled softly, realizing how vulnerable his love had made him.

GLENNA LEFT JOSEPH and went to meet the S.W.A.T. team leader. "Did Mrs. White say anything about her captors?"

"Only that they were masked and she never saw their faces."

She took a deep breath, determined to hide her disappointment. "What do we have on the suspect in custody?"

"His name is Al Tafoya, and he's a regular at Sal's Bar. The owner, Jerry Field, said that a man paid him to make regular booze deliveries to Tafoya at the motel room. He claims he didn't know a thing about the woman."

"Wait a minute. This means there are *two* eyewitnesses who saw the guy behind the kidnapping?"

"Yeah. But Al Tafoya is usually so drunk he can't even see where he's putting his feet. Jerry Field might be more help."

Glenna approached Tafoya with the photos of Professor Newton and Murphy. "Do either of these men look familiar to you?"

"I dunno," he said unsteadily. "Maybe."

"It'll go easier on you if you cooperate with us," Glenna insisted.

"Lissen, lady," he said, his words slurred. "I dun't *care* whah people look like, ya know?"

She stared at him for a minute, then decided she was wasting her time. The man faced kidnapping and conspiracy charges for keeping a woman captive, and he'd probably done it all for an unlimited supply of booze. Tafoya was lucky he remembered his own name. Maybe she'd have better luck with the other witness. She strode up to the man the officer had identified as the owner of the bar. "Do either of these men look familiar to you?" she asked, showing him the photos of Murphy and Newton.

Jerry Field studied each. "The one without the mustache resembles the guy who paid me to deliver the booze to Al. But since he was wearing dark glasses and a cowboy hat at the time, I can't tell for sure which of these guys it was, or if it was either of them. I never got that close a look at his face. About the only thing I can tell you is that he had an English accent and paid in cash." He glanced worriedly at the officer by his side. "Hey, I didn't do anything except sell liquor, and I've got a license to do that. You can't arrest me."

"You'll have to come to the station, Mr. Field. What happens there is up to the district attorney," the officer answered.

Glenna heard his protests as she left to join Murray White. "How is your wife?" she asked softly.

"Regina's fine, Agent Day," White answered. "The paramedics checked her and I'll be taking her to our own physician for a complete examination. Her worst injury is a bump on the head. The drunk tried to run, and knocked over the chair she was tied to," he explained. "She's still a little disoriented from the tranquilizers he stuck in her food, but that spared her a lot of fear when your team moved in." He shook her hand. "I can never thank you enough."

"You don't have to thank me, just give me the information I need. Mrs. White never saw her kidnappers' faces, so I need your help."

The attorney hesitated. "No," he said, at last. "I can't. You don't know these men. If I cooperate with you, they'll find me and my wife and kill us."

"I can have you both placed in protective custody."

"For how long?" White shook his head. "No, I'm acquainted with how the law protects you. I'd have to spend the rest of my life in hiding, and that's not for either of us."

"You'll be facing criminal charges as it stands now. We know you were the contact point for the people behind the theft and murder that occurred on the reservation. If I was able to offer you complete immunity in addition to protection, would that change your mind?"

He shook his head and gave her a thin smile. "I'll risk jail."

With a shrug, Glenna returned to her car. She'd have to put all her resources in the Bureau to work. Using her radio, she had a call relayed to the Phoenix office. She needed to track down Charles Murphy. She didn't like the idea of having an adversary close by, yet so well hidden. She also requested that twenty-four-hour surveillance be placed on Professor Newton.

The moon was up on a cloudless night as she entered Keams Canyon. She should have been tired, but she couldn't get her mind off the case and Joseph. He'd come to protect her, and she found the notion touching. Yet what had made him think that she couldn't take care of herself? Was he losing faith in her abilities because the investigation hadn't produced the answers he needed? The question troubled her.

She went to the motel desk and retrieved her messages. There was a sealed manila envelope from the Hopi police waiting for her. She opened it quickly. It was a copy of the lab report on the explosives used to dislodge the boulder near Joseph's house. From the residue, they'd been able to determine that it had come from a batch of explosives and detonators missing from a coal-mining operation on the Navajo Nation. The materials used in the bomb planted in her room, and to set off the fire, were also from that same theft. Secakuku had once worked for the company, and took part in the blasting operations.

A second dispatch was just as significant. Secakuku's body had been found on a remote area of the Hopi reservation. He'd apparently died of exposure, but Hopi officers were checking the site for more clues.

She stared at the report, wondering how Secakuku fit into the rest of the picture. Had he been working for Shaw or Murphy when he'd faked the destruction of the mask and robe? The evidence so far suggested he'd also been the one who'd nearly killed them with the boulder, only that had been after Shaw's murder. Perhaps he blamed their investigation, and ultimately them, for Shaw's death. Revenge was a common motive. Yet, no matter how it shaped up, she doubted Secakuku's death was accidental. She looked forward to getting the results of the autopsy.

She strode into the coffee shop, wondering if Joseph would still be there. She was much later than she'd expected. As she went inside, she saw him at the booth nearest the door.

Glenna sat across from him wordlessly. "Okay, now we have time for your long story. I hope that after I hear it, I won't be sorry that I didn't let them arrest you." She would have done all she could to have kept him out of jail, but he didn't have to know that.

"It's hard to explain," he admitted. "My mother has a special gift," he said, then went on to explain the details. "She's usually right. The hardest part is that we've never been able to prevent what's going to happen. In your case, I knew I had to try."

She gazed across the room, lost in thought. His concern touched her deeply. Yet at the same time she knew that there were certain things he'd have to understand. "Even if your motives are noble, you can't charge into situations that are my responsibility to handle. By doing that, you're showing a lack of faith in my abilities. I know and have accepted the risks that come with my job, and you have to accept that. You have no right to interfere with me and the way I choose to live my life."

He smiled wryly. "You know, the issue seems clearer when I'm dealing with someone who tries to interfere with the Hopi way of life. Now I'm beginning to see how even good intentions can cause all kinds of damage.''

"Don't do anything like that again, Joe," she said. "If you have to come to a scene, then stay on the sideline just as I would at one of your religious ceremonies. Neither of our worlds is hospitable to intruders.''

"It won't happen again. As much as I hate to admit it, you've made a good case."

"That's my job," she said. Hearing the coffee shop door jingle open, she glanced over casually. Justin Nakai stood near the entrance, looking around.

Glenna motioned for the Navajo agent to join them in the booth. The men greeted each other cordially, and Justin gave Joseph Gilbert's pocketknife. Joseph accepted it gratefully.

"What brings you here?" Glenna asked Nakai.

"I have some information for you concerning your inquiry on Murphy and Penhalligon. The Bureau office in Albuquerque, New Mexico, faxed me directly and asked me to come find you. They've located both men. They're somewhere on a ranch near Ladron Peak. That's west of Socorro, in a section of New Mexico comprised mostly of rugged, marginal grazing land and old abandoned mines. Since it's your case, it's your call. We need to know how you plan to proceed and if you'll need backup."

"First tell me about the professor. Do our people have him under surveillance?"

"Newton dropped out of sight. Our guys followed him inside one of the university anthropology buildings, then lost him when a big class let out. They've been trying to track him down ever since, but so far they're batting zero.''

Glenna nodded thoughtfully. "Okay. Let me tell you how I want to handle this. Until I can find out if Murphy has the missing Hopi artifacts, I'd like to keep my interest in him low profile. Are you familiar with the area surrounding the ranch?" Seeing Justin nod, she continued. "Is it accessible to hiking?"

"Sure. There aren't many trees to speak of, it's typical southwestern brush and grass. But the land's fairly contoured, and the ranch is on the foothills of a solitary peak, so you won't be a sitting duck. Still, Penhalligon is bound to have security. Our sources tell us Murphy is a former British commando. Their skills have to be top notch and include extensive training in the use of explosives. Some of the stolen dynamite could be in his hands, so he might have some elaborate booby traps around the ranch. If I were you, I wouldn't underestimate him.''

"I won't," she assured. "My plan is to move into the area, stake out the place, and gather information. Then I'll decide what to do next. By the way, I'm going to need topographical maps of the area. Do you have any?''

"Yeah, I had a case that took me there not long ago, and I kept everything. But wouldn't you prefer that I come along with you? I could guide you around and at the same time provide you with backup.''

"You two won't have much of a cover story if you get spotted," Joe interrupted. "But I've got an idea that just might work.''

"What is it?" Justin asked skeptically.

"The Hopis have a very special need for snakes, since the stock we use for our ceremonies has been dwindling for years. I could claim to be one of the priests of the Snake Dance, and Glenna could pose as a herpetologist from the university helping me search dens for new breeding stock.''

Justin nodded slowly. He hated to admit it, but it had just enough off-beat credibility that it could be a workable cover. "What do you think?" he asked Glenna.

She thought about it for a minute. "It sounds pretty good to me." She leaned back in her seat. "We'll leave here before sunrise tomorrow. On the chance that Gilbert's transmitter is still operable, we'll take the duplicate receiver Joe had the technician make for him. The time's come to put it to good use. If the bug is still working, it'll help us pinpoint the location of the objects." Glenna met Nakai's gaze. "I'd like to go over those maps with you tonight, if you have the time.''

Glenna spent several hours learning as much as she could about the area from Nakai. By the time she set off to Ladron Peak the following morning, she felt the confidence that came from knowing that she'd prepared thoroughly for the task. If Justin didn't hear from her in twelve hours, the entire mountain would be teeming with Bureau agents and local police.

They drove south toward Socorro on I-25 in a four-wheel-drive vehicle borrowed from the University of New Mexico.

"There's something I have to tell you. You remember when you asked me if the cure that enabled my mother to have children could also work for you?" Seeing her nod, Joseph continued. "I went to her and asked if there was something she could do. She said that she would petition the Kwan." He explained the society's function. "When I saw her earlier this evening, she told me they've agreed to hold a healing ceremony for you tonight. You do not have to be present for this, and remember that it is your right to get results."

Her spirits soared, but soon another emotion clouded her expectations. She'd tried so hard and had been disappointed so many times. By hoping once again, would she be setting herself up for more heartbreak? She took a deep breath. "I will hold onto one thing. My needs will be met," she said confidently.

"You're getting all the help that's necessary. Now let go and just trust. What worked once will work again."

As difficult as it was to push the matter from her mind, she forced herself to concentrate on the task that lay ahead. There were responsibilities that needed their attention now.

Glenna went over the details with Joseph. "If we get caught, use your phony identity and try to remember that I'm Elise Brown, a herpetologist from U.N.M. I have fake ID inside my wallet and if they decide to run a check on it, the university will vouch for me. I've also done some quick cramming and know enough about snakes to bluff my way through almost anything, including an encounter with a den of rattlers. What I'd like to know is more about the snake ceremony."

"No problem," he replied. "We believe that prayers for rain must be carried to the Underworld—where the spirits dwell—by messengers who live beneath the earth and are familiar with that region. To transmit the message, the priest must hold the snakes in their mouths and circle the plaza in a traditional dance. The priests spend days in preparation for the ritual. Many outsiders have tried to figure out what our people do to keep the snakes from biting, but that's known only to the snake priests. I can tell you this much, they don't milk them of venom. They consider the snakes their little brothers and to take something away from them would be unthinkable."

"Maybe the snakes know they have nothing to fear," she suggested, and saw him smile.

Turning west at the Bernardo exit, they drove off the short stretch of pavement onto a dirt and gravel road. Loose sand made giant dust clouds, and the winds carried news of their passage.

She parked at the base of a hillside covered with boulders the size of compact cars. Working together, Glenna and Joseph got their gear out of the car and assembled it quickly. Glenna strapped on a small rucksack that contained a pair of binoculars, the radio receiver, and a canteen of water. Included as part of her cover were two well-used herpetology reference books and a gunny sack. She wore a .38 revolver at her belt, and in addition to regular ammunition, had several snake-load cartridges. No one would believe that they'd come looking for snake dens without a weapon, so that wouldn't destroy their cover. Like Joseph, she carried a snake capture stick with a wire loop at one end.

"Justin Nakai pointed out the location of the ranch to me on the map," she said. "It's only a few miles from here, but it's going to be an uphill climb since we need to stick to areas that will provide us with plenty of cover."

They hiked along ridges pocked with mine shafts that looked like deep, dark wounds leading into the center of the earth. Most had not been boarded up, hikers being rare in the desolate countryside. Dry arroyos curved downward from the Ladron Peak foothills. From their position, she could tell that the north sides of the canyons still had traces of snow. As they reached the next rise, Glenna began to slow down. "Stay low. According to what Nakai said, the ranch should be visible downslope from here."

"I admit that the crest of a ridge is a great surveillance spot, but maybe we should pick some other place that doesn't outline us against the sky."

"Tactically speaking, I'd agree, but we need to make sure there's nothing between us and the ranch house that could interfere with the signal. Besides, we're still some distance outside their fenced perimeter, so we'll be okay. Just make sure you stay close to the ground and behind the rocks whenever possible."

Joseph crept up the hillside, using the massive boulders that littered the terrain for cover. "Let me have the receiver."

Glenna fished it out of her pack and handed it to him. As they peaked the ridge, she spotted the ranch house in the distance. "I was under the impression it would be closer than this," Glenna commented, surprised. She grabbed her binoculars and sighted in on the area below. "There's a man in a wheelchair sitting by the shade of that old apple tree." She changed the focus on the lenses. "I can't see his face very well, but from the way the others are catering to him, I'd say that's Nigel Penhalligon."

He turned on the radio transmitter and pulled out the antenna. The technician, like Gilbert, had modified a small transistor radio. No suspicions would be raised, even if someone saw him holding it. "We're either too far away, or the signal isn't there," he said after a few moments. "I think we should find out which it is by moving in a bit closer."

She hesitated, then finally nodded. "Okay. We'll slip beneath the range fencing, and then edge in along that arroyo on the south side. Once we reach the high ground about a quarter of a mile above the main building, we'll stop and give it another try. If we don't get anything from there, then we'll leave and try to come up with another plan. We're not going anywhere near the main house without backup. There's no telling what we'll encounter.''

They hiked slowly downhill toward the arroyo they had singled out. Once inside the wash, they advanced cautiously. They'd be invisible to anyone inside the house, but unfortunately they couldn't see out of the wash, either.

Joseph watched the birds and tried to listen to the sounds of the desert, alert to anything unusual. The hair on the back of his neck was standing up on end. He could feel someone watching them but he couldn't see anyone. He was about to signal Glenna that they should turn back when the distinctive click of a rifle being cocked echoed in the narrow confines of the rocky arroyo.

"You should have stopped when you were back at the fence." Still hidden, the gunman's voice rang out from behind a cluster of low junipers on the side of the wash. "It's too bad you two didn't know when to quit."

Chapter Twenty-Two

"What's the meaning of this?" Glenna challenged, though she made sure her body remained rock still. "This isn't posted land."

She heard the sound of a hand-held radio and the man snapping a few crisp orders. Suddenly he emerged. "On the ground, face down."

"I demand to know—"

"You demand nothing, lady," he said, and with a sweep of his leg, knocked her to the ground.

She allowed herself to fall, although she could have countered the move. As much as she would have loved to unhinge his freshly shaved jawline, she forced herself to act like an outraged citizen.

Joseph started to move toward the man, then wisely lowered himself to the ground, setting his snake collecting sack down beside him.

"We were hoping to reach the house and get some directions," Glenna said as rough hands removed her revolver. "It's easy to get turned around here."

"You always go hiking packing a pistol?" the man mocked.

"When I'm looking for snakes, you bet I do. The head of the department makes it available for anyone doing fieldwork. It's easier to carry than a rifle. Look, my wallet's in my rucksack, get it out. I have my ID in there, too.

My name is Elise Brown and I'm a herpetologist from the University of New Mexico.''

"A herbi what?''

"I'm an expert in the study of reptiles.''

"And he's one, too?''

"No, he's a member of the Hopi Indian tribe. Surely you've heard of the Snake Dance?'' She went through her cover story. "Now let us get up, will you?''

"Okay, but if either of you try anything, I won't hesitate to shoot you. Is that clear?''

"Eminently.'' She stood up slowly, and dusted herself off. Joseph went through the motions of examining his capture stick, checking to make sure it still worked. As it had in the past, his coolness and common sense impressed her.

"We didn't want any trouble,'' she said, studying the man before her, "just a few snakes. I don't usually meet people who are so fond of them that they'd kill anyone who tried to take a few off their property.''

The man chuckled softly. "You've got a point lady, but I'm just following an established procedure. My supervisor will be here in a few minutes, I can hear the Jeep now. Just stay cool and we'll get this straightened out.''

Joe started to move around, as if searching for snakes, when the man trained his rifle on him. "Do that very slowly, buddy.''

"No problem,'' he answered. "Just don't get nervous with that thing, will ya? I'm unarmed, unless you count my capture stick and gunnysack.''

Glenna watched the way the man held the Winchester hunting rifle. He must have been a soldier once, because he handled the scoped rifle and sling with the ease of an expert. She had no doubt that if she made the slightest aggressive move she'd be dead before she hit the ground.

"Please, let us locate a few snake dens, give us directions on the quickest way off your property, and you'll never see us again,'' she pleaded. "If there's any trouble, the university's going to cancel my grant.''

The man shrugged. "That's not my problem.''

As two others arrived in a Jeep, Glenna glanced at Joe. His face was set in hard lines. There was an air of confidence about him that hinted at an ability to skillfully defend himself. She noticed how the men watched him, and realized that they weren't eager to tangle with him at all.

A tall man wearing khaki pants and a gray windbreaker climbed out of the open-topped Jeep. "We're going to take you to the house. You'll be safe, but we have a few things to check out. If you create problems, we'll tie you up or use Mace on you. Either way, your visit will become extremely unpleasant. I'd advise you to act with all the courtesy expected of a guest."

"What the heck have we trespassed on?" Glenna asked, feigning bewilderment. "Wait, let me reword that. Exactly who's guest are we?"

"Mr. Nigel Penhalligon. I'm sure you've heard of him. A man of his stature in the businessworld can't be too careful, so I'm sure you'll understand."

They were led inside an unheated cinder block room, part of a workshop adjacent to the ranch house. Their gear was taken away, and a guard left by the door.

Joseph glanced around the second the men left. "There are no windows and no way out," he muttered. "Who'd have thought we'd end up with so many snakes to worry about."

"The two-legged kind is usually the worst," she admitted. She glanced at him, and mouthed the words "stay alert."

He nodded. They both realized the room could be bugged. He leaned against the wall, and faced the door. "All they have to do is check out your ID. That shouldn't take long, right?"

"It'll just take one phone call," she assured, guessing his real question was how quickly they could expect backup.

They heard footsteps coming, then suddenly the door opened. "We've searched your gear, and you do seem legit."

He escorted them to a separate, larger heated office at the front of the building. "There's your gear, everything's back inside. You better get a decent radio if you're coming to a place like this. Cheap ones like that have a hard time picking up the signal.''

"Yeah, I've noticed," Joe said, picking up the large sack he'd carried, ostensibly for snakes.

They put on their gear and turned for the door when a tall man with light brown hair and blue eyes, appeared. He blocked their way and smiled slowly, much like a predator eyeing its prey. "Well, this certainly is a pleasant surprise," he said, his English accent adding a certain polish and flair to the simple statement.

Glenna stared at him. It was no use reaching for her gun, the man was holding a 9 mm Browning on them. His left hand was expertly bandaged in a wound dressing. She strongly suspected he'd been the one she'd shot in the helicopter. The game was up! She could only hope that the security man had actually called the university. That would have tipped off Justin Nakai and the other agents standing by. "Charles Murphy, right? I saw you on the cable news network. I see you've dispensed with your mustache once again."

"Oh, how observant!" He laughed. Murphy signaled the security man, who stepped up quickly from behind and removed her .38 from its holster. "I do hope you weren't planning to release them. That would have created an irrevocable stain on your employment record."

"I was going to ask you to make the final decision, sir," the man said.

Glenna knew he was lying, but had she been confronted with Murphy under similar circumstances, she might have made up an excuse, too. If she was any judge of character, Murphy was more dangerous than any ordinary professional soldier gone awry. His expressions all held the same lack of emotion she'd seen on serial killers interviewed on film for Bureau seminars.

Murphy gestured to the tall man who'd taken them prisoner. "Put them back inside, lock the door, and make sure you have someone guarding them. When you're done, send me their rucksacks."

Glenna was shoved hard into the room, nearly colliding with Joseph as the guard scrambled to do Murphy's bidding.

Joe gave her a worried glance. "How thoroughly do you think they checked out your credentials?"

"Who knows?" she answered, aware of what he meant. "Our only hope is that they won't do anything right under Penhalligon's nose—too close to home, that sort of thing. That'll buy us some time."

"I wouldn't count on getting any breaks from Murphy," Joe said slowly. "He doesn't seem the type."

Glenna had no doubt that Murphy would discover the purpose of that receiver before long. A cold chill passed over her. Unless Justin Nakai brought the cavalry soon, she didn't give great odds on the chance that they'd live to see the next sunrise.

Ten minutes later Glenna heard footsteps coming toward her. Murphy appeared at the door. "Mr. Penhalligon would like to see both of you." He held the fourteen-shot, semiautomatic Browning in his hand and gestured for them to walk ahead of him. "By the way, that was a handy little tracking receiver you had there. I wish Shaw had found it when he searched in Payestewa's workshop for me. I was so curious to see it. Unfortunately for you, bringing it was a waste of time. I examined the Hopi items rather well before bringing them to my employer and found that nasty little transmitter. I smashed it immediately, of course."

They were ushered into a large, sparsely decorated living room with a room-length picture window. A fragile-looking old man sat in a wheelchair staring at the mountains outside. Murphy ordered them to remain standing, then waited.

The room was deathly quiet except for a slight squeak in the wheel chair as Penhalligon turned around. He studied Glenna and Joe through weary, heavy-lidded eyes. "I'm not exactly the formidable threat you expected," he observed, reading their expressions. "My days of personal intimidation are over. Now I hire people to do that for me.'' He gestured for them to have a seat on the sofa.

As Glenna sat down, she noticed that Murphy's gun remained trained on them. She had no doubt that even sneezing at the wrong time would have dire consequences.

"The FBI knows you're here, Mr. Penhalligon, and that we came to see you." Glenna kept her tone soft, trying to convey confidence and reason. "There's no reason to continue playing this out."

"The objects that you have taken from my tribe are extremely powerful," Joe warned. "The power of the Hopi kachinas will destroy you."

"I have nothing to lose," Penhalligon said wearily, his head almost too heavy for his neck to support. "I have an inoperable cancer, just as the mercenaries in the tabloids have reported endlessly. That's what is causing my paralysis. Very soon, it will kill me. My resources are extensive, so I've sought every medical cure money can buy. There's nothing else left for me. I needed a miracle, and knew of only one place to find it."

"Do you know what you've stolen?" Joe insisted. "The mask of the god of death is extremely powerful, but the results you'll get are not what you're searching for."

"*Masau'u* is the god of death, but there's a relationship between him and new life. In your culture, physical death is seen only as a stage in a never-ending life cycle. That's why *Masau'u* is a kachina who appears in the Spring rituals celebrating new birth, and why he's said to own all the crops."

"You know us well, but not well enough," Joe answered. "You've forgotten the place purity of heart and mind play in our rituals. That comes only to a person through a life of prayer and devotion to duty. There are no shortcuts, no matter how badly you may want to believe there are. You can't fake a metaphysical event, or deceive the gods."

"Forty years ago, as an anthropology student, I secretly penetrated a kiva and witnessed a healing ceremony where the *Masau'u* was used. I was curious about the societies and their alleged ability to cure certain diseases, but I never really thought that any of them would work. I supposed they functioned mainly as a psychological aid. That's the reason I was so completely unprepared for what happened. An old man, so weak and wasted away that he couldn't even stand, was carried into the kiva. The society did a long elaborate curing ceremony, which I secretly documented. The next morning he was taken away, only by then he was already walking around and joking with the others. A few weeks later, I saw the same man out alone, hauling firewood. I followed it up, and went to the hospital in Keams Canyon. I learned then that the man had been diagnosed as having cancer, much like what I have now. I saw his medical records and considered writing a paper, but figured no one would believe me. So I wrote it down in my journal and kept it for my own reference. That man lived another two decades. Do you believe it? I'd settle for six months. It's no wonder that I've never forgotten that night.''

''If you believe in our Way, then you must also know that you've brought this illness down on yourself. All society members purify themselves by a rite called *Navotciwa* before leaving the kiva. Otherwise the whip they control will afflict them. That whip will also contaminate persons who trespass on ceremonial rites or come into contact with religious objects.''

''I know that the mask is invested with the transmittable spirit and power of the actual kachina. That's why I've had it brought to me. I will do nothing to dishonor that. In fact, I intend to use it to duplicate the healing ritual I saw. Afterward, I'll discharm myself with ashes. I've also managed to get a recording of the discharming song, you see.''

''Professor Newton?'' she observed.

''He's a very resourceful man,'' Penhalligon answered. ''The irony of all this is that in the nineteen twenties I might have had a chance of getting the Hopi people to let me enter their kiva and avail myself of their healing methods. Unfortunately they've suffered so much betrayal at the hands of the white population, that they've shut the doors to that side of their culture."

"So you steal from us like the rest," Joe observed.

"Your tribe gave me no other choice. I tried to offer your people money, cars, land."

"You've tried to buy something that can never be for sale, and when that failed, you decided to take it by force. But this isn't the type of thing that can be taken forcibly. When your actions harm someone else, those same actions will end up harming you. That, too, is part of the Hopi Way."

"Whether or not you believe that part, Mr. Penhalligon," Glenna interjected, "there are a few facts you should know. I'd already discovered that Murphy was responsible for the thefts, that's what brought me here. I'd also learned that Murphy arranged for Murray White's wife to be kidnapped in order to ensure White's silence. It worked, too, except that the owner of the bar—whom Murphy paid to provide liquor—recognized him despite his disguise," she said, stretching the truth. "I'm just the tip of the spear. Unless I check in with certain people soon, this area is going to be overrun with special agents and the police."

"You can't threaten me with death, I'm already facing it," Penhalligon answered. "Legal consequences don't matter when weighed against that." He glanced at Joseph. "What might persuade me to let you both go, is information. Tell me all you know about the *Kwan* ritual. I know your mother is the keeper of the mask and robe of *Masau'u,* and her brother impersonates the deity. What can you tell me about the curing ceremony itself that may save your life? And keep in mind that if you lie, I'll know. I already have quite a bit of information."

"I can't tell you anything, because I don't know. I belong to another society. Blood ties don't necessarily link us to a particular group. But I could find out if you let us go."

With a wave of his hand, Penhalligon dismissed them and gestured for Murphy to take them away.

Murphy led them across the back of the house to a low, thick adobe storage shed off by itself. She didn't like the implication. "So what happens now?"

"You'll be kept alive, at least for a while. You might be useful to us as hostages if something were to go wrong with our plans," he said casually. "It's really too bad you didn't believe that the artifacts were lost in the explosion that almost killed that incompetent Secakuku. Shaw really tried his best to mislead you, I have to admit that. If he'd just had enough sense to stay away from that penny-ante smuggling, my employer might have granted him clemency."

"Was Secakuku in league with you?" Glenna asked.

"Actually, he was Shaw's man, and for that reason we had to get him out of the way. We weren't sure how much he knew, or whether he'd try to bring a mountain down on us next."

As they were hustled into the adobe shed, Murphy allowed them to turn around. "You've been worthy adversaries. I tried to gain a bit of time by getting you out of the way, but you managed to avoid my shotgun blast that night on the road, then the bomb I planted in your room. And Ms.—excuse me—*Agent* Day, I must reluctantly congratulate you on your fine shooting at our 'liberated' helicopter. I now have a nine millimeter hole clear through the palm of my hand, thanks to your bullet. A few inches higher, it would have been my head."

"Did you kill the old man at the hogan and the young desk clerk, too?" Glenna wished she had been shooting high that day.

"No, one of my overeager assistants accomplished that barbaric act while I was outside disabling their truck. I was simply going to relocate them for a while, until I was done here." He shrugged, then continued as if the deaths were nothing more than the unfortunate outcome of circumstances.

"I must say, you've made this operation exciting," Murphy added. "You even got close to capturing me in that sting operation you set up with the medicine man. You obviously didn't have the man wired or you would have had me. Did he refuse to allow a microphone? He *was* stubborn.''

"You resemble Professor Newton," Joe commented, preempting Glenna's response. "Are you two related?"

Murphy smiled, but didn't answer. "Nigel will conduct his healing ceremony tonight, and by daybreak we'll be on our way to England. I'm very sorry to say that you will have outlived your usefulness then, and you simply know too much to stay alive. I do, however, promise you a quick death and a deep, albeit unmarked grave. You can count on my efficiency, I assure you.'' He stepped back out of the shed. "I'm wiring one of Shaw's remaining sticks of dynamite to the door, just in case you get any ideas about breaking out. Do try not to set it off. It would create a great deal of noise, and Nigel will be much too busy to be interrupted by your deaths.''

The room was dark when the heavy door was shut, and it took several seconds for their eyes to adjust to the gloom. Glenna ran her hands along the walls. "There's no holes or cracks where the light is getting through. The only spot that might be vulnerable is the door.''

"And that's out of the question," Joe finished for her, "if we're to believe Murphy. We'll have to make our move when someone comes to…finish us off.'' Joseph sat down on the cool, hard-packed earthen floor. "Do you think Nakai has someone looking for us by now?''

Glenna exhaled softly and sat down beside him. "Not yet, not unless they telephoned to check on my ID. I wasn't supposed to call in until late tonight, so he won't be on the alert until then. Even so, he's sure to give us a grace period just in case we're late getting to a telephone.''

"When can we expect help, then?"

"Probably just before sunrise, when it's best to stage a raid.''

"That's cutting it close."

"I'm aware of that," she said slowly. "Joe, if I could have bargained my life for yours, I would have. I wish you weren't here with me now.''

"I'm glad I am," he answered with heartbreaking honesty. "I know that perhaps this isn't the most romantic spot to ask you this, but if we get out of this alive, will you marry me?"

"It's the darkness, right?" she joked. "It makes you whisper all sorts of promises."

"Glenna, I've never been more serious in my life." He brushed his palm over her cheek in a light caress. "I've spent years searching for someone who could take your place in my heart and it hasn't worked. Maybe I'm just a one-woman man. I love you and life's too short to waste any more of it. We've been given another chance. Let's not throw one dream aside because we're worried about the ones that may not come true."

"I won't marry you, Joe, because I love you too much. You'd be better off with a woman from your tribe who could give you children of your own." Her words were strangled as a pain as deep and encompassing as her soul engulfed her.

"I want you because I love you, not because of what you can or can't give us. If we're meant to have children, then it'll happen. Whether you follow the Hopi Way or some other path, it all comes down to the same thing. You have to believe that evil is not the master of good. You have a right to ask for what will make you happy and to expect good results. You said once that you believe in a power that watches over us all. Hold to that, and know you'll receive whatever you need."

"But Joe, even if I was able to bear children, they'd never be considered Hopi. So you·see, no matter where we turn, there are obstacles."

"There's a way for them to be part of my clan and the tribe." He explained what his mother had told him. "Stop seeing the problems, Glenna. Open your heart to love and let that guide you." He gathered her against him and claimed her mouth in a deep kiss.

In the darkness he could feel her growing soft in his arms as his own body grew taut. The sweet and delicious female scent of her body surrounded him.

He broke the kiss slowly. He wanted her more than ever, but there would be few chances, if any, to make their escape. They had to stay alert. Whether or not she would admit it, his future was joined with hers. They belonged to each other and he wanted them to be able to share far more than a common unmarked grave.

"We've got to find a way out of here," she said, her voice unsteady.

They discussed possible plans of action, working each one out and discarding those ideas that seemed less likely to succeed. Hours passed, but they heard no change in the activity going on outside.

Joseph finally stood and walked to the door. It had been dark for a long time now, and although he was tired, he wasn't sleepy. "Something's going on out there. You can hear people running about. Listen."

She heard car doors opening and closing and vehicles driving by. Standing beside him, she put her ear to the door. "My guess is they're packing up. Something must have gone wrong for them to be evacuating now, though. It's not dawn, and that's when they were scheduled to leave."

They heard a man snap an order, then running footsteps heading directly toward the shed. The sound stopped, and a man's voice rang out clearly just on the other side of the door. "I'm going to disconnect the dynamite," he shouted. "Move back to the far wall. If you try anything now, we'll all go up in smoke."

Glenna's body tensed, a plan coming to mind. She moved to the far side of the shack, placing as much distance between her and Joe as possible. "Be ready," she whispered. "He'll have a gun, but if we stay separated, he won't be able to aim at both of us."

The door swung open, and a man entered. He held a battery-powered lantern in one hand and a semiautomatic pistol equipped with a silencer in the other. The guard waited in the doorway and gestured for them to move closer. "Don't get cute. I can give you a fast death or one that's painfully slow. The choice is yours."

Chapter Twenty-Three

The guard held the gun steady, his eyes trained on them as they reluctantly moved to the center of the room. "That's right, come together. We'll make it nice and neat that way. Personally, I'd have just as soon triggered that dynamite, but Mr. Murphy was concerned that the noise would be heard for miles, and it would attract too much attention. We believe your FBI friends are in the area and we don't want to have them descend on us quite yet."

"You'll need hostages," Glenna countered.

"No, we're through here. Holding hostages would only complicate matters if anyone stopped us."

Knowing she only had seconds, Glenna looked at Joe, then glanced at the ground to his left. Joe read her cue quickly. Remembering one of their contingency plans, he stumbled and collapsed to the ground.

As the man shifted the pistol directly toward him, Glenna kicked out, knocking the weapon out of his hand.

The gunman swung around with the lantern, catching her extended leg and knocking her to the ground hard. As she rolled quickly away, she felt a sharp pain in her abdomen that nearly doubled her over. For a moment she was barely able to move. The guard raised the lantern to strike her again, but before he could complete the action, Joseph launched himself against his midsection. The guard crashed backward into the adobe wall, and the lantern flew to one side.

Recovering in the blink of an eye, the man grabbed Joseph, who was scrambling to his feet, and continued the fight. Trying to move around the two grappling men, Glenna searched for the gun in the flickering light of the damaged lantern.

The guard butted with his head, landing a hard blow against Joseph's chest. As Joe reeled back, the distinctive slap of rotor blades told them a helicopter had just touched down outside. Before Joseph could retaliate, the guard was out the door. Joe ran after him.

Giving up her search for the gun, Glenna rushed outside. "Joe. Stop! Let him go!"

"No! He might be our last chance to find the mask and robe."

The guard ran full speed toward the helicopter, which was hovering above ground in a cloud of dust.

Glenna dashed after both men, the pain in her abdomen receding to a dull throb. In the gathering dawn, it looked as if everyone had already packed up and left; not a vehicle was in sight. She saw Joe narrowing the distance between him and the guard as she also closed in. Then, through the open doorway of the helicopter, Glenna saw Murphy bring his assault rifle to bear. He gave her a quick look to make sure she wasn't armed, then trained his sights on Joseph, who was about ten feet behind the guard.

Glenna knew she couldn't shout a warning over the sound of the chopper's engine, and she'd never catch up to Joe in time. Trying, despite the odds, she raced forward hoping to stop the inevitable from happening.

A few feet from the guard, Joe glanced at the helicopter. Suddenly he dove into the swirling dust, away from Murphy's line of fire.

Glenna breathed again. As the aircraft began to rise, she saw the guard grab onto the helicopter's skid. Leaning out, Murphy pulled him up into the helicopter.

Glenna looked around, hoping to find a weapon, but without a gun, there was nothing she could do to prevent their escape. Her heart suddenly froze as she saw Murphy raise his rifle once again and train his sights on her. Caught

out in the open, she knew her time had come. She'd never
be able to outrun a bullet.

A heartbeat later, Murphy lowered the barrel and gave
her a snappy salute, honoring his adversary.

Weak at the knees, she watched the helicopter skim away
just above the boulders, then finally climb toward the
peak.

Joseph joined her. "It looks like you owe him one."

"I prefer to think that we're even. By not killing a federal cop, he saved himself lots of grief," she said, uncomfortable with his observation.

As the sound of the helicopter dwindled to nothing, they
walked to the ranch house, not knowing what to expect.
"The ritual shouldn't have worked for Penhalligon, so why
did they change their plans?" Glenna said. "They weren't
supposed to move until daybreak, and it's barely that
now."

"Maybe they spotted the search parties and got worried." Joe looked around for motion in the brush.

"If Nakai was close by, we would have heard more action. My guess is that our support teams are still some distance away."

As she went inside the house, she found the emptiness
oppressive. Her footsteps against the brick floor sounded
unnaturally loud in the stillness. As she stepped inside the
library, she stopped in her tracks. The empty wheelchair
stood sentinel over Nigel Penhalligon, who lay face-down
on the floor. The flowing *Masau'u* robe could not quite
hide the hideous slant of his legs, which were bent from the
knees at unnatural angles away from his body. It was i...
he'd tried to walk, but the effects had been disastrous. The
kachina mask was only inches from his fingertips, leading
her to believe that he'd tried to reach out to it in the throe...
of death.

Joseph crouched by the medicine pouch, which was stil
attached to the dead man's waist. Someone with wolf
colored eyes had died, as his mother had predicted. Pen
halligon's eyes had been a very light brown, wolf-colored
though not as striking as Glenna's. "I tried to warn him

Prayer isn't granted unless a man's heart and thinking are clearly in line with the good of all."

They heard virtually simultaneous crashes as the back and front doors of the house were kicked open. "FBI! This is a raid. Drop all weapons and raise your hands immediately. You're completely surrounded!" Justin Nakai's voice could be heard clearly.

"Nakai—this is Glenna, we're in the library!" she shouted back. "Well, it looks like our backup has arrived," she said, turning to Joseph with a wry smile.

Minutes later Nakai met Glenna and Joe in the living room. "By the way, the members of Penhalligon's staff who escaped by car have all been captured. Only his personal security team escaped. We know that Murphy and his men used two helicopters to make their getaway, but so far those remain at large."

"Without Penhalligon, they have no employer or mission. If we don't catch them leaving our borders, then I doubt we'll ever see them again," Glenna said.

"We're going to do our best to intercept them before they leave the country."

Glenna ambled slowly to an awaiting Jeep with Justin and Joseph. She tried to ignore the discomfort in her abdomen. The implications were grave. She'd been warned in the past that it was a sign of very serious trouble for someone with her medical history. She swallowed the giant lump in her throat. Maybe it was better never to dream or to hope.

With effort, she forced her mind back on the case. "I still can't get over the resemblance between Newton and Murphy. It's not as if they're twins, but it was sure enough to confuse us."

"They're cousins," Nakai answered. "I got an update on Newton a few hours ago. Since they're still trying to locate him, the Bureau compiled a list of relatives and associates, and Murphy's name turned up."

JOSEPH AND GLENNA DROVE back to Albuquerque, the closest big city. While Joseph gave written statements,

Glenna left the Bureau offices. The pain in her abdomen had lessened, but she knew it was not something she could afford to ignore. It took two hours for her to contact her physician and have the local hospital clinic perform the required tests. Yet Joseph was only just finishing by the time she returned.

"The Hopi Tribal Council contacted Arizona's Congressional Delegation," Joseph informed her, "and they've managed to expedite the return of our artifacts. They've even made a private plane available to us." He gave her a hard look. "Where were you?"

"I had to get something checked out," she said, avoiding the whole truth. There was no use in worrying him now before she had definite answers; she'd know soon enough anyway. She'd asked that the results be faxed to Dr. Wanda Shapiro as soon as they were available.

A few hours later they landed at a small airstrip near Keams Canyon, then drove to Joe's village. Joseph carried the mask, robe and medicine pouch back inside the house, and presented them to his mother.

Wilma smiled and sat up. Color seemed to flood back into her face. Exchanging a few quick words with her son in their native tongue, she handed the objects back to him. As Joe returned them to their rightful place, there was a knock at the door.

Glenna went to answer it, giving the family a few minutes together. A Hopi officer stood outside. "How can I help you?" she asked.

"I was asked to come and take you to Keams Canyon. Doc Shapiro has a lot of connections around here, and she called the captain. She's just received some medical information she claims you have to know about."

Glenna felt the blood drain from her face. She had started to go with the officer when Joe came forward and reached for her arm. "Does this have something to do with your absence in Albuquerque?" Seeing her nod, he turned to the officer. "We'll follow you. She and I have things to talk about."

Glenna explained about the tests as they drove toward the Hopi clinic. "So you see, I didn't want to worry you until I knew."

His mother's prediction about someone with wolf-colored eyes echoed in his mind. She'd said that it would be someone with a secret that ate at them from the inside. Glenna had amber eyes, and she'd held a secret. Had the ritual failed completely? His hands trembled as they gripped the steering wheel.

"No matter what lies ahead, we'll face it together—as husband and wife. As soon as we can manage it, I want you to marry me."

"I can't let you do that. You have no idea what might be in store for either of us."

"Whatever it is, I know we can deal with it. My brother's future was cut short before he ever realized all the good things he had. Let's not waste the opportunity that's been given to us. The chance to make dreams come true doesn't come often. Let's grab onto it and not let go. We can face anything as long as we can face it together."

When they arrived at the clinic, she parked the car and turned to face him. "Joe..." Unable to find words, she touched his face in a light caress, and kissed him. When she finally pulled away, she caught a glimpse of Doc Shapiro standing by the clinic door waiting for them.

Glenna walked to the entrance with Joe at her side. "We came as soon as we heard," she said.

Wanda nodded. "I was told by your physician that you were quite concerned about these tests and I should relay the news to you as soon as possible." She stood in front of Joe, blocking his way when he tried to follow them into her office. "Where do you think you're going?" Wanda demanded.

Glenna smiled. "It's okay, Doc. This is going to affect him directly. We're getting married." She looked into Joe's eyes and saw herself reflected in the tenderness of his gaze.

Wanda shut the door, then waited for them to seat themselves. Taking her time, she walked behind her desk and sat down. Suddenly she smiled broadly. "I really enjoy keeping people in suspense, particularly when I've got good news.''

"What do you mean?" Glenna sat forward.

"I'm not sure how it happened, kiddo, but all those benign growths you've had for such a long time are gone. In fact, they couldn't even find signs of the scarring that should have been there from the operation you had before."

"You mean . . ."

"Well, let me put it this way. You two are going to need to practice birth control. Otherwise, as young and healthy as you are, you're going to end up with a *very* big family."

Glenna choked. With a smile, Joe pulled her out of her chair and into his arms.

A satisfied smile spread over Wanda Shapiro's weathered face. Quietly, she slipped out of the room.

HARLEQUIN
INTRIGUE®

A SPAULDING AND DARIEN MYSTERY

This month read the heart-stopping conclusion to the exciting four-book series of Spaulding and Darien mysteries, #197 WHEN SHE WAS BAD. An engaging pair of amateur sleuths—writer Jenny Spaulding and lawyer Peter Darien—were introduced to Harlequin Intrigue readers in three previous books. Be sure not to miss any books in this outstanding series:

#147 BUTTON, BUTTON: When Jenny and Peter first met, they had nothing in common—except a hunch that Jenny's father's death was not a suicide. But would they live long enough to prove it was murder?

#159 DOUBLE DARE: Jenny and Peter solve the disappearance of a popular TV sitcom star, unraveling the tangled web of Tinseltown's intrigues.

#171 ALL FALL DOWN: In an isolated storm-besieged inn, the guests are being murdered one by one. Jenny and Peter must find the killer before they become the next victims.

#197 WHEN SHE WAS BAD: Jenny and Peter are getting ready to walk down the aisle, but unless they can thwart a deadly enemy masquerading as a friend, there won't be a wedding. Or a bride.

You can order #147 *Button, Button,* #159 *Double Dare,* #171 *All Fall Down* and #197 *When She Was Bad* by sending your name, address, zip or postal code, along with a check or money order for $2.50 for book #147, $2.75 for book #159, $2.79 for book #171 or $2.89 for book #197, plus 75¢ postage and handling ($1.00 in Canada), payable to Harlequin Reader Service, to:

In the U.S.	In Canada
3010 Walden Avenue	P.O. Box 609
P.O. Box 1325	Fort Erie, Ontario
Buffalo, NY 14269-1325	L2A 5X3

Please specify book title(s) with your order.
Canadian residents add applicable federal and provincial taxes.

SDRE

HE CROSSED TIME FOR HER

Captain Richard Colter rode the high seas, brandished a sword and pillaged treasure ships. A swashbuckling privateer, he was a man with voracious appetites and a lust for living. And in the eighteenth century, any woman swooned at his feet for the favor of his wild passion. History had it that Captain Richard Colter went down with his ship, the *Black Cutter,* in a dazzling sea battle off the Florida coast in 1792.

Then what was he doing washed ashore on a Key West beach in 1992—alive?

MARGARET ST. GEORGE brings you an extraspecial love story next month, about an extraordinary man who would do anything for the woman he loved:

#462 THE PIRATE AND HIS LADY
by Margaret St. George
November 1992

When love is meant to be, nothing can stand in its way . . . not even time.

Don't miss American Romance
#462 THE PIRATE AND HIS LADY.
It's a love story you'll never forget.

PAL

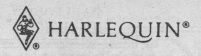 HARLEQUIN®

THE TAGGARTS OF TEXAS!

Harlequin's Ruth Jean Dale brings you
THE TAGGARTS OF TEXAS!

Those Taggart men—strong, sexy and hard to resist...

You've met Jesse James Taggart in FIREWORKS!
Harlequin Romance #3205 (July 1992)

Now meet Trey Smith—he's THE RED-BLOODED YANKEE!
Harlequin Temptation #413 (October 1992)

Then there's Daniel Boone Taggart in SHOWDOWN!
Harlequin Romance #3242 (January 1993)

And finally the Taggarts who started it all—in LEGEND!
Harlequin Historical #168 (April 1993)

Read all the Taggart romances!
Meet all the Taggart men!

Available wherever Harlequin books are sold.

HARLEQUIN HISTORICAL

· STORIES · 1992 ·

Capture the magic and romance of Christmas in the 1800s
with HARLEQUIN HISTORICAL CHRISTMAS STORIES
1992—a collection of three stories by celebrated
historical authors. The perfect Christmas gift!

Don't miss these heartwarming stories, available in
November wherever Harlequin books are sold:

**MISS MONTRACHET REQUESTS by Maura Seger
CHRISTMAS BOUNTY by Erin Yorke
A PROMISE KEPT by Bronwyn Williams**

Plus, this Christmas you can also receive a FREE
keepsake Christmas ornament. Watch for details in all
November and December Harlequin books.

**DISCOVER THE ROMANCE AND MAGIC OF THE
HOLIDAY SEASON WITH HARLEQUIN HISTORICAL
CHRISTMAS STORIES!**